TRANSITION

WANDERER OF WORLDS

BOOK THREE

ACKNOWLEDGEMENTS

We must thank our wonderful beta readers who read, reported on, interrogated and questioned every detail of our final draft. Their questions led to our book being five months overdue but we wouldn't have it any other way—quality is more important than speed. It's because of their keen eyes and love of stories like ours that have allowed us to improve. So thanks must go to David Woodward, David Strange, Sue Strathdee, Kylie Crase, Nicole Hary, Fiona Moran and Jodie Lane.

DEDICATION

For David and the supportive staff
of Stretton State College

For David

TABLE OF CONTENTS

THE STORY SO FAR

Hawke Donovan is abducted as a child and stolen out of his world by Wanderers because of his Shielder blood. He is taken in by the Authorities and placed in their care. Lieutenant Cayden (later to become a Division General) promises Hawke a life of his own making. Howard Ellis proposes that Hawke works for him instead. Hawke signs up with the Authorities, eventually becoming a Hunter—a specialised rank trained to track and assassinate rogue Wanderers. After seeking out the final member of the group that kidnapped him, he returns to his long-time girlfriend, Brita.

While travelling to Stonehearth to sell his ruined farm, Daeson touches a strange pillar of light. It transports him into a foreign world where he learns of his Wanderer Healer blood. Taken in by a group of criminals, his second ability to detect lies makes him especially useful. The woman in charge—Omerri—seduces him to keep him close.

Synjan, a Wanderer Navigator, has worked for Howard Ellis all her life. He has raised her as a capable and intelligent weapon. Her rational mind knows she needs more out of life but her obligation and fear of the unknown keep her tethered. On a mission at the Authority base, Synjan is shot and brought to Daeson, who Heals her from the brink of death.

When Daeson leaves Omerri, Synjan is sent to bring him back but she delivers him to the Portal instead. On a whim, she leaves with him, uninvited.

CHAPTER ONE

Island Of The Gods

EHIND closed eyes, Synjan's awareness rose like groundwater. Aromas of moist earth and humidity filled her lungs as she inhaled. Dappled sunlight played across her face, creating nuances of shadow and light, enticing her to look. When she licked her lips, she tasted the pungency of a rich forest and sultry air. Everything was poised, waiting for her next breath, her next heartbeat, coaxing her to join the sounds of life pulsing around her. She needed to wake up and become part of the unfolding story.

Synjan blinked her surroundings into focus. They were queer and upside down; her back was arched over an enormous lump. Being upended made her feel ill and the queasiness didn't go when she swallowed. All she could see was greenish light filtered through leaves, mottled with pockets of shadow. A distant breeze whispered through the canopy far above and sunlight momentarily seared her eyes. She flinched away then dug the heels of her boots into the ground for leverage. Slowly, she rolled off her backpack, extracting her arms awkwardly from its straps.

She landed on all fours and was filled with wonder as her hands sank into a damp cushion of leaf litter. It was cool and ticklish against her palms. Her fingers searched and she marvelled at the darkness of the dirt and the wet sensation of leaves clinging to her skin as she explored. A little black and white worm the size of her smallest fingernail was flicked onto the back of her hand, curling into a tight circle then uncurling, repeating the process as it writhed around, seeking the safety of its home again. When it fell back into obscurity, she looked up and around herself.

Synjan was in a small clearing encircled by thriving rainforest. The wall of foliage around her was defined by gnarled tree roots, mossy vines and plant-choked trunks. She absorbed its emerald beauty while she got her bearings.

She'd finally Wandered out of Trent! Into the next world. Its strangeness was both expected and overwhelming. She straightened up onto her knees, her palms resting on her thighs as she inhaled the complexity of the moment. It was imposing.

An alien feeling swelled in her chest, filling it with impossible radiance, threatening to crush her heart with its enormity. She was made giddy by its power, swaying as something unexpected bubbled up and erupted out of her—laughter. She tipped her head back to release the sound. It amplified the feeling of joy inside her, echoing back from the wooden skins of the trees. This tingling warmth was a pure, blissful happiness of a magnitude her cautious and rational self could never have contemplated.

Movement to her left had her looking that way, still chuckling. Daeson walked towards her, his feet kicking up dead leaves in little swishes with each step. The way he was looking at her... he seemed perplexed by her laughter but his expression didn't discourage her jubilation. If anything, his face made her want to laugh harder.

"What's funny?" he asked.

She smiled bashfully, realising he probably thought

her insane to be kneeling here, laughing at trees. When he frowned and glanced around uneasily, she recognised his concern and did her best to quell her exuberance; she felt like her eyes might be glowing, so bright was the sensation inside her. She needed to reassure him.

"Nothing, really," she demurred. "I'm just... happy."

"Oh," he said in a tone that declared he didn't share her sentiment. He watched her for a moment. "I didn't know you were coming with me."

His diplomatic statement impacted her good mood slightly. "Ah. Well, neither did I?" she offered, her tone apologetic.

He didn't look satisfied with her words and she couldn't blame him. She'd had no conscious intention of Wandering with him but there was obviously a part of her that had understood she needed to. She'd packed her things—too many things—and she'd stolen money from Ellis, subconsciously walking away from a life that had never consisted of living and had almost ended her.

The thought was sobering and the urge to laugh left as she recalled the lure of death. Daeson had returned her from the brink but there was something that had irrevocably broken that day; the tether that had kept her in that world.

No longer would she consent to exist in a role for a purpose she hated, paying off a debt that grew daily, surrounded by people she couldn't define. Love? Had she loved them? Was that why she'd stayed? It didn't feel like that was the right answer but it was all she could come up with. Why else would a sane, intelligent woman take twenty-four years to start living for herself? Perhaps it was loyalty. It didn't seem worth it, in hindsight.

She regretted that Daeson had fallen victim to her impulse but she didn't regret doing it. The reward of living was something she'd earned.

His expression told her he wasn't in the mood to be thanked for saving her again, even if she could explain how this time he'd helped rescue her from herself. She didn't think there *was* a way to show how profoundly grateful she was to him for his intervention but she resolved to try.

Daeson's posture changed as he peered into the depths of the forest.

"What is it?" Synjan asked.

"Singing."

She heard nothing beyond the cadence of industrious insects and an indefinable rumbling in the distance. She closed her eyes and mentally sought around them.

Three people were close, snatching her attention. She hovered over them, assessing their patterns and guessing their intent. Two men—one with a solid orange pattern and the other with a purple, blue and ochre pattern—and a woman defined by soft green and lemon yellow. They walked single file and all held something in one of their hands. Weapons?

Heart hammering, Synjan scrambled to her feet, attracting Daeson's startled gaze. His eyes widened as she reached beneath her shirt and withdrew the small gun she carried in her bra—her other weapons were in her backpack.

"There are three people coming," she told Daeson as she grabbed his arm to keep him in place. She stepped in front of him, holding her gun behind her back. "Two men, one woman."

Every cell in her body lit up with recrimination, grating like a rusted saw. Why had she been so slow to map? Why had she been so relaxed? She'd lolled about like nothing could possibly hurt them in this lovely new world, as if all danger had been left behind. Who was she to assume they were *safe*? How stupid could she be? Safe meant secure and she'd done nothing to secure their position. Freddie would be mortified; her heart cringed as she pictured her trainer's disappointment.

She was acutely aware of how big Daeson was and what an inadequate shield she made. The top of her head didn't reach his chin and he was twice as wide as her; she was hardly concealing him. He had no training. It was her job to protect him. She was going to fail at the first hurdle because she'd been too busy feeling good after Wandering.

"Where?" he asked, confusion evident in his voice.

"There," she pointed.

"I don't see—"

"Soon," she snapped. She reached back and briefly grasped his fingers, trying to soothe him and the barrage of condemnation in her head.

They would get better at this. She'd do better next time.

Synjan wouldn't have been able to articulate what she was expecting of the approaching strangers but when they stepped silently from the foliage, they were beyond anything she could have imagined. They were almost naked. Looking them over made her acutely aware of the layer of sweat coating her whole body and every place her thick, heavy clothing clung.

The first man was huge. He was taller than Daeson, his brown skin smooth beneath its sheen of sweat. He had brown eyes, dark brown hair cut uniformly close to his head and held a stone axe in his hand. His torso was covered by a large grass panel woven in an overlapping pattern. A matching shield hanging off a string-like belt covered his genitals. His bare limbs were roped with muscle and looked powerful as he came to a stop opposite them.

The woman was attired similarly except she wore fibrous-looking woven underwear. Her small breasts were bare behind her grass armour, the shield secured to her belt to accommodate their curvature.

Both men had welcoming expressions but the female assessed Synjan and Daeson carefully. She had very dark eyes and long, straight black hair tied in multiple braids. When she saw Synjan observing her just as closely, she nonchalantly (but purposely, Synjan thought) shifted her grip on the short sickle-type weapon she held. It was made of bone.

The third in the trio carried a stone-tipped spear and was dressed the same as the first but that was where the similarities between them ended. This man seemed younger and he was not as tall. His skin wasn't quite as dark and he had light brown hair that was almost blonde on top—possibly from spending a lot of time in the sun. His bare limbs were long and lithe, his build athletic and sinewy. His eyes were outstanding; they were the colour of sunlight radiating through leaves.

Synjan was reminded of Ellis' deep green eyes and immediately squashed that thought. The man near her was young, his expression curious and receptive. Even though his twinkling eyes were green, they were pale and vibrant. He was nothing like her past.

The two men exchanged glances and sang a short tune to one another. The woman added to their song, sounding less enthusiastic but more melodic.

Daeson stepped around Synjan. Though something fearful in her clenched up, she didn't hold him back. Instinct told her that these people—despite carrying weapons— meant them no harm. Their body language was too open.

"Hello! I'm Daeson, this is Synjan. Do you speak Authoritan?"

His greeting was met with more excited singing and a few gestures before the smaller man dropped his spear and walked around the compact clearing, looking up at the nearby trees. After a few steps, he must have seen whatever he was looking for because he leapt at a tree and shimmied up the trunk so quickly it looked like he wasn't even holding on. Synjan had never seen anything like it but she was distracted from her amazed staring when the other two strangers left the clearing. It was baffling how silently they could slip into a space dense with foliage and disappear.

Daeson leant close. "Put your gun away," he ordered quietly.

Synjan blinked up at him. She resented that he was telling her what to do when she'd only been acting in his best interests. He obviously didn't like her having a gun ready to protect them. She thought he would've felt differently if the strangers had been hostile. As far as she knew, he couldn't fight and it wasn't like he could Heal them into submission.

"I was just—" When Daeson looked directly at her, all justifications fled. It seemed petty to argue with him, especially when she'd been about to put the gun away anyway. "Never mind," she mumbled and slid the weapon back into her bra.

The climber dropped agilely out of the tree and approached them with two golden fruits that dwarfed his hands. The larger end had a blush of red burgeoning to life on the soft skin. He held one out to each of them and sang some grand and beautiful notes. Synjan took hers, offering a smile and a head dip of gratitude before she brought the gift up to her nose. It smelled sweet and her mouth flooded with saliva.

"I think this is a fruit," she told Daeson.

"Yes, it's a mango," he responded and she could only nod. She felt curiously overwhelmed upon hearing that the mango was something he'd had experience with. She guessed he'd had it in his home world but couldn't explain why that simple act of serendipity made her feel so awkward and ignorant.

The other two returned as quietly as they'd left, their hands filled with white flowers bearing bright blue stamens. Synjan and Daeson each received a bouquet while being serenaded.

Nodding and smiling as she accepted her flowers, Synjan wished she could respond in a better way than with simple facial expressions.

"I'm in trouble," she said through gritted teeth.

"Why?" Daeson asked.

"Because they keep singing. I think they sing their language and I can't sing."

"Maybe you'll improve."

"I doubt it. I also wish I could thank them for their gifts."

"Let's give them something then," Daeson suggested and approached his backpack, setting down the flowers and mango beside it. He opened the main zip and thrust both hands inside, stirring up the innards Synjan had so carefully arranged back in Trent—it didn't feel like something that had happened a few hours ago... it felt like days.

Daeson straightened up holding a red T-shirt, opening it out in order to size it against the strangers. He moved in front of the giant.

"This should fit you," he announced and held it out towards the lucky recipient. The stranger's dark eyes lit up and he grabbed the garment, inspecting it before enthusiastically pushing his head and arms through the correct holes. It snagged on his chest armour but he was not to be deterred—Daeson helped him pull the stretchy material as far down as it would go. It clung awkwardly at his waist.

All gazes swivelled toward Synjan. It was her turn to produce something. She strode to her bag, trying to recall all the objects she'd flung into it and rejecting most before she'd even crouched over the yawning mouth of her pack. She did her best not to look up as she felt through her belongings, aware of their expectant stares. She found something she could part with—she'd apparently thrown an awful lot of cutlery in her bag. The metal clinked as she assessed it blindly, her counting revealing that she had at least one small and one large spoon to spare.

Relieved, she put the mango and flowers in her pack and removed the gifts she was willing to offer. Hurrying back to the empty-handed indigenes, she held them out with a tight smile.

The woman took the small spoon cautiously but the man snatched the one in front of him, singing something at the other male as he held his metal prize aloft. The woman's gaze shifted off her teaspoon to his dessert spoon, then back to hers. With the sickle still in hand, she punched the man in his unprotected ribs, coming dangerously close to cutting him. The thud of her knuckles cut his song short and his arm flinched downward. His spoon was plucked out of his fist and the woman shoved her teaspoon at him negligently. She gave Synjan a triumphant smirk before examining her reflection in the larger surface area of her gift.

Synjan's eyes widened. She looked at the man now in possession of the smaller spoon, regretting causing conflict between him and the woman. He pouted but cheered up when he saw Synjan looking at him. He tucked the metal object into something behind his back—she assumed there was a pouch there—and picked up his abandoned spear. He sang and gestured encouragingly at her.

He pointed at an area of forest opposite from the direction they'd arrived. Synjan was perplexed but could tell he wanted her to go with him. Had she and Daeson landed in the middle of their forest trek and now they wanted to take them along? Lead them to safety? Were they in danger? His companions didn't seem to think that whatever he was suggesting was a good idea. He was unperturbed by their refusal and skipped towards the other side of the clearing, making grabbing motions at Synjan that reminded her of the

Gredann fisherfolk hauling in their laden nets.

"I'm going to go and see what he wants to show us. See if there's a problem," she told Daeson as she picked up her backpack and followed.

She didn't hear if he replied and it was difficult to keep track of where her target had gone. She found herself mapping to be sure he was still ahead of her because he was so quiet and there was no obvious path.

After a hectic chase, Synjan broke free of the forest's tangled clutches and emerged beside a beautiful lagoon. Her mouth fell open as she squinted up at a waterfall gushing from a modest height into a pool of water that looked pristine and invitingly cool. It held the rainforest at bay with a border of long, thick grass and dark rocks. Where she'd arrived, there was a gently sloping path of mud that led straight into the pool. Clusters of broad leaves and vivid flowers floated on its surface, bobbing in the wake created by the waterfall's churning waters. Now she understood the distant rumbling sound she'd heard since waking.

Her attention was dragged from the picturesque scene by the dancing movements of her companion. First went his spear onto the grass, followed by his belt, spoon and lower armour before he peeled his grass chest plate over his head and dropped that, too. Synjan noted that his genitals were cupped by the same cloth-like woven material that made up the female's underwear. As he turned and sprinted into the water, she also noted that it only serviced his front, as his buttocks were on display until he dived beneath the surface.

By the time he appeared in the middle of the lagoon, singing and beckoning to her, she'd already dropped her bag, stripped off her boots and socks and was working on her denim pants. Even though it had been summer in Gredann just a few hours (minutes?) before, her home world's weather was much milder. Here, the humidity was stifling and she was forced to peel her thick pants off. Her upper garments were similarly bonded to her skin but she wrenched them over her head with great relish, unconcerned that a stranger was seeing her in her underwear—her covering was far more modest than his, after all.

"It's just a swimming hole!" Synjan yelled, believing they weren't too far away for Daeson to hear her. "Come and cool off!"

Once she'd unclipped the holstered gun from the centre gore of her bra, she stashed it in her backpack. Eagerly, she ran into the lagoon, losing her breath momentarily as she submerged. It was as exquisite and cool as it had looked from the edge. Despite there being no cover, the trees encroached and leant over in places, affording patches of shade and keeping the water chilled.

Had this been the destination of the three strangers all along? Why were the other two not interested in coming with their companion, then? Perhaps a swim delayed their mission. With her innate sense of direction, Synjan compared the sun's relative position to the shade she was swimming through and guessed the time to be mid to late morning. Perhaps the indigenous trio had somewhere to be?

Thinking about time shifts made something inside her feel fluttery with uncertainty. They'd left Trent in the late afternoon but it was now earlier in the day. Had time reversed here or had they been asleep for a night and part of the next day? Perhaps it was even longer than that, or only a matter of seconds after they'd Wandered. The different worlds might not spin in perfect synchronicity. The Authorities would have a better idea—they wouldn't know about Wanderer Portals, though. It was a quandary she filed away to discuss with Daeson when they got some time.

She was stroking towards the swirling water at the

base of the waterfall when the other three emerged from the forest. There wasn't enough room for them to stand comfortably in a group so there was some shuffling while they fanned out. The two locals yelled at the man swimming with her. To Synjan, their words sounded especially obnoxious because they were sung. One word was repeated often enough that it registered as significant.

"Are you Tagan?" she grinned, pointing at the male doing a lazy backstroke in front of her.

His eyes lit up and he grinned, singing the word back at her.

"TAY-gan," she repeated, trying to make the word more melodic as well as put emphasis on the first syllable like he had.

He laughed at her and she took it as confirmation. He pointed near her nose.

"Me? Synjan," she answered, wondering if she should invent a progression of notes for her name. The idea was dismissed as quickly as it had come.

"MeSynjan," he echoed, matching the way she'd said it. She understood now why he'd laughed at her pronunciation of his name; a familiar word spoken by a foreign tongue was a unique and dissociative experience. Was she the same person if her name was said differently? She knew she was but she was enchanted by the notion of reinvention.

Laughing, she corrected him, being careful not to add extra words. When he repeated her name a few times, Tagan decided to share his information. He swam towards the shore where their onlookers stood and sang her name amongst some other words. The reception wasn't quite what she expected.

"Synjan," the woman sang gruffly, pointing at the bank near her feet before she sang something even more gruffly at Tagan. The other man also made the reeling-in gesture at her.

"They don't seem happy you're in there," Daeson remarked. "Maybe there's something in the water."

Synjan hurried out without comment, feeling the weight of Daeson's disapproval but unsure of its origin. She deliberately kept her eyes averted so that she couldn't see his reaction to her emerging in her underwear, guessing that wouldn't impress him, either. His first question when she woke up made her realise he was more than just surprised that she'd come along. He was angry with her. Did that mean he wanted to separate? Her heart skipped faster as she crouched by her backpack and searched for some more appropriate clothes.

It was unwise to make assumptions but she couldn't understand why Daeson would want to split up. They'd make an excellent team and not just because of their Wanderer talents. She was fit, highly trained and astute. He had experience Wandering and living alone. Both of them had no idea about the situation they'd got themselves into. They'd complement each other, she was sure of it. She just had to make *him* sure of it.

The abrasive singing exchange continued as she found a pair of denim shorts and pulled them on. Tagan was still in the water and deliberately antagonising his companions. She couldn't fathom why but he was definitely smirking as he paddled about. The other two continued to sing-yell from the bank. Synjan wondered if there was some sort of reverence attached to this body of water. If so, Tagan seemed to have no respect for it and, by following him in, she'd demonstrated the same quality. Great. She'd have to choose her actions more carefully in future; she had a lot of atoning to do.

The only short-sleeved shirt she had was a white tailored blouse with decorative cuffs that snugly enclosed her arms above her biceps. It also had pleated sleeves that caused the material on her shoulders to puff slightly and opalescent buttons in the shape of flowers. It was too pretty for her current environment but she couldn't afford to worry about that; it was made from a natural material that kept her cool and that was her main priority. She'd have given a great deal to exchange it for something less fitted and more resilient but she'd apparently been in business-mode when she was sent to collect Daeson and chosen clothes that might impress, rather than being practical.

By the time she'd tied her boots, replaced the gifts she'd received and hoisted her backpack on, Tagan had left the lagoon and was ready to go.

"I think the natives want us to follow them," Daeson told her as the group jostled for position on the narrow bank by the lagoon.

"Natives?" she asked, querying his language choice.

"The native-born of this world."

"Ah," she nodded. "Then I guess we should." She paused to look at him. "You're not going to change clothes?" she asked.

"No." He didn't elaborate.

Tagan led the way, prodded by the woman. Daeson fell second last in line behind Synjan, the shirt-wearing native bringing up the rear. They moved back the way they'd come, immediately ensconced in green foliage that grabbed at the impostors but not their bare-skinned guides. The drumming of the waterfall receded as they went, giving way to the sound of Daeson's heavy footfalls and the persistent whine of various winged insects excited by their visit. Looking down, Synjan wrinkled her nose at the dark spots covering her breasts; she swished a hand at them but the insects merely rose into a swirling cloud for a moment before reattaching themselves. A few others were content to alight on her exposed arms and her infrequent slaps seemed especially loud now that no-one was singing or talking. As her skin started to itch, she wondered if changing her clothes had been a smart idea after all.

Since their immediate future was set, Synjan felt secure enough to divide her senses as they walked. She couldn't close her eyes to map but that didn't stop part of her mind lifting away from their current position to get a better idea of the world they'd landed in.

Right away, she felt how distant the Portal was. The sensation of yearning pulsed weakly within her and she was dismayed by how far she had to push towards it; she mentally withdrew before she found an exact location. The worst discovery was the composition of the landscape between them and their escape; the part of the world they'd landed in was predominantly oceanic with islands of varying sizes sprinkled across it. At the very least, they'd need to sail to get to the Portal. The topography was baffling because it was unexpected.

There had been many times in her past when she'd readied herself to Wander alone, just to be free of Ellis. She knew the official world order and Femme was listed after Trent. All information she'd read on Femme had talked about what a scientifically advanced world it was, governed by women who kept men as slaves. They had agriculture and machines listed in the brochures that she couldn't even imagine and the growing population supposedly lived in flourishing, technologically-sophisticated cities. The whole world was touted as an immersive experience of organic genius and civic harmony, an unparalleled example of progress and peace. It had sounded wonderful. Moreover, it had sounded like a heavily populated world.

It was possible she and Daeson had landed in a particularly remote region but her instincts told her that wasn't the case. These natives carried crude weaponry and treated one another as equals. The islands were too sparse, there was too much ocean around them and the only notable populations she detected were in the vicinity of the island upon which they currently stood. She wasn't sure how she'd confirm it, but she didn't think this was Femme.

Where in all the worlds were they? Synjan's focus shifted to the immediate area, needing something definite to ground her.

They were walking northward on a small island that appeared, when she hovered above it, to be like the small dot at the bottom of an exclamation mark. It was circular and modest in size. There was an elongated island to the north that was much larger than the land mass they were crossing. The long, thin island was the only one close enough to swim to.

Synjan sighed, frustrated by a question she had no answer to and intimidated by the prospect of successfully navigating the barriers of this world. She wasn't even sure she had an ally by her side and for the first time, she felt small and helpless. The confusion and inability to decide how to move forward threatened to swallow her whole. It sat on her chest, making it hard to take a breath. She stumbled, not noticing a root the pair ahead of her had stepped over. When she flung a hand out to steady herself, it was grabbed by Daeson. His grip on her sweaty arm was firm and reassuring as he helped her stay upright.

"Synjan! Are you alright?" he asked.

She met the gaze of the woman ahead of her—who'd turned to see what the commotion was about—before she looked back at Daeson. "I'm fine. Thanks," she told him quietly and he released her once she was steady on her feet. She reached around and unclipped the metal flask of water attached to the outside of her pack. With a practised hand, she unfastened the lid and took a long drink to calm herself. "I wasn't watching where I was going properly. There's a nasty root lurking somewhere around here, waiting to take advantage of distracted people." She recapped the flask, eyeing the ground between them.

When she looked up at him, his blue eyes were clear of malice and relief washed through her. Concern was etched on his face. He might be angry with her and maybe he was sorry she'd come but he didn't hate her. He cared that she'd nearly fallen over. He'd helped her instinctively. His Healer nature was likely her saving grace. She offered him a tight smile and turned away, aware that their guides weren't keen to halt progress and that she needed to keep following. When her feet began moving again, she was no longer mentally divided.

Everything about this life would be a jumble for a while. The cursory glance she'd had of the world told her it would be difficult to negotiate and she didn't have the skills necessary to do it easily. She wasn't used to failing or relying on others but she'd have to adapt; she'd have to get used to the panicky feeling of being out of control for a little while. The only thing she could depend on was Daeson. Whether he liked it or not, they were in this situation together so he would become her focus. For support *and* protection.

Just as the press of the forest became stifling and Synjan's limbs and face raw from grabby foliage or her own scratching hands, the trail ended. She followed her female guide out of the green-hued oven and into brilliant, infinite space; her humidity-laden breath was rejuvenated and then snatched by brisk ocean wind. It was so dazzling, Synjan brought her hand up to shade her eyes, blinking repeatedly to allow her overwhelmed vision to adjust. She took a few tentative steps out of Daeson's way while she did, aware now that they were on the edge of a cliff looming grandly above the ocean. The island was much taller than she'd anticipated.

The sun shone down from close to its zenith, the sky above a deep, vibrant blue. A few fluffy white clouds trailed lazily across its broad expanse, impervious to the vast depths of the ocean below. A bird's cry was carried to her on the wind and her pulse leapt—the cry was familiar! The connection to the home she'd always carry in her heart was small but it made things seem not quite so dire. Her arm still shielding her eyes, she looked around with greater interest, smiling to herself.

Their small party was perched atop a grassy area that looked like it had been deliberately cleared of forest to make space for a huge rope bridge. It spanned the distance between their dot island and the longer exclamation one. They couldn't swim between the two and there was no way down off this cliff. Three trunks had been sunk into the ground to support the bridge; two for the handrail ropes and a third—set closer to the forest than the others—for the rope that ran down the middle.

After a brief singing exchange, the female native set off across the bridge and Synjan studied her. She noted how the structure swayed and bounced beneath spritely bare feet and what the taller woman did to counteract and cooperate with it. The bridge was more air than substance and Synjan was keen to try it. In no time at all, their guide was across the gap and Synjan fought the urge to applaud her skill. She closed her eyes and tipped up her face to bask in the light of a brand new sun.

CHAPTER TWO

The Rope Bridge

ONE moment Daeson was picking his way over unsteady ground—careful not to scratch himself on branches or have his face swiped by wet leaves—and the next he stood near a cliff's edge, staring at a rope bridge as a warm flurry of air rippled his clothes.

It wasn't the kind of rope bridge that he'd used on his home-world, where planks of wood were roped together to cross burbling creeks. Those bridges, though useful, could be bypassed with some careful stone-stepping or bank jumping.

This bridge was an entirely different creature, created from braided vines that creaked and rustled. The drop was a harrowing plunge to the ocean below and Daeson imagined a smattering of jagged rocks poking out of the water's surface to greet whoever had misstepped.

He was passed by the t-shirt wearing native and could see large patches of sweat colouring his underarms and striping his back. Daeson thought now his gift had been cruel rather than kind. Ahead of him was Synjan, who stopped to swipe an arm across her brow. He was angry at her for running off into the jungle without him, following after an unknown man. Was this the type of woman he was travelling with? She'd done it twice already, running after men she didn't know. Sweat trickled down his back and stuck his clothes to his skin. His spiteful refusal to strip had backfired. Inside of the jungle, the heat was a physical thing, like a giant's hand pressing on him, making every step difficult as he sweltered beneath a blanket of oppressive humidity. It was better now, in the open, but even though he had a chance to change clothes, he wouldn't. It would look like he'd made a hasty decision; to strip now would be to admit his mistake. He could put up with the heat.

The woman was the first to scurry across, walking foot over foot because the bridge was too narrow to place feet together. Daeson faced the bridge directly and thought of it as a letter V. The central rope was a thick braid that made the point of the V. Two thinner ropes formed the railings and zigzag patterns of thin flaxen braids connected the railing to the central rope.

It looked like something he could easily get tangled in and fall through. It didn't look strong or trustworthy. He thought about the constant strain from the buffeting wind. How many times had this bridge been lashed by a storm? How many days had the sun baked it, drying the vines until they were brittle?

Daeson's stomach churned. His bladder felt tight and full. His gaze returned to Synjan who was adjusting the items clipped to the outside of her pack, presumably so nothing would get caught in the ropes while crossing. She didn't look worried.

"I have to go," he mumbled while turning away. The native with green eyes—Daeson remembered his name was Tagan—sang to him and grabbed his wrist, tugging him closer to the bridge. Daeson wrenched away. "I need a toilet!" he insisted before disappearing into the foliage. There was a moment of insanity when he considered returning to the waterfall and lagoon. It had been nice there. With plentiful supplies of fruit and water, he could live there quite well.

As good as it sounded, it wouldn't work. He would have to face the bridge at some point.

When Daeson unzipped, he found his nerves had a tighter hold on his body than expected, forcing him to think of other things to relax. He focussed on the smell of the plants around him, their sweet scent clinging to the air like perfume. He took deep breaths until he managed to get a flow going.

A glossy-shelled beetle trundled a path down the tree that he was watering. Daeson watched as it carefully negotiated its way around the cracks in the trunk. The beetle was a pretty, shiny thing and he could feel his anxiety lessening as he watched its progress. By the time he was ready to return to the bridge, he felt calmer.

After he broke through the foliage once more, he saw his backpack was gone. Synjan stood nearby, wearing hers.

"The big guy took your pack across for you," she explained.

Daeson stared at the bridge, feeling his chest tighten at the thought of stepping out. He was aware his hands had fisted and forced them to uncurl. He took a step towards the bridge and hesitated. Synjan must've seen something in his face.

"Would you like to go together?"

"Yes, let's go together," Daeson replied, echoing her words. He was grateful that she was both perceptive enough to notice his nervousness and compassionate enough to offer help. Tagan said something that Daeson didn't understand, but his body language spoke of impatience. When Daeson gestured for him to go first, Tagan refused and sang more urgently, flapping his hands towards the bridge.

"I don't like how he's rushing me," Daeson said. "Can you go behind me? I don't want him to push me."

"Okay."

As Daeson approached the bridge, he was aware he'd never experienced this kind of fear; it made his insides squirm and his legs feel weak. Heights had never bothered him before; he'd scrambled up trees as a boy, he'd climbed onto the roof of his cottage—and fallen through it—and he'd looked out the window of the topmost floor of the Queen. None of those times had made him dry mouthed or nauseous, so why now?

Daeson walked between the large, thick posts hammered into the ground that supported the bridge. He gave each one a firm push. All of them were immovable. Satisfied, Daeson gripped the side ropes tightly and placed his foot onto the rope. One step forward would have him hovering over the ocean.

The breeze on his face was warm and mostly constant, not like the bullying and frigid gusts that had tried shoving him around the back alley of the Queen. He was relieved that he wouldn't have to battle hostile weather. He didn't think he would be able to cross under anything less than perfect conditions—like today. He looked across to the far side; it was impossibly distant. How had the natives managed to build a bridge this long? Who had cast the rope? How had they tied it up? Had someone climbed down the cliff, swum across and then climbed up the other side, carrying a rope?

He heard Synjan gently urging him forward. He was delaying, he knew. Omerri had mentioned a few times that the first step of a journey was the hardest. He thought he knew what she meant now, though he suspected it wasn't meant to be taken so literally.

Daeson lifted a foot and had to look down to see where he was putting it. The bottom rope, as thick as it was, was too narrow to be useful. His boot dwarfed it when he stepped down, making it difficult to balance. He felt himself tipping and he yanked on the opposite railing to compensate. Both railings shifted only slightly, but enough to give him the impression that once he was farther out on the bridge, the railings would be free to swing wildly when he pulled on them. He made a fearful noise.

"Swivel your foot. Your foot. Daeson, listen! Turn your foot so your toes point out."

Daeson did as told, turning his foot so that the toes of his boots pointed outward. He found it easier to balance. He waited a moment, willing his heart rate to slow down. He would not get through this if he panicked. He wished the breeze blowing onto his face was cooler.

Daeson took another step. It wasn't so bad when he focussed on the rope beneath his feet and did the duck-like walk that Synjan described. His third step brought him to the zigzag of thin braids connecting the railings to the central rope. With great care, he lifted his foot and moved it forward before turning it sideways and stepping back down. He repeated the process; foot up, forward, turn, down. Foot up, forward, turn, down. Each step was excruciatingly slow.

"Good work. Easy does it," Synjan commended behind him. "There's no rush, take your time."

Daeson was moving his right foot forward when it got stuck on something. He felt the railing tremble beneath his hold and tightened his grip.

"It's just your boot lace caught," Synjan said. "If you wiggle your foot, it'll come free."

He followed her advice and felt the lace unhitch. He might've put the hindrance out of his mind, except his focus shifted off his feet and into the space beyond.

The ocean was a meaningless plunge below but the white caps dotting the waves exposed how high he was. Panic—never too far away—slunk from his chest where it had lain in wait and lodged in his throat, making it difficult to breathe. The railings wobbled violently beneath his hold. His legs shook and were no longer able to carry him—his arms were doing most of the work and he was aware now that his shoulders, neck and jaw were aching. He could taste something slimy and acrid at the back of his throat and the need to pee returned.

"Keep moving forward, you can do it," Synjan encouraged.

"I can't! I can't move!" Daeson yelled, even though he'd heard her softly spoken instructions easily. Once he started yelling, it was difficult to stop. "Let's go back! I want to go back!"

The bridge jiggled as Synjan moved behind him. As the ropes shifted beneath her motion, he gripped them tighter still and they swayed alarmingly to one side.

"Stop moving! Stop moving!"

"Alright, I'm not moving," she said quickly. He froze, paralysed with fear. The bridge and its railings stopped swinging. There was a long silence before Synjan spoke up. "Do you want me to go back?"

"No! Just... just wait."

Daeson felt like he was tipped to one side. He focussed on unclenching his muscles and letting his legs take his weight. The more he relaxed, the more the railings righted themselves. After a few deep breaths, he lifted a foot to take another step just as the bridge began rocking on its own. Screaming, Daeson dropped to a crouch.

"Stop it! SYNJAN STOP IT!" It felt like his skin was tightening.

Synjan spoke to him in a gentle tone. "It's not me, it's the guy behind me. I'll stop him." He heard her yelling at the native, sharp and angry.

The bouncing stopped. In his crouched position, looking at the waves below, he could easily imagine himself toppling through the flaxen railing. His ears throbbed with the *whomp-whomp* of his heartbeat, so loud that he couldn't hear anything else.

"Is he gone?" Daeson asked.

"Yes. I don't think he knows what you're going through."

The lie sat in his stomach, barely having an impact amongst the fear that was already knotting his insides. Daeson's good will towards the inhabitants of this world vanished.

"Do you think you can stand up now?" Synjan asked.

"Not yet."

He closed his eyes but that was worse so he opened them and focussed on the bridge instead. He could see where small strands of flax had unravelled, like a wayward thread begging to be pulled from a sweater. He saw where some pieces had rotted away and rubbed off, forming imperfect dips and knots. In other places, he could see where the bridge had been patched or mended with newer, fresher vines.

"Daeson, it's okay. Would you like me to help you up?"

"No."

He couldn't move. His knees were locked in position and his elbows braced. Synjan continued speaking to him, softly, calmly. She asked him to focus on her voice, to listen to her words, to let her help him and they would cross this bridge together.

The noise of the ocean fell into the background as he concentrated on Synjan, listening as she talked him through every step. First, he stood. Then, he moved forward.

After what seemed a long time, Synjan spoke her encouragement. "We're almost there."

He looked up, certain that he was about to step off the bridge onto the other side. His gut wrenched when he realised her 'almost there' was farther away than his 'almost there'. He faltered. Synjan continued to soothe him until he found his rhythm again. Her voice filled his world. Foot over foot, everything beyond the bridge blurred into insignificance.

Finally, the rope met with solid ground. Daeson sped the last few steps, instinctively reaching for one of the posts as he moved past. He was horrified when it shifted. His stomach knotted again and he stumbled forward, half falling, half sitting on the grass. His stomach heaved once, twice, then settled.

Synjan crouched beside him, her hand on his shoulder.

"You did it, it's over. Let's have some water."

Daeson looked at Synjan with gratitude and admiration as she took off her backpack to retrieve a bottle. She'd said and done exactly what he'd needed to get through that horrible encounter. He didn't think he'd have managed to cross the bridge without her.

Synjan handed him a bottle of water and he drank it greedily. Beyond it, the native couple were silently watching in a way that made him feel a mixture of indignation and embarrassment. He handed the bottle back to her, half empty.

"Sorry," he said. Now that he was safe, he felt foolish. "Thank you for helping me."

"It's okay," she said. The truth of her simple statement humbled him.

An excited voice coming from the bridge drew his attention. Tagan ran across it, lightly holding the rails. When he joined them, he laughingly dropped into a crouch, hooting as he mimicked Daeson's fear.

Daeson scowled.

"You're an asshole," Synjan bristled. "*Stop* it."

Tagan looked confused by their reactions, glancing from one to the other before he made a gesture neither of them understood. Then he appealed to the woman who made their trio. She listened without expression before disappearing into the jungle. Tagan followed immediately after her. The muscular native picked up Daeson's pack and held it above his head before singing to them.

"Are you right to keep going?" Synjan asked, shouldering her pack.

"Sounds good to me," Daeson replied and stood. Synjan smiled before she entered the forest. He followed closely behind but had to look back to see if the large native was still with them. Other than his and Synjan's movements, he couldn't hear anyone.

Daeson had expected a well-used path but there was none that he could see. He followed Synjan closely, stepping over mossy logs and ducking under vines. Synjan paused a few times to look to her right. Daeson followed her stare but couldn't see anything.

They trekked for a long time and progress was slow. The land sloped downward and they were led along a meandering line by the woman in front. With a sickle in her hand, Daeson didn't understand why she didn't just hack at whatever was in her way.

They entered a newly created clearing, made obvious by the fresh smell of chopped greenery. Stripped logs lay in a row surrounded by the upheaval of shrubbery. Flung soil and discarded branches littered the ground. His memory superimposed the indignity of his ravaged garden on Kharltae; the criminal act that had forced this life upon him.

The three natives sang angrily at each other and the large man set down Daeson's backpack in order to approach a nearby tree, weeping with sap. He placed his hand upon the wound as though to stop the bleeding and looked imploringly at Daeson and Synjan. The other two natives investigated the area as though it were a travesty.

The forest must be sacred to these people. It made sense now why the woman in front hadn't chopped vines or branches away while finding their path. Someone else had cut the trees down to make logs, but it wasn't obvious who or why.

They didn't linger. The woman ordered everyone to follow her and disappeared into the dense foliage. Daeson shouldered his pack and fell back into place. Lots of prickly and sap-sticky plants rubbed against his clothes. Twice he'd brushed against a nettle-like tree that pinched his arms through his sleeves. It was when he felt a potent thirst after the second time that he realised what such a thing meant.

"Synjan, be careful of that purpley-red tree. It's poisonous." He pointed at the plant coming up on her left and was satisfied when she skirted around it.

She looked over her shoulder at him. "How did you know?"

"It got me a couple of times," he admitted.

Synjan lapsed into a thoughtful silence.

Their exit from the jungle was sudden. The forest floor immediately changed from leaf-littered dirt to soft, loose sand and the tree-line followed its stark progression. The sun's brightness assaulted Daeson as he stepped out of the forest depths and into the light. It took a few blinks for the sunspots to clear away and he was left staring at an immaculate white-gold beach and the peaceful, sparkling ocean beyond.

Three canoes had been pulled onto the beach—two were long and simple with a peculiar bowl-type boat attached to them by rope. The third was shorter but rested on two oblong buoys.

Catamaran, he identified. He'd learned a lot about the different types of boats from his visits to the vacation world of Mwavey. The catamarans there had been large and sleek. This one was small and rough but even so, it looked sturdier and better made than the canoes.

Three more natives were on the beach, singing to

one another as they emptied armfuls of items into the bowl boats. The large native stepped forward, his deep voice booming across the sand and attracting the others. They gathered around him, touching his new red shirt. Tagan ran in amongst them, holding up his teaspoon.

Daeson took off his backpack and set it down on the sand so he could reach around and unstick his shirt from his back. When he moved forward, Synjan fell into step with him. They approached the boats together.

Daeson looked in the closest bowl boat and saw a collection of fruits, plants and nuts. "Looks like this group was a foraging trio," he said.

"Or a hunting trio," Synjan replied, pointing at the catamaran. Now that they were closer, Daeson could see the hulking body of a huge brown pig in the centre. He was surprised only three people had brought an animal that size down.

A smiling woman with short hair approached. She carried a calico tote bag and upended its contents of leaves and berries into the bowl boat beside them. Daeson was stunned to see faded Authoritan writing on the bag's side like it had come from a shop. He turned to gauge Synjan's reaction and to discuss with her what such a thing meant, but she was staring at the tree-line instead. The intensity of her gaze was disarming.

"What are you looking at?"

"There are people up there. Others. Same sort of build as these natives. Two of them."

"What are they doing?" he asked, trying to figure out where she was looking and unable to see anything but tree trunks and shadows.

"Just watching."

"I can't see them."

Synjan gazed at the group working on the boats nearby and then up at Daeson. Her expression was confused and wary. "No, neither can I. Not with my eyes, anyway... but I can map them. They're there."

She looked at the trees again. Daeson was unsettled. They were being watched by people who were so good at blending in with their environment that they were invisible. What was more disturbing was their newfound friends had no idea they were being watched. If they did, would things be less casual? Surely friends wouldn't hide in the bushes watching? Did these others pose a danger? Were they the ones who'd cut down the trees and lined them up? He was frustrated that he couldn't communicate with their rescuers.

Synjan took a step forward and Daeson grabbed her arm to stop her. She gave him a questioning look.

"If we make a fuss about them, they might not just watch us go. They might... interfere."

He watched her expression change as she thought it over. "Okay."

Daeson dropped his hand and they stared at one other. Her agreement made him feel obliged to fill in the silence. "So... how far is the Portal?"

"*Really* far away," she told him grimly. "The world between the Portal and us is filled with deep ocean waters and sporadic islands. It'd take us *months* to get there. I haven't mapped it properly but I know it won't be easy to get to."

"Oh." He wanted to say something uplifting but he didn't feel it inside of him. His inability to lie also took away his ability to provide comfort. The best he could do was change the subject. He looked across the water. A section of the sky was dark and angry, promising an incoming storm. Beneath it but not far from them was a pillar of rock. It looked strange; a towering column in the middle of the ocean.

"Is that where they've come from?" Daeson asked, pointing.

Synjan's eyelids fluttered closed and she lapsed into silence. It gave him a chance to observe her. Her skin and hair were as fair as the natives were dark but her height and strong build were a match for theirs. There was something about her that reminded Daeson of the farmer women on Kharltae, the ones that bore no nonsense and got the work done. She also reminded him of Jade with the way she'd filled the silence with her chatter when driving him to the Portal and so far she'd rarely lied. All of these things painted a positive picture of her.

Except she also reminded him of Nick when she'd immediately pulled out her gun. She'd kept it out of sight but it was a reminder of the world she'd come from. She'd spoken to him of escape—and he couldn't really blame her—but was she escaping her world or was she bringing it into this one? What possessed a person to join a stranger on a life-changing journey?

It stumped him, what could be going on in her mind. They hadn't a chance to talk before being discovered. There was no time for it now, they needed to be able to sit down and chat somewhere safe. It felt unnatural, to be dependent on her so quickly. He didn't like it.

He regretted sharing his truth-telling ability with her. Why had he done that? He barely remembered the conversation they'd had on the farm... had it been yesterday or earlier this morning? It felt both recent and stretched in time. Perhaps that was something else the Portal did; it stretched time. He remembered her offer to help him Wander instead of taking him back to Omerri. He remembered her talking about Wandering to the next world. Had it been his idea or hers? He certainly didn't remember agreeing to take her.

Synjan's eyes opened, her pupils contracting rapidly in the sudden wash of daylight. "I *think* that's where we're headed—these canoes seem like they've come from there—but there's another group of people on an island that way," Synjan said, pointing behind them. "It's farther away than the one we can see and there are a lot more people on it. Closer to two hundred or more squashed together." She gestured with her hands and Daeson thought it looked like she was moulding a clay vase.

"I think they want to take us to their home," Daeson said.

Synjan nodded and giggled, sparing him a wry look. "That's bad news for me."

"Why?"

"Daeson," she sighed melodramatically as she clapped a hand on his upper arm, "you might've thought your fear of heights was bad but you haven't seen *anything* yet. Wait 'til you see me on the water."

Her change in attitude surprised him. It felt like she was adopting a role. He'd seen and heard that change in people's voices when they were preparing to tell a joke. Daeson wasn't fond of jokes since they were lies told with the intention of being funny. He only forgave those who told good jokes, the kind that made him laugh enough to trump the unpleasantness in his belly.

"Why? What happens when you're on the water?" he asked, figuring it was easier just to play along with her riddle and get it out of the way.

"I get insufferably sick," she said and her hand fell away.

It wasn't the punch line he'd expected. He wondered why she'd spoken so strangely before telling him.

"You get sick," he repeated.

She laughed like *he'd* told the joke. "Yeah, and I'm sorry in advance but I'm going to vomit the whole way there."

"You get *sea*-sick," he said, realisation dawning.

"Very," she grinned. "I'm sure our teaspoon friend will be making fun of me, next," she mused, looking across the sand. Daeson followed her gaze to Tagan, helping to centre Daeson's backpack in a canoe.

"They've already decided we're going with them," he

said. "Have *we*?"

Synjan looked at the tree-line where nobody was visible and then they looked at one another.

"I don't think we have any other choice." Her words were a sour truth.

They were interrupted by Tagan, walking across the sand towards them, singing. When he drew near, he reached for Synjan's pack but she moved away. Tagan huffed and sang harshly. Daeson looked at the group of people huddled around the other canoe, watching and possibly waiting for Tagan to bring over Synjan's pack. Daeson thought they wanted to put the two backpacks together.

"Are you going into the same boat as your pack?" Daeson asked when Tagan stormed away. She'd taken it with her when she'd gone to the lagoon and had carried it herself across the bridge. Now she was actively refusing to part with it.

"Of course," she said, throwing him a peculiar look. He wondered why she believed her things were of such great importance that she would hold onto them stubbornly. Did she think the natives would take all of her cutlery?

He turned at the sound of activity and watched as the catamaran was pushed into the ocean, bouncing over each rolling wave. Two of the women leapt in and started paddling, the dead pig their only passenger.

"It looks like they want to get going," he said. Synjan grunted a positive note and Daeson left her to join the pair waiting for him. He took off his boots and socks and threw them into the canoe beside his pack before he helped to carry the canoe into the waves. He was urged to get in even though they were barely ankle deep. Not wanting to argue, Daeson climbed in and sat down, noticing the impressive progress of the catamaran ahead, already a distance away.

Daeson had to draw his knees up to his chest in

order to make enough room for both men to climb in. He could already tell this wasn't going to be a comfortable trip. There wasn't an extra oar for him so Daeson just watched the native paddling in front of him, the muscles in his bare back working as he swept the boat forward with each stroke. Behind Daeson was Tagan. The canoe had looked and felt sturdy on the beach but there was a distinctive sideways roll as each wave hit. Daeson's fingers clenched on the sides, seeing they were taking on a lot of water. Once they rowed past the shallows, the boat stabilised and he relaxed.

He wondered how Synjan was doing.

She was huddled in her canoe as well, most of the room taken up by the t-shirted native paddling at the back. These canoes could easily fit three people if there weren't packs the size of small children with them. Her face was turned up to the sky and he was close enough to see her exaggerated motions of deep breathing. He looked ahead for stormy skies and couldn't find where the dark clouds had moved to. The storm must have changed direction. They were lucky to have a peaceful ocean row.

The motion of his own canoe was slight but constant. He wondered if it would be enough for her to handle. To her credit, Synjan managed to contain her illness until they were about halfway, then she was hanging off the side, retching.

He felt guilty for not suggesting they travel together. He could've taken up one of the forward paddling positions on the boat, healing her when she needed it. Part of him doubted that she would've allowed herself to be separated from her bag in order to try it, but he hadn't given her the chance to consider it.

"Get closer. Closer." Daeson turned as much as he was able, looking over his shoulder at Tagan who was responsible for steering. He gestured with his hands, hoping the native would understand the signal. The ocean was gentle enough that the canoes could paddle fairly close to one another and he could reach across and Heal Synjan.

Tagan sang something fast and paddled them farther away from Synjan's boat, laughing and making sick sounds in mockery.

Daeson didn't like Tagan.

CHAPTER THREE

Convolution

YNJAN clambered out of the wobbling canoe with all the grace of a drunken toddler. The sun-heated rock she exited onto was rough and sharp enough to cut her but she lay down and pressed her cheek to it regardless. Land. Glorious, flat, unmoving land.

Someone gingerly lifted her hands and pulled the backpack off her body but all she managed to do to help them was open her eyes. She saw a gentle smile from Daeson's shirt buddy, the guy that had rowed her across a truly deceptive stretch of sea for the past... she squinted at her watch. It was still on Gredann time and completely useless in that sense but it told her how long the sail-of-torture had taken; two hours. She'd have sworn in front of an Authority firing squad that it had been twice that.

He crouched beside her belongings, peering worriedly at her. Gritting her teeth, she ignored the pinch of her aching muscles and sat up, smiling at the attentive native. "Thank you," she said, gesturing towards her bag.

Her guide had another agenda in mind. "Synjan?" he queried, his features arranged in such a hopeful way that it tugged at something vulnerable inside her.

"Yes," she agreed tiredly. "Synjan." She touched her chest at the same time.

"Bo," he sang, his voice as rich and deep as the ocean.

"Oh, shit. I am *never* going to be able to copy that," she muttered, knowing she'd have to try. "Bo?"

He beamed at her, signalling that her attempt at his name was adequate and Synjan was relieved. Her view was momentarily disrupted as a pair of long female legs walked deliberately between them, on their way to unloading some items that had been brought back. The legs belonged to the woman who'd met them.

"What's her name?" Synjan pointed at the woman's retreating back and then looked enquiringly at Bo, knowing he couldn't understand her words but needing to speak anyway.

"Paki," he supplied, proving he was on the same wavelength.

She and Daeson had been discovered by Tagan, Bo and Paki. It felt right to know their names first. She saw Daeson coming towards her.

"Daeson," she said, acknowledging his name for Bo and his presence for herself. "This is Bo," she introduced.

They exchanged greetings and then Daeson crouched near her as well, placing his hands on her shoulders. Instantly, pervasive warmth spread through her, radiating into her chest and then everywhere at once. Her inflamed skin cooled. Her roiling stomach settled and the bone-invading exhaustion from spending the last hour or so vomiting over the side of a rolling canoe was dispelled. She felt invigorated and sat up straighter, her eyes alight with the peculiar pleasure of being Healed.

"Thank you!" she cried and then winced as her fast movements twinged her overworked abdomen. Apparently, Healing couldn't fix muscle fatigue. "That journey looked short from the beach but it was torturous."

Daeson held out a plastic bottle towards her. "Have a drink," he advised.

She took it and drank two large swallows. "Thanks," she said, handing it back because he'd done the Healing and should be drinking as well. In a world so filled with salt water, fresh water might be a precious commodity. They probably shouldn't waste any. Synjan got to her feet and turned to surveil where they'd landed. "I wonder how they get water up *there*," she breathed and Daeson followed her gaze.

This was home, judging from the way the people moved confidently upon the broad shelf of rock that constituted its base. The rocky foundation curved around the foot of an enormous cliff that towered over them. The face was craggy, stretching so far above her that, when she looked up, Synjan thought it was many times the height of the tallest building she'd ever seen in Bardon City. Though that structure was legendary in their part of Trent, this monster cliff was probably just 'kind of high' in this world.

When she'd mapped earlier, she'd noted that the bridged islands they'd explored were like a giant exclamation mark. Oddly, the island their hosts inhabited was vastly smaller—more of a pillar than an island, really—and strongly resembled a flipped comma or apostrophe. She mentally dubbed the archipelago the 'Punctuation Islands'.

Currently, they stood on a platform of rock that hugged the long back of the comma. To her left, at the fatter end of the island, was an innovative pulley system designed to transport large objects to the top. Synjan marvelled as the huge boar they'd brought back was carried to the base of the bluff and placed in one of the small half-shell boats. The boat sat on a net that was stretched up and around it. The net was slotted over a giant hook which hung at the end of a vine-rope down the cliff face.

About halfway up, a jutting shelf in front of a shallow cave served as the mid-point and a heavy-looking wooden tripod had been erected there. As she watched, the netted boat holding the pig began to ascend the precipice at a quick pace, pulled by the sure hands of natives standing on the ledge above. A similar system was rigged from the top, as she could see another hook and rope dangling above the halfway point. She supposed this world wasn't sophisticated enough to build a device that could stretch the entire length from clifftop to base. She wondered how they'd even managed to design *this* pulley system.

A scraping noise to the right drew her attention. Synjan turned and saw that the canoes they'd rowed from the Exclamation Islands had all been divested of their bounty. They were being stowed at the end of the rocky ledge upon which she stood. She guessed the tide must bring the water high enough to need the boats moored because they were being tied to hooks that jutted out of the cliff.

Beyond the modest marina, she saw with her eyes what her mind had stumbled over when she'd mapped for Daeson—a truth she'd spared him because she hadn't wanted to frighten him. The reality was no reassurance. People were *climbing* the towering escarpment using just their hands and feet. There was no vine bridge or ladder here; the primary way the natives got up to their home atop the rock face was to scale it. She could even see children climbing, though the smaller ones had some sort of vine wrapped around them for support or safety, and a parent climbing alongside.

Synjan glanced at Daeson and saw he'd followed her gaze. The tightness in his jawline declared his feelings. There was no way he was going to climb up like the locals did. Could *she* even make it? What alternatives were available? The shelf of rock that served as a natural jetty was broad enough to hold twenty people but featureless and uncomfortable. They couldn't camp here. Besides, the moored boats told her that the tide was low now but the rock would eventually be awash with water. Going elsewhere wasn't an option, she couldn't face another two hours of rowing—and that was to the island that was closest. Ellis' voice echoed through her memory: *Choice is necessity cloaked by the illusion of desire.*

Except she couldn't see anything desirable. Their future in this place was uncertain.

In her estimation, there were a hundred people living here as one group and the rocky pillar they were climbing wasn't particularly large. They were no doubt used to it but she was flummoxed by the notion of such a perilous climb completed on a regular basis in order to reach what had to be cramped conditions. It didn't make much sense when there was a lush and spacious island close by. What was so special about it that they cried over its trees and didn't live there? It would be a damned sight easier than living *here*!

While Daeson glared at the rocky wall dotted with climbers, Synjan realised Bo had sent her backpack over to the base of the pulley rope and it was being arranged alongside Daeson's in a half boat. It was clear their belongings would go up next. Should she allow their gear to go to the top of this massive cliff? How in the name of all the Gods would they get up there after it?

"There are stairs there!" Daeson exclaimed, sounding excited.

Synjan looked at where he was pointing and she was surprised to see a rough set of steps carved into the base of the cliff. They immediately curved behind a wall of rock so she couldn't tell where they led. Daeson set off for them and she took a step to follow when a hand on her forearm detained her. Synjan frowned up at Bo, unsure why he'd stopped her but not compelled to break out of his hold when he sang a short, harsh word. She looked back at Daeson and two other natives were also singing sharply at him, trying to stop him from going up the stairs. He shook their grasping hands off and strode determinedly up the stone steps, ignoring the loud, worried men that followed him.

Within a minute, he came back down, fuming.

"The stairs don't go anywhere. What's the point of stairs that don't go anywhere?" he complained as he stalked back to Synjan. Her heart sank and she forgave him his thunderous expression. She'd had a very difficult time getting him across that bridge. This cliff was bound to be his nightmare.

She had another solution for him. "Do you think you'd be alright to go up in that boat and net thing? Could you close your eyes and hang on?"

Daeson watched the boat with their bags being pulled up and then dragged onto the halfway shelf. "I could do that."

Synjan took his hand and walked over with him. Bo followed silently.

"Daeson's next," Synjan announced to no-one in particular, knowing they wouldn't understand her but needing to get their attention.

Oblivious to the dirt and spots of congealed blood on the bottom of the small boat, Daeson side-stepped the net holders and into the land-stricken watercraft. He crossed his legs and wedged himself in, making it clear he wasn't going anywhere but up. He made the vessel look especially small.

A chorus of surprised singing, confused looks and the same word—"Bin!"—met his bold move. They didn't seem angry so much as surprised and they didn't evict Daeson while they sang at one another in an effort to figure out what was going on.

Synjan turned to Bo. "Please! Tell them how nervous heights make him!" she appealed. She didn't know how to make Bo understand that the only way Daeson was getting up the cliff was being pulled up in this boat but she did her best with hand gestures and sad expressions anyway.

Bo's deep voice cut through the excited melodies of the other workers, commanding their attention immediately. There was a brief exchange but then it seemed their guide had become their ally and his singing convinced the winchers to go ahead and haul Daeson up. They started working to put the net up around her broad-shouldered Wandering partner, squashing him even more as the vine mesh was secured on the hook and most of his head room disappeared.

"Will you take the next one?" he asked, peering through gaps in the net in order to maintain eye contact. Synjan knew the journey up the cliff would still be tough for him but she also knew it was a necessity.

"I think I can climb, I'll be fine," she demurred, wanting to reassure him.

He gave her a dubious look. "Are you sure?" he asked firmly. It felt like the most serious question she'd ever been asked and appreciation for his concern welled up inside her chest. The last thing he needed to worry about was how she'd get to the top.

"I don't want to push our friendship with these people. If we're too much trouble, they might not let us stay with them. Don't worry, I'll be careful," she promised.

When the net started lifting with Daeson in it, she smiled at him before turning to Bo. "Thank you again." She gave his hand a squeeze.

He looked down at where their hands were connected. Synjan couldn't read his expression but thought perhaps the contact too much so she hastily let go. When she met his gaze, he was smiling, his dark eyes dancing. He made the now-familiar grabbing motion that told her he wanted her to follow, so she did.

Bo led her away from the cargo lifting area, past the boats to where it seemed everyone started their climb up the cliff. She looked up and up, leaning back in an attempt to take the whole height in. It was impossible, though she could see enough to reassure herself that it was not sheer. Here and there, tufts of grass or small, tenacious trees took hold in larger nooks. The rock in front of her had scuff marks from countless hands and feet on the little outcroppings near her head. She touched it tentatively; the warm and gritty cliff was made of lots of tiny brown-black rocks all melted together. Up close Synjan could see clear flecks of red and amber, cloudy chunks of beige and green and glassy streaks of shiny black. The cliff was as harsh and beautiful as the world they'd landed in.

Bo wrapped a vine around her body and showed her how to loop it under her armpits. She was to wear it like a lasso, leaving her arms free but hanging in front of her. She thought it might hinder her climb. She played with the vine when Bo gestured for her to test it out, finding—much to her surprise—that the tough, rope-like harness was slightly elasticised. When she leant back it stretched, indicating that if she fell and had to rely on this item to save her, it would catch and bounce with her until she could reclaim her grip on the cliff. Slightly reassuring.

Synjan glanced up at Daeson who was already floating up the second half of the rock face. She winced at the way his transport was being twisted and swung by the winds whipping around the upper reaches of the island. She would be nudged by them as well, but she'd have much less reliable equipment to keep her on track. The clouds that had moved overhead and the rising humidity also boded ill.

She took a deep breath and shook out her hands,

kicking her legs as well. It was a good thing Daeson had Healed her, she might not have been able to tackle the climb otherwise.

Bo was an invaluable guide. He climbed parallel to her, pointing at places for her hands to grip and nudging her feet onto jutting ledges that could support her boots. She understood very quickly why the indigenous people wore grass shields on their chests—it was nothing to do with modesty and everything to do with protection while climbing. Within ten minutes, her decorative blouse ripped open, buttons popping off when she lifted her body weight over the sharp obstacles of the cliff face. Her bra was repeatedly scuffed by the rock and her chest was scratched, her skin weeping streaks of blood that she couldn't afford to worry about as the distance between her and the ground below grew. Not for the first time, she wished her breasts were smaller; they hindered her progress enormously.

Hold after hold, Bo patiently clung to the rock beside her, guiding and singing. She envied his bare feet, feeling her boots clunky and inhibitive. Of course, they were also very protective and her hands—callused and fight-worn as they were—would have benefitted from some sort of covering as well. The cuts stung but weren't important; she wiped the blood onto the seat of her shorts when it started to drip. After a while, Bo changed her lasso vine for her, careful to replace the new one before taking the other one away. She didn't see where it went; her gaze only ever drifted up or sideways, always seeking an appropriate grip. Her years of training put her in good stead to maintain the focus necessary to scale a giant, rugged beast like this cliff. She was also glad that she was small and limber, able to support her body weight with her hands. She could only imagine the strain Bo experienced, being so much larger and heavier, though it was probably relative. His muscles were large for a reason.

Even though she began the climb with all the focus and enthusiasm she could muster, determination alone was not enough to get her to the top. The ache in her shoulders came first, the burn of lactic acid and exhaustion causing a tremble down her arms that was difficult to counteract. Sweat dripped into her eyes constantly, stinging and blurring her vision at the least opportune times and her legs shook from the repeated motion of rising up, finding footing and pushing her into a new place to search for hand holds. She didn't have the reach Bo expected her to so she frequently pulled herself up with a weak grip that caused her joints to cry out. At one point, rain swept over them all but it was only there long enough to saturate her clothes and make the cliff slippery; the temporary coolness evaporated quickly in the heat of exertion.

She began to lag. Her breathing was ragged and sounded extra loud as she found a place where she could stand with both feet together and her hands in front of her. She paused, closing her eyes and pressing against the rock.

"I just... need a minute... to catch... my breath," she puffed, afraid to look in any direction. She guessed she was about two-thirds of the way up but couldn't confirm it. If she looked down, she might fall and if she looked up, she'd see how much of this punishing climb was still ahead of her. Neither option appealed.

To her surprise, Bo climbed past her.

Her eyes sprang open and she shouted an apology at him but it was snatched by the wind. Adrenaline shot through her, spurring her forward in an effort to not be left alone on the inhospitable cliff face but he was well experienced and soon pulled far ahead of her. Dismay nipped at her heightened emotions, summoning tears she was glad he wouldn't see and she told herself how silly she was being. She'd got the hang of climbing by now. She knew how to look for holds within her reach and pull herself up or select places for her feet to push off from. She didn't need him.

A short while later, just as she was looking for another spot to rest, the reason for Bo's departure became apparent. The vine rope around her tightened slowly but persistently, forcing her to hook her arms over it or have it wrenched off.

He'd climbed away from her in order to pull her up.

A rush of relief and gratitude brought a fresh wave of tears as she grabbed hold of the vine with both hands. The trip was jerky and she banged into the cliff a couple of times but her ascent was swift and wonderful. She quickly learned to brace herself with her feet and walk up the rock, grinning at Bo as he peered down to be sure she rose safely.

At the top, she again found herself flopping gracelessly onto an unknown surface but this time she was helped by many hands. Laughing, she rolled onto her back and then sat up as another familiar face grinned at her—Tagan. He pulled the lasso vine off her.

"Thank you!" she told Bo, reaching out a shaky hand to grasp his steely forearm. Bo shared a warm smile then startled her when he sang something sharp at Tagan. The fairer native's fingers had disposed of the vine and begun curiously exploring the texture of her gaping shirt and bra.

Synjan stepped out of his reach as he sang back at Bo indignantly. She looked around herself instead of getting involved, trying to settle her harried nerves. The island was as compact as she'd expected from below. It seemed exceptionally crowded at the skinny end of it, with many people gathering around—most of whom seemed to be strong men Bo had enlisted to help pull her up. An irrational vision of being pushed off the edge persisted, despite telling herself she was just suffering from the climb.

She saw numerous tree stumps driven into the ground a respectable distance from the edge. They looked the same as the columns that had supported the bridge. The ones to her left had the safety vine ropes tied around them, though they only spanned a part of the width of the climbing area. With chagrin, she realised that the section with the vines was for children to learn on. And newcomers, apparently.

The stumps on her right continued in a longer line, stretching along the length of the inside curve of the comma. They were all looped with thick vine ropes, too. She had no idea what they were for but she was distracted from them when she spied Daeson, surrounded by a small group of children. They were singing eagerly as he grinned at them. Adults were gathering around him as well so she circled Bo and Tagan (still singing crankily at each other) to get to her Wandering partner. Daeson's admirers noticed her approaching before he did and parted for her before encircling them both.

A few were pawing at him and she smirked when he slapped their hands away.

"Don't touch me there, that's not right! You stop it too, go away."

His rejection became the cue for his fans to get handsy with her instead. "Hey!" she announced as someone stroked her bottom and another person patted a breast. She did her best to pull the sagging edges of her blouse back together and elbowed away new attempts to touch her. She was afraid to get too aggressive in case she hurt someone and they were forced to leave.

"How was the boat ride?" she asked Daeson, attempting to maintain a normal conversation while the throng intensified.

"It was better than I expected. How was your climb?" he asked, slapping someone's hand before it could reach his hair.

"It took me an hour and a hagfish, but I made it, thanks to Bo," she laughed. From Daeson's expression, she gathered that he hadn't spent enough time in Dockside to have heard the phrase and her wide grin became sombre. "It took a long time," she translated, checking her watch again. When she calculated that she'd climbed for ninety minutes, she understood why her body was quivering with fatigue. How long would it have taken if Bo hadn't intervened?

"Is that blood?" Daeson asked, looking at her chest.

"Um, yeah, just a few scratches," she dismissed, feeling her stomach flip beneath his gaze. He nodded and looked away and she couldn't decide if she was pleased or disappointed that he hadn't offered to heal the meagre wounds.

A woman nearby sang something loud and attention-getting. When she repeated her call, everyone fell silent. Once she was sure everyone was watching, she made the 'come' gesture at Daeson and Synjan and sang at them. With some murmured melodies of response, the crowd moved towards the larger end of the island. Synjan and Daeson were swept along with them.

The area at the top was not generous but it was flat and easily negotiated as it opened out before them. Near the cliff where she'd climbed up, the ground was worn down to dirt but as they moved along, grasses swayed, tickling Synjan's calves. Just beyond where the line of posted anchors to her right stopped, a grove of four large and unusual trees stood on her left, drawing Synjan's gaze.

The trunks and boughs were distinctly hand-like, with the main trunk as the wrist breaking off into five or six thick boughs—the fingers—that supported lanky, drooping vines. The trees were reminiscent of willows except without leaves; they possessed bunches of green vines instead, and the straggly bits of green string sprouting along their lengths made them look hairy.

Daeson looked as fascinated as she felt; he moved against the current of the crowd towards the little forest, reaching out to touch a low vine when he got close enough. He pulled on it and discovered what Synjan had at the start of her climb—the plant flexed and stretched, even when still attached to the branch it was growing from. When he let go, it bounced back with a swish that prompted delighted laughs from the children.

Synjan was dismayed to see that their bags had been tied up in the fourth tree. There were other things hanging with their backpacks but her gear was all she was really worried about. What would these people do if they went into her gear and found one of her guns and her knife? She turned her alarmed gaze to Daeson.

"They've hung our bags up in a tree?" she queried. He'd been upon the plateau longer than she had; perhaps the residents had asked his permission to string them up.

"Maybe there are predators around that would get into them." His tone was dismissive.

"Maybe but... do you think we're allowed to get our stuff? Like, we can pull it down if we want it?"

He cast a wary eye at her. "It's a single rope looped over a branch that we can untie from the ground."

"So it should be easy to get to when we need it," she nodded, trying to reassure herself that if no-one had gone into the bags already, they were unlikely to do so in future.

"I'm sure it will be." Daeson's words were clipped and she got the impression he was not interested in pursuing the discussion any longer.

Synjan couldn't understand why he was getting uptight. His attitude towards his belongings was different to hers but she expected that, considering he wasn't carrying live ammunition and weapons in *his* pack. Still, he seemed irrationally angry.

They were ushered away from the quartet of vine trees by smiling faces, nodding heads and curling hands. One set belonged to a teenaged girl who, Synjan was astonished to see, was wearing purple shorts. Where had she got *them*? The girl was lost in the crowd of the island dwellers swarming around them before Synjan was able to attempt a question.

As they walked, it began to rain again but it wasn't like the rain she was used to. Back in Gredann, when it rained it tended to settle in for hours and fall heavily. It was always cold and uncomfortable to get caught in. People scurried to find shelter and did their best to stay out of it until it passed but here, no-one seemed bothered by it. In fact, Synjan wasn't entirely sure it *was* rain, it seemed more like consolidated mist cloaking everyone simultaneously. Perhaps it was just a cloud passing through, coating everyone in vapour before it continued on. She marvelled as the bare, brown skins around her glistened with dewy drops. The usual, unpleasant humidity returned as soon the rain cleared up.

It didn't take long to reach their destination. Everyone was travelling towards a white circular pit that filled the broader end of the island. The natives fanned out around the pit, sitting in groups on woven grass mats or on the edge of it, with their legs comfortably resting on the white dirt below.

The gradual departure of the mass of people gave Synjan a better chance to look around. There wasn't much to see. The space between the four trees and this communal area had been covered with grass but this dug-out pit was obviously the area that saw the greatest amount of traffic because it was all dirt. She had no idea where everyone slept but the aged fire pit in the centre of this space implied it was where everyone ate and socialised.

Synjan, Daeson and their guide walked around the pit after the rest of the people were seated. The first thing they passed was a handmade water tank. It was a knee-high wooden fence arranged in a rough circle with a canvas sheet as its base. Looking into the clear water, she could see the straight, white edges of fabric overlapping on the bottom; it appeared to be *two* bits of material. Their straight edges proclaimed that they weren't custom made for this purpose. In some places, the fabric hung over the edge towards the ground, flapped gently in the occasional breeze.

The pool or tank was deliberately built to hold water on this barren pillar but it presented yet another question. How could barely-clothed people manage to create a waterproof liner when there was clearly no mechanical way they could produce such an object? There weren't even any plants around that could be harvested and sewn into such a thing! The sophistication of the pulley and the water storage was completely at odds with the rudimental presentation of the people around her.

Beyond the water tank, a gnarled slab of rock was layered around a large part of the outside curve of the island, eliminating more living space. It was crevassed and pocketed, shadows beneath overhanging lintels hinting at little niches within. She didn't get a chance to look closely at it as they were herded to the end of the rock, where a simple wooden frame stood. The ground within was covered with woven grass mats whose deep green colour declared them to be freshly made. A clay water container and some cups sat to the side. The roof of the frame was made of woven grass and decorated with three hard, reflective discs that hung along the front like talismans. As they approached, the discs spun and flashed in the sun.

Their guide placed two grass mats on the ground in front of the hut and indicated that Synjan and Daeson should sit, singing a pretty tune as she gestured. As the Wanderers complied, two people moved to stand in front of the lean-to. One was a man, one a woman, both with greying hair, minimalistic clothing and wrinkles on their smiling faces.

They sang something at the crowd that raised a melodic cheer, then sang at Synjan and Daeson. Three children jumped to their feet and ran off in different directions, drawing Synjan's attention momentarily. The man and woman then sang together, their body posture straight and tall with their chins held up, making complicated gestures with their hands before they sat down as well. Synjan felt like she'd just witnessed a welcome or declaration speech of some sort, acknowledging she and Daeson as visitors to their home.

Two of the children returned with long woven trays of fruit. Both of the official welcomers stood, making a show of presenting the contents to them.

"We're going to run out of things to give away," Daeson told her quietly, in amongst their nods of acknowledgement and thanks.

She laughed her agreement and examined the offering in her lap as the natives—the leaders of the group?—sat again and looked contentedly at them. There were five different kinds of fruit, each of them a unique shape, colour and texture. She picked up a small green one with a furry skin and began peeling it, wanting to show her hosts that she was pleased with their offering—plus she was starving. Daeson picked up the same furry fruit and bit straight into it.

Synjan's eyebrows lifted as she watched him. He was doing his best to remain stoic but it was obvious that eating the furry fruit wasn't a pleasant experience. She giggled when he looked at her. He said nothing but did peel the fruit before taking another bite.

The officials remained quiet while they ate but when

the other child came walking back a moment later, they looked more animated. The boy wasn't alone. A grizzled woman, as brown and wrinkled as a raisin, hobbled after him. She was bent forward at an awkward angle but walked unsupported. She was definitely the eldest person Synjan had ever seen and she found it hard to drag her gaze off the ancient little woman.

A fifth grass mat was placed between the visitors and the welcomers and the old woman sat in amongst a flurry of cracking bones and wheezing grunts. She peered out at them from the depths of her crinkled face, her eyes so dark they were almost black. She grinned, her few remaining teeth winking at them as she said, "Hello."

Synjan almost leapt off her mat with excitement, exchanging an energised look with Daeson before they returned the greeting.

Unfortunately, all they got in return was another, "Hello!" It sounded almost as eager as they had, but it showed a greeting learned by rote rather than true understanding.

"I don't think she speaks *that* much Authoritan," Synjan sighed and Daeson hummed his agreement. Still, the old woman was not as ignorant as they were supposing.

"Good come Mukake," she declared, her voice maintaining a spoken rhythm rather than a sung one.

"Thank you," Daeson replied.

"Mukake?" Synjan queried, gesturing at the crowd of people nearby.

A toothless smile. "Mukake," she said many times, pointing at a different person each time. She pointed at Synjan after the fourth 'Mukake' and said, "Wandruh." She then pointed at Daeson and again said, "Wandruh."

"They know we're Wanderers!" Synjan exclaimed.

"It seems so," Daeson declared, sounding stupefied by the notion.

"I thought I saw shorts on that girl! And the pulley and the canvas in that water tank! They've had Wanderers here before."

"That's where that shop bag came from," Daeson said.

Synjan looked back at the old woman. "Synjan," she said clearly, tapping her chest. "Daeson," she introduced, touching his arm before she pointed at the woman and made an enquiring face.

"Hiyani," came the answer and this time it was sung. Each syllable seemed to have its own progression of pretty notes that blended together into a truly lovely melody.

"Hiyani," Synjan attempted, her voice inaccurately pitched and flat.

"Bin, bin. Hiyani," came the careful correction.

Again, Synjan tried to match the notes she could hear but even she could tell that what came out of her mouth was nothing like the lovely name she was hearing. After repeating the process three times, Synjan was heavily discouraged.

"I think 'bin' means 'no'," she told Daeson, wishing to take some sort of learning experience away from this exchange.

"I think so too," he agreed before he perfectly sang the old woman's name to her.

Synjan's lower lip protruded but she wasn't about to bother trying to get the woman's name right again.

Hiyani showed her gums once more in a grin before she said their names to them. Next, she pointed at the grey-haired man and woman sitting quietly in the shade structure. "Shinu. Shinu," she announced.

Daeson mimicked the names perfectly, nodding at the people in question. Hiyani smiled her approval. "They both have the same name," he said slowly, obviously working through a thought.

"I don't think it's their name. I think it's a word that

means leader or boss," Synjan hazarded.

"Yes, that makes sense," Daeson agreed. He seemed pleased to have his confusion cleared up by such a tidy theory.

"So if we've been welcomed by the bosses, they must not mind us staying with them?" Synjan guessed, looking at Daeson.

While their conversation was going on in Authoritan, Hiyani started speaking with the Shinu. Their singing was pleasant but when Hiyani rose (with surprising ease) to her feet and took a step away, the tone of the conversation changed.

Hiyani didn't walk away immediately, she paused to sing something quite snappy back. Both Shinu objected but Hiyani sang, 'bin' to each of them. She stalked away, leaving Synjan and Daeson with the two Shinu and the tribe behind them sing-whispering to one another. It sounded like a musical theatre warm-up.

The Shinu looked at each other, a whole different conversation silently communicated in the harsh lines of their mouths and the flush of their cheeks. Synjan exchanged a glance with Daeson, wondering what in the worlds had just gone wrong and, most of all, how it was going to affect their stay with the Mukake people.

Synjan and Daeson were invited to share the shade of their leadership structure. Grateful for the shade, they sat shoulder to shoulder on one side while the Shinu did the same on the other. As the minutes rolled by, they tried to communicate but it was an ongoing struggle. Synjan realised that the leaders weren't committed to learning any of their Authoritan words, yet they expected the Wanderers to learn their language. Synjan didn't approve of the leaders expecting others to make the effort but she was hardly in a position to debate the relative merits and drawbacks of a flawed leadership position with them. It was an unwelcome reminder of Ellis.

Daeson was able to conform to their expectations. He sang so well that Synjan often found herself just staring at him, at his throat, at his beautiful lips, trying to fathom how he could make the lovely sounds he could. At least once, something in his voice vibrated through her until tears sprang to her eyes; other times he sounded so joyful she wished she could listen to him all afternoon.

His success only made it more obvious that it was going to be a long and difficult stay for her. She stumbled across notes every now and then that would cause Daeson's deep blue eyes to light up with approval but whenever she tried to repeat it, she couldn't. She told herself that she had many other skills and talents that were life-saving and important but she couldn't think of anything more essential for survival in their current situation than communicating. It was a deflating realisation.

Not long after they'd made the move into the Shinu's dwelling, a woman and her daughter—who looked to be about seven or eight—brought food to the Shinu. They also carried a woven grass platter boasting a collection of berries, a mound of salted meat, a large strip of steaming grilled fish, some flat bread-like strips and some fragrant yellow beans, which they offered to Synjan and Daeson.

They thanked the woman profusely and exchanged names—she was Kahu and her daughter's name was Malahu. It was only when Kahu gestured after Synjan's wellbeing that she realised the native woman had been the one rowing with Paki in the unusual, double-hulled vessel. Synjan thanked her again and assured her as best she could that she'd recovered from her ordeal.

Others came and introduced themselves in a steady stream after that, though most didn't bring more food. The exchanges were always lively between the Mukake and Daeson and a little more strained with Synjan.

Despite her inability to communicate with ease, she felt comfortable on the island. Enough that she didn't think they'd need to leave until they got their bearings properly.

After yet another family came to the Shinu's leadership space to meet with the Wanderers and left with smiles and visible excitement on their faces, Synjan felt confident. "It looks like we're welcome here," she stated, encouraged by the endless procession of positive interactions.

"For now," Daeson agreed.

CHAPTER FOUR

Bitter Realisations

FINGER trails of colour blazed through the sky as the sun set over the water. Daeson had never seen pinks and oranges and purples so vivid. They looked artificial. The sky could've featured in one of the many paintings Omerri had displayed in her house, the ones that had been too valuable for the penthouse. When he'd been shown around, he recalled marvelling at the expensive furniture and admiring the paintings featured on the walls. The house was her facade, a respectable place for her more important guests to visit when they wanted to meet with her, so they wouldn't have to approach the brothel. Daeson realised everything about Omerri was like that; a different face for different people. He'd seen only what she'd allowed him to see.

The thought came with another nipping at its heels; he'd been a willing participant, blind to her true nature, accepting her practised smiles and warm compliments, receptive to her lingering touches and soft kisses.

Thinking of her brought a mixture of emotions to the surface; he could feel them tightening his throat, choking him with a surplus of guilt, anger and loss that he hadn't dealt with. Her memory blurred his vision, pressing heavily on his temples and inside his chest. He looked upward as he walked, thinking it wrong that he should associate a new sky with Omerri, worse to consider that every time he looked up at dusk, he would recall her house, her face, her smell. He dallied so he could admire the colours a little longer, wanting to force a new association upon it... one that would smell of the ocean and remind him of welcoming people. It was no good. Dusk belonged to her now, its magical light and fading colour somehow poetic in its portrayal.

Ahead of him, Synjan walked with the Mukake woman named Kahu and her small daughter. He supposed she was leading them to their sleeping quarters. He hadn't seen any huts so wondered where the natives slept. Had they made burrows? They had pulleys to bring large things up the cliff... what clever structure had they made for shelter?

He was concerned when they neared the edge of the cliff but his heart didn't sink until they stopped. Nearby were thick posts dug into the ground at strange angles, looking like a broken jaw with haggard teeth. A number of ropes were tethered around them. Daeson could see that a few cords were in use while others lay available with a lasso at the end. He understood without being told what was expected.

"No," he protested, stepping backwards. He hadn't yet neared the edge and wasn't intending to. "I'm not doing this again."

Synjan turned and offered him a sympathetic look. The woman with them indicated for him to take a harness and Daeson shook his head again. He remembered the word for no.

"Bin, bin," he sang to Kahu. She tilted her head in confusion and he hated her for it. He hated her not-so-simple request that he should climb over the cliff's edge. He hated this difficult world and he hated Synjan for talking him into coming here. He hated the Portal for being so far away, taunting him with an impossible escape. He hated himself for running away. Again. Oh, his hatred was unreasonable, he knew it in his head and even a little bit in his heart, but it didn't matter. He hated everyone and everything here.

He needed time alone. Daeson faced Synjan and did his best to control his tone, though he still sounded terse to his own ears. "We'll meet up again in the morning."

When he walked away, he heard Synjan bid him goodnight to his back. He threw her the return over his shoulder but didn't stop. She'd seen him at his most vulnerable and it was humiliating to constantly face his fear. Her seasickness wasn't a match to his inability to look down from a height. She couldn't help her nausea; it was a physical reaction. Being scared of heights was… absurd.

Half a dozen people were assembled at the strange-looking large trees. He angled in their direction. As he drew nearer, he realised that they were all elders except for a heavily pregnant woman. Daeson presumed they were no longer able to scramble up and down the mountainside. He watched as they helped each other into a different variation of the climbing harnesses that Daeson had seen so far—their ones looked to be more supportive. Instead of a lasso, it was a kind of saddle that they sat in, with holes for their legs. The vines were secured in such a way that they didn't need to hold on.

The elders—who were already harnessed—scampered up the trees. Daeson gaped at their skill, more accomplished than his own. He watched as the climbers crawled onto the boughs and secured their stretchy ropes before lowering themselves, hanging among the branches. They ended up hanging in mid-air, reminding Daeson strongly of bats. They weren't upside down but the resemblance was too close for him to dismiss.

As Daeson watched them arrange themselves for sleep, Hiyani approached and took his hand. She sang a few soft words and gestured for him to take a harness and climb up. Her face was compassionate, her expression much like Synjan's at the cliff-side. Daeson was kind but firm when he said 'bin' to her and pulled away. He wasn't afraid of being up a tree but didn't think he could sleep like that.

He wondered where the very young children slept, the ones who couldn't climb by themselves. He'd noticed some babies and toddlers strapped on their mothers' backs. Older children scurried up and down the cliff, some with cords around their middles, some without. There had to be a place for the children too small to climb... unless that was how it worked here. One day a child would be attached to their mother, the next they'd be tied up with a stretchy vine and made to climb the cliff themselves. So it must only be him and the elders up here.

No, he'd seen goats throughout the day, cavorting on the rocks. Surely they would have shelter and not be hoisted up a tree? He looked around for them but couldn't see them anywhere. The colours of the sky had rapidly darkened into blended hues of blue. Night was taking over and he had nowhere to sleep. He wished he'd thought to set up his tent. It had been years since he'd last done so. All he remembered of the experience was that it had been difficult to set up in the dark.

A bleat caught his attention. Daeson followed the sound to the opposite end of the pillar, to a natural rock shelter that housed four goats. There was a long, low overhang that protected them from the elements. He curled up as best he could, pushing against goats too stubborn to move out of his way. They huddled together, exchanging warmth.

It was more comforting than he'd expected, to curl up with goats. He was reminded of the farm. If he hadn't been distracted by the Wanderer Portal, he would've reached Stonehearth and sold his land for a good amount of coin. What would he have done with himself afterwards? Two years had passed since he'd left his home world but it felt like a great deal more. It had taken on the quality of unreality, something that he'd heard about, not lived through. His memories were vivid, though more of his father and the farm than any part of the world itself. He hadn't seen much beyond the village of Cloverlea and regretted being unable to. Now he would never know what secrets Kharltae had to offer.

He didn't know that much about Trent either, beyond the city of Gredann. Omerri had travelled to different cities but hadn't taken him, touting that he wouldn't be safe. He'd been penned at the Queen of Hearts, only sometimes allowed to visit the local parks, shops or taken on a drive to the lookout where she'd first shown him the ocean. She'd been at his side each time and his whole world had become her.

An ache of inconceivable depth lodged itself in his chest. How could he miss her so intensely? He thought her betrayal would nullify his love but here he was, pining for her company and wanting to be in her bed. It was foolish, to wish for something he knew he shouldn't want. His arms ached to hold her, to rest his head on a pillow and have his nose tickled by her hair. It had annoyed him so much, that she would sweep her hair into his face when he was trying to get to sleep... now he wanted to be annoyed by it again. If he'd known that the last time she'd flicked her hair onto his face would be the last time she would ever do it, he wouldn't have been so irritated. He would have cherished the smell of her shampoo and the wispy strands of her long black hair stroking his cheek.

Daeson uttered a strange sound that fell between a cough and a sob and he did his best to squash the rest down. The most he could suppress was the noise, not the tears themselves. He swiped at his eyes and a goat bleated at him.

He would *not* mourn the loss of a tainted relationship. He would *not* think of Omerri when all it brought was pain. He *would* go to sleep and face the day fresh and new.

Daeson closed his eyes and took in a deep breath, blowing it out slowly as he focussed on relaxing himself. Today had been gruelling and now he would rest. This world would test him, he knew, and sleep would be his only escape from it, for now.

CHAPTER FIVE

Rocks And Hard Places

WATCHING Daeson walk away shrouded Synjan in despair. She wanted to call him back or follow him but neither option seemed appropriate. He was temperamental and the time apart would probably do them both good. Besides, she hadn't a clue what she could say to make him feel better.

Synjan was extremely frustrated as well. They'd been expected to greet everyone and hadn't been allowed away from the Shinu all day, except to visit the toilet area. She and Daeson hadn't had a chance to debrief, discuss their predicament, plan or even get used to where they were staying.

She wasn't keen but felt obligated to give the Mukake's way of living a go. There were ninety-three of them living in this space—she'd counted patterns while bored with the Shinu—and their traditions seemed entrenched. Bad ideas couldn't withstand consistent testing after all this time and survive, surely?

Synjan was helped into a seat-like harness made of the same material as the lasso she'd worn. It was like a large pair of soft, stretchy grass pants, with holes for her legs to go through and a top that reached almost to her waist. Four small loops protruded at the front and back. The panel at the front was thinner than the back; she was reminded of the carnival that had come to Gredann annually. There'd been a ride there with wooden seats attached to chain harnesses and safety straps that hooked around her waist and between her legs. When the machine had started, the seats had swung around in a wide arc that had made her feel like she was flying.

Looking at the emptiness ahead of her, Synjan was about to experience the same sensation. At least she'd solved the dilemma of how the whole group slept on the pillar every night; they didn't. They slept on the side of it, in the lee of the comma's curl, where the 'tail' provided some protection from the elements. The three of them stood amongst the crooked anchor posts, preparing to descend.

While Kahu sang incomprehensible instructions and helped Synjan get into her grass seat, her daughter stepped into her own smaller harness and sat down on the edge of the cliff. Synjan's face must have given away her worry because Kahu turned to see Malahu in that position and sang firmly at her. A whiny reply came that had Kahu huffing and singing back loudly. She grabbed Synjan's hand and walked her to the cliff's lip. Kahu picked up a vine and dropped it over her daughter's head and then did the same to Synjan.

It was difficult to keep the saddle in place and get the lasso under her armpits at the same time. Once she managed, Kahu guided Synjan to sit on the edge of the cliff. She pointed downward at something but that was the moment Malahu chose to flip over and wriggle her way backwards. Kahu yelled at her but the cheeky brat laughed and sang back in a taunting manner that had her mother reacting instantly; she rolled over and started climbing down, too. Kahu was wearing a seat harness but climbed without a lasso.

Synjan's heart accelerated. She wasn't sure what to

do. She'd been getting her bearings when she was called upon to act. She had to move!

Mimicking her guide's actions, Synjan turned and supported herself on flat hands. Needing a foothold to aim for, she glanced down. Below her, a confusing amount of tree trunks (or possibly they were beams cut from wood, she couldn't tell) projected from the cliff face as far as she could see, lining the curved wall. She got an impression of spear-headed shapes and people dangling but had no time for making sense of it—the light was fading fast and it was shadowy already.

Synjan had no idea what the wooden planks wedged into the cliff were all about or where Kahu was headed (besides after her daughter) but she couldn't ask questions. Her knuckles white, she found a foothold more quickly than expected. As she found another and lowered herself down, following the route Kahu took, she passed a variegated line of footholds—different widths, depths, heights and spacings—indicating her first step hadn't been luck. This part of the cliff had been modified to make it easier to get over the edge, possibly because people might be very tired by the time they were stumbling off to bed and they needed a bit of extra assistance getting there.

Kahu caught up to her daughter quickly. The slap the child received echoed in the concave space, swiftly followed by crying. Synjan wasn't able to focus on them properly as she was too busy descending the cliff. It was a slow, careful job being executed by an inexperienced climber in diminishing light; she didn't dare look around.

Once Malahu was chastised, Kahu gave her attention to Synjan and guided her to their destination about ten metres from the top of the cliff. Synjan swung down and under one of three wooden beams embedded in the rock—they were spaced evenly apart and level with one another. There was a lower trio, the two side beams were different from the top because they were angled towards the central one and tied with vine where they connected. Synjan considered it as a roost for people to sleep in. It was very open.

Using Malahu as an example, Kahu showed Synjan that there were more of the stretchy vines tied around the higher beams, all of them ending in little carved hooks. She selected vines for Malahu and herself, then encouraged Synjan to climb up and attach herself as well. Awkwardly—and stupidly—Synjan used the vine wound around her body to pull herself up instead of climbing on the cliff and found it was the wrong move. It got tangled on one of the trunks, she lost her footing and dropped.

Adrenaline coursed through her as she fell into space but was caught by the vine within seconds. In her head, she imagined the tree it was tied to atop the cliff pulling out and flying over the edge, racing her doomed body to the rocks far below. Of course, it held. Synjan had screamed but it cut off as she bounced, dangled and then managed to scramble her feet back up onto a beam.

A deep voice sang from off to the side; Bo no doubt asking what was wrong. Kahu sang back, reassuring him that Synjan hadn't managed to plummet to her messy death just yet. Another voice (Tagan's, she was pretty sure) also sang something and there was a short time where many voices joined the discussion—punctuated frustratingly by her name—before the singing fell away and Kahu could concentrate on getting Synjan hooked onto the cliff via the four loops in her seat harness.

It took all the courage Synjan had left to let go of a beam and allow herself to swing into space. The lasso from above was additional support in case she fell and, twisting her head and looking around, she saw that it was only children in her vicinity that had it. The adults simply climbed down to their nests each night, hooked themselves in and went to sleep before unhooking themselves and climbing back up in the morning.

Synjan was certain she wasn't going to sleep in such a position. It felt odd just being upright and the longer she dangled there, her back against the stone of the cliff, the more the harness felt like it clutched the wrong places. The lasso under her arms was also annoying and she shifted many times to loop it in a position that didn't bother her. She hadn't changed her clothes and thought it might be cold but the composition of the sleeping area stopped the wind from hitting people directly. The temperature was surprisingly pleasant.

Kahu and Malahu sang softly to one another and then to Synjan.

"Goodnight Kahu, Malahu," she said, assuming they were exchanging the same thing with her.

They fell quiet and, gradually, the murmur of other voices fell away, replaced by the sound of the ocean churning into the bottom of their rocky furrow far below.

Synjan was left with her thoughts. She had never felt like a stranger before and this world was daunting in its differences. She told herself she needed to try and appreciate some of its similarities to her home as well. To trust in them. The salt of Dockside was in her blood, her veins tingling with awareness as the ocean around her sang its unique lullaby. She'd Wandered into an untenable situation but there had to be hope. The life she'd left behind was far away but fate had seen fit to shape the next part of her life's journey in surroundings that were familiar. It was something.

In seeking comfort, however, she opened herself up to thoughts she wasn't ready for—about the good things she'd left behind. Freddie's face danced behind her eyes, his voice echoed in her ears and his memory stabbed a knife through her heart so sharp she gasped and clutched at her chest. A wave of grief followed. It was so big she drowned in it, struggling to keep air flowing into her lungs as she cried for the one true love she knew for certain she *had* lost. If her family's deaths had created a hole inside her that could never be filled, then Freddie had been the salve that eased the pain of that grief. Now, he would have to be absorbed and become part of it as well.

Covering her face with her hands, she did her best to sob quietly. Freddie's voice telling her to keep perspective in the moment was a welcome irony. She focussed on that; it was easier to deal with. She no longer had a cause to keep her eye on. She was beholden to no-one but herself and, possibly, Daeson. Together, they needed to come up with what they were fighting for, what they were looking for when Wandering the worlds.

At that moment, all Synjan was looking for was change and she certainly had it. Now she needed to come to terms with her past, align it with her present and decide what she wanted to become in the future. It was an overwhelming prospect but at least it stopped her crying for Freddie.

Gazing into the dying embers of a sea set on fire by the sinking sun, Synjan finally closed her eyes and embraced the slumber only those who've known complete physical, spiritual and emotional exhaustion could find.

CHAPTER SIX

Loss And Control

ELLIS knew something was amiss when Nick slunk through the doorway after Omerri. The fact that she'd come to his office in the middle of the day was enough to set him on edge; that Nick stood at her back as she poured herself into a chair was downright alarming. Ellis didn't stand to greet them.

"What is it?" he hissed, narrowing his gaze.

Omerri chose not to answer immediately. Infuriatingly, she sat forward on her chair and crossed one leg over the other, smoothing her dress over her knee before her hands stroked her glossy black hair, twisting it into a tail over her left shoulder. Her compulsive grooming agitated him but he gritted his teeth and said nothing. Her confession would come about no sooner whether he pandered to her theatrics or not.

"Ellis, darling, I have some—*we* have some terrible news," she corrected herself, instinctively angling her body towards Nick without turning around. Their hands met as Nick touched her shoulder and Omerri grasped his fingers but her gaze remained fixed on Ellis. He held back a sneer. Their display of unity sickened him. They'd come here purposefully to ruin his day and he was ready to hate them for it. "It's about Synjan."

He sat forward, elbows on his desk and hands wound together in one tight fist. "She hasn't come home yet," he said quickly, encouraging her to be succinct.

Omerri wet her lips and when she spoke, her voice was as fragile as her bearing. "Yes, I know."

"You told me it would be quick, that the work would resolve itself shortly," he accused.

"I know, but it seems I was… wrong."

"It's been two days!"

Omerri flinched from his loud words, the knuckles on her hand turning white as she attempted to syphon every last drop of support from Nick's fingers.

"Ellis, man, calm down, we get it," Nick broke in.

"Do you?" he snapped, glaring up at the younger male.

"Of course! Synjan's important to you, you're worried."

His upper lip curled in derision. "The level of understatement in your inexcusable mewling is unfathomable," he condemned.

Nick blinked. Omerri stared. "Ellis," she breathed her reproach, but there was no conviction in it.

Ellis glared at her once more. "Just tell me," he ground out.

Her eyelashes fluttered and her throat worked as she swallowed, preparing herself. "Well… the job I sent her on *was* supposed to be quick. I asked her to drive out of the city and bring back one of my employees—"

"You told me she was doing something for *Nick*," Ellis interrupted, shifting his glare to the man standing so gallantly behind his mistress.

Predictably, Nick's expression became one of surprise, his mouth opening as he struggled to say something that wouldn't contradict his lover's false construct.

"I lied," Omerri snapped, drawing Ellis' attention once more. When they made eye contact, her bravado evaporated—or her illusion of distress was reasserted, he couldn't be sure which. "I felt you wouldn't ask questions if you thought she was with Nick," she admitted softly, her head angled downward in a manner of contrition.

"After the losses you'd *inexplicably* suffered, I assumed you'd need help," he agreed, to let her know he knew about the shooting deaths of her employees the day of the bombing.

Omerri's chin lifted and she paled, her eyes suddenly huge in her face as the implication behind Ellis' words sank in. He wasn't sure why his having an informant at the Queen would shock her so dramatically. She knew him well enough by now... was there more to it? "But you didn't indicate Synjan had left the *city*."

"I knew you wouldn't approve but she had to. That was... she had to get my employee. He'd run away without cause and I needed him *back*," she choked, managing to sound like a victim of circumstance and someone driven to desperate measures for a worthy cause. Clearly, she was the architect of her own consequences but it would take a much better man than Ellis to make her see that. "Sh-she could use her talent to locate him, you see. I gave her my limo to get to him and told her..."

A theory too horrible to voice was forming in the back of Ellis' mind and though he was fighting to keep it there, it ran through his body like iced water. His chest tightened and his heart beat in his ears. His hands—so firmly clenched together upon his desk—were slick with sweat. Omerri was right in front of him but his vision was distorting somehow and she seemed to be retreating from him, her excuses droning unintelligibly together.

"Is she dead?" he demanded, voice brittle.

Both of the faces hovering on the other side of his desk blanched at his blunt question but Ellis didn't care.

He had to know.

"No!" Omerri cried. The horror in her voice was enough to convince him that her answer was genuine.

Ellis felt like he could breathe again and the scene before him righted. Fear was quickly replaced by anger. "Then where is she? Who *is* this employee she went after?"

A frown dared to crease the skin of Omerri's brow and Ellis realised that this man was more than just an employee. He was important enough to send the Queen of Hearts herself begging for *his* heart's assistance; he was the core of this dilemma. She wasn't telling him everything.

"It's not important," Omerri dismissed.

"It is if he is with Synjan. Is he?"

"We... think so."

"Then who is he?"

"No-one you ne—"

"His name's Daeson," Nick cut in. Omerri was so startled that he broke his leash that she dropped her hand to her lap. She looked guilty and angry and unsure of which emotion to concede to.

"Daeson," Ellis tasted the name.

Omerri blinked rapidly to dispel tears. Again, she swallowed, deliberately suppressing the information he sought.

"Why is he so important that you would risk Synjan?" Ellis insisted, keeping his voice smooth and his words sedately paced. His hands separated from one another and became individual fists before him.

"Synjan wasn't at risk with him," Nick glowered.

"You didn't answer my question."

An obstinate silence greeted his polite observation and Ellis was appalled by the ghosts moving behind their eyes, taunting him with evil secrets. They'd come to cripple him and still wouldn't pay him the courtesy of honesty. A burning sensation travelled from the base of his skull, partway down his spine and across the breadth of his shoulders. The heat of it invaded his mind, buzzing through his thoughts and destroying what was left of his patience.

"Where is she?" he screamed, slamming his fists onto the desk and causing both of his visitors to jump.

"We don't know!" Omerri wailed.

"You have a theory!"

"The Authorities called me not an hour ago to report they'd found my car abandoned."

"Where?"

"In the middle of a field. South," Omerri warbled, folding one arm across her body and resting the other elbow upon it so that her hand could press against her chest.

"You are implying that Synjan has... *run away* with this Daeson?" Ellis hazarded, aware that her answers still weren't complete but unable to guess at the truth. The fact that she was still playing games infuriated yet fascinated him.

Omerri tensed. Nick glanced at the top of her head and then continued staring at Ellis. Neither of them seemed willing to commit to revealing the truth—but they knew, oh yes, they knew much more than they were saying.

Ellis was done with waiting. He settled back in his chair, resting his head on the back of it and grasping the arms loosely. He registered Omerri's look of horror before he closed his eyes.

"Ellis! *NO!*" she cried but it was too late.

Ellis pushed out of his body and into Nick's. There was a moment of resistance as Nick's will battled with his but there was no real contest. In an instant, he was standing behind Omerri and she spun in her chair to look up at him, terror contorting her beautiful face. She knew what had happened. She'd seen him do it many times before and she knew what was coming.

She should have thought of that before she decided to play games with his heart.

He glanced across at his own body, slumped in the chair behind the desk where he'd left it, vulnerable and empty. This had to be the least risky situation in which he'd employed his Controller talent. He forced Nick's hands into fists in front of him and then shifted his gaze to Omerri. She'd sprung out of her chair and was backing away from him, blubbering the word, 'No!' over and over.

"Shhh," he ordered in a voice that wasn't his, reaching out with reflexes that didn't belong to him to stop her getting away. Nick was slightly shorter than Ellis so when he grasped Omerri by the throat and wrenched her closer, their faces were almost level.

"Ellis, p-pleeease," she choked, clawing frantically at the hand wrapped around the delicate column of her neck.

He took a moment to admire her handiwork, watching as she scratched hard enough to draw blood. The pain was not quite as sharp as it should be. Something about taking Control of another person's brain allowed him to filter a percentage of what was received by the mind he'd plugged into.

Perhaps it was because he hadn't entirely evicted the usual resident consciousness, just subjugated it. Nick would still be able to see and feel what was happening; he would know his hand was throttling Omerri but he wouldn't be able to stop it. He likely wouldn't understand *what* was happening, for he wasn't privy to Ellis' consciousness inside his mind (nor was Ellis conscious of his—such was the territory of Intuits) and so he wouldn't have any understanding afterwards, either.

"Tell me," Ellis ground out in Nick's higher tone. Omerri writhed, trying to pull away. The chair she'd been sitting on was still between them; he reached down with his free hand and batted it out of the way. He walked her backwards to the nearest wall and pressed her gently to it, loosening his grip on the fragile column of her throat. It would help her talk. She winced, expecting to be slammed into the wall (now *that* was a game they hadn't played in many years).

"I don't know where she is, I swear to you!" Omerri shrieked, her makeup running and smearing as her tears fell.

"Do. Not. Lie," Ellis snarled, baring Nick's teeth as he leant his face closer to hers.

She scrunched her eyes shut and whimpered as she tried to turn away from him. "It's true! I don't know. Please, Ellis," she sobbed, "you know I love you. I'm so sorry!"

"About *what*?!"

"I didn't know they'd do it—"

"Do what?"

"I think she Wandered with him!"

It was Ellis' turn to feel as though he'd been struck. Indeed, it seemed as if all the air had suddenly rushed out of Nick's body, leaving him gasping. "Wandered?" he wheezed. "Why would she do that to me?"

"We tried to keep them apart," Omerri sniffled, one of her hands wrapped miserably around Nick's wrist, the other on his hand. Irrepressible fingers lightly scrabbled across the web by his thumb, seeking an advantage because his grip had loosened even more in shock.

"Who?"

"Daeson and Synjan."

"What about them?"

"Nick made sure they didn't meet. He was with me for two years and she didn't know."

Ellis was having a very difficult time processing her words; they didn't seem pertinent to the fact that his heart had possibly Wandered out of the world with a veritable stranger. He contemplated returning to his own body but decided to wait. Jumbled as it might be, it seemed he was now getting the information he sought. She had to make a point eventually.

"Why would she care?" he demanded exasperatedly.

Omerri gulped and then pressed her lips together, her expression wary.

"Omi?"

"You'll be mad," she squeaked.

"You'll tell me anyway," he crooned.

Her blue eyes flooded with fresh tears and renewed despair as she debated replying and Ellis knew that he was about to get to the heart of it. "Omi!" he shouted, shaking her by the throat.

She released a warbling note of fear and revealed her secret at last. "He's a Healer!"

Ellis stared at her, the tumblers of his mind falling into place like a key in an oiled lock. "You had a Wanderer *Healer* living with you for two *years* and you never *told* me?" he asked incredulously.

Omerri's mouth had begun to wobble uncontrollably as she reached up to cup his face, her fingers icy as they trembled upon his skin. "Don't be mad," she beseeched hoarsely. "I was just trying to protect him."

"From *me*?"

"I didn't want you to take him and send him to your house! We're in love!"

"If that's true, what is he doing with Synjan?"

"I don't know! I don't *know*, okay? I sent her to bring him *back* to me but it seems like she drove him to the Portal and now they're both gone! The Authorities can't find any sign of them!"

"You gave their descriptions to the *Authorities*?"

"I had to!"

"Now how am I supposed to protect her?"

"Don't be ridiculous—she's *gone*! They've known about her for years and besides, she was on the base after the bombing and they shot her. If it wasn't for Daeson Healing her, she'd be *dead* right now, so just be glad she's only Wandered away from you, not died!"

Ellis emitted a primal bellow of rage and pulled Omerri forward so he could slam her head against the wall and shut her up. The need to split things apart with his bare hands was overwhelming and she was available.

Wild, desperate screams spilt out of her and she began to fight in earnest, trying to get away from him… but he wouldn't allow it. He balled his free hand and punched her smartly in the mouth, satisfied when blood spewed out of her cut lip. It didn't bother him that she was attempting to stab Nick's eyes with her nails or rip his throat open. The Ellis that occupied his body relished the sting of torn skin. He was beyond reason and beyond love. Rage and despair so deep and black the stars themselves would be absorbed into his orbit hummed through him, ensconcing him in welcome numbness.

Omerri and Nick had harboured a Healer, had taken Synjan to the Authority base, had got her almost killed and *then* sent her to meet the Wanderer who'd saved her? They'd practically *forced* her to leave Trent. She hadn't been feeling well when last Ellis had been with her; she'd been confused and in shock and he hadn't recognised it. He hadn't been there for her because of all the secrets that had been kept from him.

A knee to the groin registered and Ellis staggered under the weight of intense, consuming pain. As the white haze cleared from his vision and throbbed potently in his pelvis, he found his rage anew and swung Omerri around. He flung her across the room. Her feet left the carpet and she flew through the air briefly before she struck the other chair in front of his desk. It impeded her flight with an unnameable crunch and she fell heavily onto the floor while the chair bounced away.

Ellis advanced on her and kicked hard into the softness of her belly, causing her to gasp for breath. "You betrayed me," he snarled as she tried drunkenly to get onto her hands and knees, her hands patting the carpet unsteadily. He lifted a foot and sank the heel of Nick's boot into her ribs, using it for leverage to shove her over onto her back.

She cried out pitifully, struggling to sit up but seeming unsure about which way she should move. She sobbed his name but he ignored it. His anger was a bright red cocoon, compelling him to punish her.

"You betrayed me!" he repeated, straddling her. He leant down and punched her again. Blood and snot bubbled from her broken nose, propelled by her whimpering and ragged breaths. Another punch rocked her head to the side, the skin around her eye instantly red and swelling. She reached a hand blindly between them, attempting to fend him off. He slapped it aside and grabbed her by the face, his nails digging into her puffy skin as he yanked her up to Nick's visage. "YOU BETRAYED ME!" he thundered at her, feeling the agony of that betrayal like a sword through his heart. All was lost and this, the woman he'd loved the longest, had been the instrument of his agony.

Ellis threw her down like the garbage she was and pulled away from Nick. He entered his own body and stood, leaning his fists on his desk in order to see what happened on the other side.

Nick was disoriented when he got control of his body again. He staggered over Omerri and backed away, staring at Ellis with haunted eyes. He held his hands in front of him and looked at them as if he was trying to process what they'd done to his lover. When his eyes met Ellis' again, they were awash with guilt... but the light of awareness was there, too.

Omerri emitted a wet, gurgling noise that might have

been a cough, drawing Nick's attention. Instinctively, he crouched to help her but when she realised he was close enough to touch her again she shied away from him with a keening lament that didn't die down. She curled into a rocking ball, bawling unevenly.

Nick shot Ellis a kicked dog glare, filled with hatred and subservience. There was a healthy dose of fear in it, too.

"Get her out of here," Ellis ordered, his voice devoid of emotion now that the rage inside him had given way to mourning. Synjan was still lost and the only consolation he had was that he'd hopefully destroyed Omerri's ability to accept Nick being close to her ever again. It was not a victory he'd tout.

Nick didn't need to be told twice. Overcoming his apparent devastation that Omerri was cowering from him, he scooped her up and cradled her against his chest. He scuttled out of the room on shaky legs, leaving Ellis alone to consider how he might possibly salvage his heart from the wreckage Omerri had made of it.

Oceangate Base appeared as it always did but Ellis found signs of increased security once he was close enough. The portal-phones were in a building just beyond Access Point Delta, where members of the public could access them. Getting in had previously required walking past a couple of soldiers but it seemed the process would never be so simple again. He was directed to pass through a metal detector and had to swipe his Citizen I.D. Card before he was allowed onto the base.

The new system rankled but he didn't allow his disapproval to show as he proceeded to his destination. Taking exception to the world's advancement was futile; though he'd long enjoyed the cloistered nature of Trent, it was only a matter of time before the Authority influence affected it more obviously. It would soon be like his home world, Fendror. He was prepared to move on if he had to, but he'd never expected to face that decision alone... he pushed thoughts of Synjan away determinedly.

A pair of tinted glass doors slid open to reveal a room lined with cubicles. All of them were green-lit, indicating they were vacant. Ellis walked in, noting the soldiers standing at either end of the room but not making eye contact. He chose a cubicle at random—he never used the same telephone consecutively—and locked the door behind him.

Ellis sat on the stool before the telephone. He withdrew his wallet from the inside pocket of his jacket and thumbed through it. He inserted his credit card into the machine and watched as payment was accepted before rifling through his wallet again. From a well-concealed slot, he removed a business card. Although it had smooth edges, it was discoloured. The back was covered in aggressive penmanship; not his writing. He neatly placed the card and wallet on the shelf beneath the telephone before lifting the handset and dialling 0005, the world code written on the card.

"Welcome to Auth-net. What number, please?"

Ellis carefully read the number to the woman on the other end of the line. His heart was beating too quickly and he was inexplicably short of breath, both hands wringing the heavy handset as if it would make this call easier. Nothing could. His thoughts were not so easily dampened now that he was in this tiny booth, contemplating what he would say.

After many rings, the woman's voice cut in once more, startling him. "Your party doesn't appear to be answering. Do you have an alternate number?"

"Uh... yes," Ellis stammered, feeling more

fragmented as each minute passed. He peered at the card—truthfully, he hadn't expected the first call to be answered, yet he'd hoped for something to go more easily in this disastrous day. "It's for a different world, though, code 0021."

"What number, please?"

Ellis read the new number, unsurprised when it was answered after just one ring but feeling unprepared all the same.

"Blackmoor Base, how may I direct your call?"

"I need to speak with Division Lieutenant Frederickson."

"Transferring you."

His call was answered by yet another soldier secretary assigned the task of impeding his progress.

"Who may I say is calling?"

His oldest friend had given him a code. "Just tell him Corona."

A moment of silence followed his instruction before he was asked to repeat the key word for clarity. This little underling was obviously trained because he didn't ask any more questions, he just moved Ellis' call to where it needed to go. The next voice he heard belonged to the man he sought.

"Hello?"

"Freddie," he breathed his relief into the handset, beginning to feel like everything might not be completely doomed after all.

"What's wrong?"

"Can you talk?"

"I came to my office when I heard it was you. I'm good."

"You need to come here."

Freddie took a moment to digest this instruction and Ellis waited; after forty years of friendship, he was fairly confident he knew what was going through the soldier's mind. Ellis wouldn't identify himself or where 'here' was because they were both aware that calls on Authority lines were screened. Nor would he give details about why he'd called. The fact that he'd requested Freddie's presence—the fact that he'd even *made* this call—meant that the situation was serious and it concerned one of three things; Ellis, Synjan or Tiln.

"Time frame?"

"Immediately."

Freddie exhaled, obviously feeling pressured and uncertain he could prioritise Ellis' wishes over whatever else was going on in his life. Ellis needed to tip his hand, he needed to get his friend to Trent so that he could tell him that Synjan had Wandered. Freddie was the only one that could save her—he could talk to Hawke and ensure she wasn't Hunted. It was the only option.

"She's gone, Fred," he said and his voice broke at the admission. His hands continued to wring the handset, pressing it so hard to his ear that it burned. The words scratched his throat and squeezed his heart, tears gathering in his eyes. "And... I'm afraid. The predators will follow and... we'll never get her back."

"Fuck," Freddie said. "How long?"

"A day. Perhaps two."

"Fuck!"

"Will you be able to confirm?"

"I—guh, I dunno, I think so—yes! Yes, I'll get confirmation before I come—actually... *should* I come?"

Ellis was momentarily baffled, wondering why the conversation was going around in circles but then he understood what was being asked. Freddie was a smart man. He was asking if he should come to Trent to get details or should he just go for Hawke's help instead? The less portal trips the faster everything would go.

"You're saying... ?"

"I'm saying I'll go for confirmation and intercession

at the same time."

"I admire the efficiency but... no. Come here first. There's more." Like the fact that Synjan had Wandered with a Healer named Daeson; it would be necessary for Hawke to understand that detail if he was going to help them get Synjan back. Ellis couldn't even hint at that over an open line.

"Fuck. Okay. Jesus. I'll be there as soon as I can," he promised and hung up.

Ellis did the same and sat there quietly, thinking. His core felt more substantial now, less like he was unravelling from the inside out. Freddie would come and Ellis would tell him all the horrible things Omerri had hidden from them and then Freddie would go off to see Hawke and ask for his help. Hawke would somehow be able to capture Synjan and bring her back to him— although, Authority portals weren't going to work for such a task. They'd imprison her.

Realising there were still many details to organise, Ellis gathered his belongings and left the base, his jumbled thoughts all that he could stand to keep him company until Freddie arrived.

CHAPTER SEVEN

Of Wanderers Past

DAESON was rudely awoken by a sharp pain in his side. One of the goats must have kicked him, upset about their new houseguest. Melodious yelling before another strike to his ribs proved his first guess wrong

"Stop, stop!" he called out. "Hey!" he protested when the blows changed from his body to his head. He covered his face, rolled over and wormed out from the rocky alcove. He smacked the foot aside when it came for him again and heard a surprised squawk. Bitter glee brought a smirk to his lips but it disappeared when blows were cast upon his head once more. Daeson scrambled to his feet and took a few running steps away. Goats scattered out of the shelter, bleating as they bounded around a small elderly woman. Daeson blinked in disbelief, thinking the pre-dawn light was fooling him. *This* woman was the one who'd pummelled him? She must be made of nothing but wiry muscles and small, hard fists.

Her song and expression were fierce as she stormed toward him, waving a fist menacingly above her head. Daeson skipped out of her reach and around some rocks. Instead of chasing him, the woman turned her complaints to someone approaching. Daeson recognised Hiyani from the greeting ceremony the day before—she'd spoken in faltering Authoritan. Right now she wasn't saying much of anything as she clutched her stomach and laughed shrilly. Hiyani's laughter turned into an alarming series of barks and coughs. Between her gasps for breath, she managed to sing a short phrase while pointing at Daeson.

"Neh-neh-ma."

The angry woman looked surprised before she turned an assessing stare his way.

"Neh-neh-ma?" she repeated, the phrase calming her considerably. Daeson committed the words to memory. He watched, feeling misplaced as the two old women conversed musically with one another. He considered leaving them and finding his own way around but Hiyani was someone he wanted to speak with. If anybody was going to have answers for him about the Wanderers who'd previously come through this world, it was her.

The old woman began rounding up the goats, leaving him alone with Hiyani.

"Wanderers," Daeson said, then switched to the way she'd pronounced it the other night. "Wandruh?" His stomach gurgled and Hiyani seemed more interested in answering that sound than the question he'd posed.

"Wandruh," she repeated while pointing at him, as though he hadn't already introduced himself. "Drink. Food." She made a gesture that looked like she was drinking soup from a ladle before beckoning Daeson to follow. She sang two words to him and repeated 'drink' and 'food'. Was she translating for him? He was positive he'd heard the phrase mentioned already but his lessons with the Shinu had been fast and overwhelming, interjected with long sentences.

"Wandruh? More Wandruh?" he spread his arms out but Hiyani was already on her way. She looked back and beckoned. For a woman who couldn't manage more than a shuffle, she was surprisingly fast. When he caught up to her, he changed tactic.

"Synjan? Where is Synjan?" he asked.

Hiyani sang something short and continued walking. Perhaps Synjan was already awake and breakfasting. Many voices were raised in song, their melodies overlapping from different directions. The natives were already tending to their tasks before the sun had fully lifted from the horizon. Perhaps fisher people woke earlier than farmers?

"I could help make a vegetable patch. I used to have a farm," he offered. Hiyani glanced at him and offered a gapped smile, her face wrinkling heavily.

"Food," she said.

Perhaps she hadn't heard properly. Being so old, it was possible her hearing had deteriorated. Daeson remembered the ear-funnels that the elderly people in Cloverlea had carried around with them. They would hold it up against their best ear while a person spoke into it.

"Farm. Farming," he said without conviction and was ignored.

They arrived at the place where he and Synjan had been welcomed yesterday. About twenty natives— almost all of them old—sat on green mats in the main circle. Woven items were before them in various states of completion. Daeson could see coils of rope, bowls and the squares that formed their climbing armour.

Hiyani made distance on him while he gawked. He hurried after her, seeing her heading for a spread laid out on a table low enough to kneel at. When he got closer, he saw that the table was made of planks of wood balanced on logs. Fresh water was in a large wooden bowl with spouted wooden cups beside them, along with a stack of woven baskets and a pile of mats. Daeson slaked his thirst before picking at the meal, breakfasting on fruit and a peculiar kind of porridge. He discovered some crunchy black things in a bowl that were salty and strangely addictive. He'd munched through half of them by the time Hiyani collected him. He was led to his own sitting mat, beside hers. On his other side was a pregnant woman named Rana, who picked up a handful of long, thin leaves and offered them to Daeson. Her smile was broad and filled with crooked teeth. He sat down cross-legged and took them while thanking her, unsure what he was supposed to do with them.

"Neh-neh-ma." Hiyani demonstrated a weaving pattern for Daeson to copy. He was pleased to find the task easy and soon both Rana and Hiyani showed him more complicated weaves that were tighter and involved knots. It didn't take long for him to make a decent-looking bowl with knotted handles. He thought that Omerri would have loved to sit here and craft something like this with him.

Thinking of her stilled his hands and roused another pang in his chest. Conflicting emotions surged together; love and betrayal, resentment and guilt. There were others as well, too subtle to take apart and analyse. Omerri had snuck up in his thoughts, smacking him with her easy reappearance. He exhaled in frustration, wanting his desire to be with her to disappear.

A hand on his arm brought his attention back to the present. Hiyani slowly repeated two words that Daeson didn't understand. With a finger, she tapped her chest and then pretended to throw something into the sky. He was dazzled by her gesture. Had she understood his pain? Did she know he was suffering heartache? Was she trying to tell him to release it? He focussed on his task once more; he'd been given a basket to copy and he allowed his mind to rest while he concentrated on the simple task of weaving strands of narrow leaves together.

When Daeson finished his basket, he showed it to

Rana. She sang in a manner he interpreted as praise. When he presented his basket to Hiyani, she took it off him and began undoing it.

"It looked good enough to me," he told her before she handed it back, half of it undone.

"Loa," she sang, gesturing a hand in a circular motion. "Loa."

"Loa. Again," Daeson said, but she might've meant *tighter* or *wrong*.

Weaving baskets and other items with the natives might be fine for him to contribute to their society but he thought learning how to communicate with them was more important. He wanted to ask about the Wanderers who'd come through here. Hiyani knew a few words in Authoritan but not enough for them to have a full conversation. If he could speak with them, he would be able to ask more specific questions. He had a theory about the structure of the language after spending time listening to the Shinu yesterday.

Daeson set the basket down and turned to Hiyani. She frowned at the basket and then at him.

"Arm," he told her, motioning from his shoulder to his hand. "Elbow. Hand. Fingers. Fingernails." He pointed to each in turn while Hiyani stared blankly. Daeson did it again, going through each of them in turn and in the same order. By the third time, he saw the spark of comprehension and she told him what they were in her language.

"Oneta," she sang low, indicating her arm. "Oneta," she sang again, but this time a note higher, pointing to her elbow. "Oneta," she waved a hand while singing higher still. "Oneta." Higher again for her fingers. "Oneta," she sang softly on a high note while pointing to her fingernails.

One word. The entire arm and its components had been a single word with different notes. Singing the right note was crucial. His theory had been correct.

"Oneta?" Daeson slapped his leg.

"Bin," Hiyani touched her own leg. "Onali," she sang at the lowest note.

Before she went back to her weaving, Daeson watched Hiyani massage the fingers of her left hand as though they caused her pain. Her knuckles were swollen and he recognised them as an affliction known as Old Scourge. His father had been pained by it in his final years. Gratitude drove Daeson to take her hand in both of his and wish the Scourge away. He felt the familiar warmth radiating out of his hands and into hers. He pictured the warmth moving along her fingers, gathering at her joints. When it was over, he released her and noticed that the weavers around them had stopped what they were doing to watch.

"Drink," he said, having already forgotten the word. He uncrossed his legs and stood up. His movement broke the trance that had settled over the natives and they sang excitedly to one another, likely about what they'd just witnessed. He expected a pack of them to follow him to the meal table but they continued singing and weaving. Only Hiyani joined him, so she could demonstrate how well she could use her hand, opening and closing it for him.

"Mela neh-neh-ma," she sang and cackled, thumping him on the back. He grinned at her while wondering if his newly discovered talent would be put to use here the same way Nick had sought to use it with his men. He wasn't sure how he'd feel about that. Denying them of Healing would be selfish and he wouldn't reject whoever needed his help, but he didn't want to go back to being used for his talents. A simple gesture had become a dilemma.

Hiyani didn't seem so at odds. She ushered Daeson back to his spot on the grass and handed him his half-woven basket.

"Loa," she prompted, waving her hand in a circle.

Daeson was relieved and surprised. As he re-wove his basket, he became curious about why they weren't taking advantage of him, why Rana wasn't requesting that he heal her maligned teeth, why others weren't approaching him with their health problems. Surely there were those who were sick and could use his help? He speculated about the Wanderers who'd passed through before, the ones who'd taught Hiyani to speak Authoritan, who'd lent their shorts and possibly helped construct the pulley system. Had one of them tried to cut stairs into the cliff-side? What had happened, that they'd only managed to shape thirty-something stairs? Had they left or died?

"Wandruh, Wandruh," he said, tapping Hiyani on the arm until she looked his way, annoyed. He threw his hands out and looked around himself. "Wandruh?" he asked, though he didn't think a questioning tone meant anything to her.

"Wandruh kapu piangi," she sang while mimicking paddling. Rana sang something and he turned to look at her. She looked sad and made the reverse signal for 'come here', her hands letting out an invisible rope instead of pulling one in. He turned to Hiyani again who was looking at him carefully. "Daeson kapu amn piangi lo-lo bdy pongi."

"I don't understand," he said.

"Kapu." Hiyani mimicked paddling.

"Kapu. Canoe or boat, I think. Okay."

"Piangi," she sang, her hands doing the same letting out gesture that Rana had just made. Daeson understood the word as 'go' so he nodded, though the head movement meant nothing to the Mukake people. As far as he knew, they didn't have a word for 'yes'. "Lo-lo pongi?" she asked, her hands now pulling in. *Pongi* must mean 'come'. The two words were strikingly similar for opposites.

"You're asking me if I will leave or stay," he realised.

He didn't see comprehension in Hiyani's eyes but he didn't need it. "Wandruh piangi?" he asked, figuring the Wanderers they'd hosted in the past had left them.

"Wandruh piangi!" Hiyani repeated then pounded Daeson's shoulder. He assumed this meant he'd done well. "Daeson piangi?" she said again. He could see she was expecting an answer.

"Daeson… pongi. For a while, anyway, because the Portal is so far."

"Portoh! Portoh kapu piangi Wandruh-ma! Daeson pongi bin Portoh, neh-neh bin wibu amn." Hiyani batted Daeson's shoulder again and cackled before she returned to her weaving.

It was frustrating that he knew only bits and pieces of what she'd said. He was fairly sure she'd repeated 'Portal' back to him a few times, though he'd also heard his name and the word for no in there. She'd sung the other words too quickly for him to understand and so he went back to twisting blades of grass in his fingers, threading them in and out, thinking about the Wanderers who'd come and gone from this place.

Movement caught his attention and he looked up to see Synjan and Tagan. Both of them carried their breakfast with them in baskets and on small woven mats instead of eating at the table like he had—was he supposed to have done the same? Daeson was surprised by how glad he was to see her, considering his angry thoughts about her last night. The urge to share what he'd learned about the Mukake language was strong but he didn't want to launch straight into it without letting her get settled first. He couldn't think properly without a full stomach and assumed she would be the same.

"Hi, Synjan. I hope your morning started better than mine," he said with a smile, certain that being kicked awake was the worst that could have happened.

She flinched before pulling a face. "Well…"

CHAPTER EIGHT

Settling In

FALLING! *She was falling!*

Jerked awake by the sensation of plunging downward, Synjan thrashed wildly, bucking and flailing through open space, desperately trying to get hold of something to stop her mad descent. A whirl of rocks and ocean swung incomprehensibly as she slammed into the cliff, cutting the back of her head on a sharp bit of rock. Reeling with pain and fear, she clawed and lunged at the monolith.

As suddenly as the sensation accosted her, it stopped. She wasn't falling. She'd swung herself farther away from the cliff while sleeping and something instinctual had tried to send her back, only to have her distressed mind spring into action and send her off balance instead.

Synjan's ragged breathing calmed and she became aware of the wide-eyed observers by her side. She was too relieved that she was still alive to worry about being embarrassed.

"This is a horrific place to sleep. I think you're all fucking insane," she told Kahu and her daughter, her speech distorted by the way she was pressing her face to the cliff. She added a harrowed laugh at the end that was more a release of tension than genuine amusement.

They cooed soothingly at her and Malahu completed some sort of manoeuvre Synjan was glad she couldn't see properly, because she was suddenly on the other side, patting her arm sympathetically. Reluctantly, Synjan let go of the cliff and breathed through the anxiety caused by swinging freely over the ocean. Her stomach took a circuitous route before it settled but even then, she knew two things for certain. One—she was not going back to sleep. Two—she was not *ever* sleeping here again.

"I think... is it time to go up? Up?" she asked Kahu, gesturing to the cliff top.

Malahu sang something questioning to her mother but the answering song seemed to negate whatever had been asked. Kahu must have understood that Synjan wanted to climb back up because she started singing and pointing at places for her to get holds, helping her out of the security lines she'd slept in. When Synjan didn't see or was too slow to follow, her limb was grabbed and placed where Kahu wanted it to go.

While they began an unsteady ascent, Malahu climbed assuredly ahead and went over the lip well ahead of them. Kahu was distracted enough to sing sternly at the child—which caused her cheeky offspring to lean over the edge on her stomach and laugh down at them, much to Kahu's visible frustration—but this time, she stayed with Synjan.

When she finally got to the top, Synjan realised why. Crawling unsteadily away from the rim of the sleeping area, she became aware of how watery her limbs were. She was in some sort of residual shock. Plus, there was the blood. Given that she was still wearing her denim shorts and blouse, quite a bit of her body had been left bare. She was scratched and bleeding in some places because of how she'd clutched at the sharp rocks. Now that she was paying attention, it stung madly.

She thanked Kahu, grateful for her assistance and

was left behind to rest while the young mother chased Malahu down. Synjan wasn't sure why she worried so much about where her sprat was, the island wasn't big enough to lose her and the kid could climb better than some adults—though that was likely the problem. Perhaps she was concerned that Malahu would climb down to the ocean unsupervised. Her missing father figure probably had something to do with Kahu's anxiety levels as well, but Synjan couldn't ask.

Her convalescence was cut short by a looming shadow that grabbed her hand. "Synjan!" Tagan sang, tugging her to her feet.

She winced as he squeezed her lacerated flesh and hastened to keep up with him—if only to lessen the pain. "Ow, Tagan," she told him. He spared her a look over his shoulder but didn't slow down, leading her determinedly towards the central area. She almost resisted her guide's directions when she noticed Daeson on the outskirts but then she realised she was being shown to where there was food so she relented.

She picked up a small basket and began filling it with protein, taking several tentacles of freshly cooked octopus, some dried pieces of fish with crispy skin, some nuts and many different types of fruit. Satisfied with her collection, she was about to walk away when she saw a meagre amount of black beetles left in a bowl. She'd had some of them at dinner while they were still warm and she liked them even better than nuts (despite their tiny legs and antennae, which got caught in her teeth). Handing Tagan her cup of water, she took the whole beetle bowl and placed it on her food mat.

Assured that Tagan would follow with her water, Synjan headed towards where Daeson was weaving. There was space in front of him so she lowered herself into a cross-legged position facing him, keeping her food balanced as she sat.

"Hi, Synjan. I hope your morning started better than

mine," he said, watching her careful descent.

When she was settled, she looked up. She was pleased to see his smile. The way they'd left things the night before had probably added to the restless sleep she'd had. His question was intriguing but she shuddered and pulled a face when thinking about her start to the day. "Well..." she warbled, lifting both arms to show him their scraped and bleeding undersides, "I've had better."

"Let me get that," Daeson insisted, encircling each of her wrists in his hands.

As it had with Tagan, the contact stung but his grasp was gentler. Daeson's face was expressionless so she peered downward at her wounded arms. She was disappointed that she couldn't see the Heal happening—she wasn't sure what she'd expected, some sort of glow or something—but there was only the sensation. A familiar warmth worked its way down her arms, along the back of her head and then into her legs, sealing lacerations and soothing away all her stings and aches.

Daeson gave her healed limbs a cursory inspection before sitting back and looking around furtively. Synjan followed his gaze, noticing that the women either side of him and quite a few others nearby were watching the process. Although she sensed that their observation was approving, it was uncomfortably intense.

"Thank you," she said quietly and offered him her cup of water.

"You're welcome," he replied as he took it and drank.

"Do you... think you shouldn't Heal me in front of everyone?"

"No, it's alright," he said, handing her empty cup back to her.

Synjan nodded, emitting a little sigh as the Heal's delicious aftermath worked its way through her body. While she savoured it, her arm was commandeered by

Tagan, who pulled it close to get a good look at where there was blood but no wound. She watched his expression change from confused to amazed before she was able to pull away. He stared between the two Wanderers while she finally got a chance to eat.

"So, what went wrong with your morning?" she asked after she swallowed a mouthful of octopus.

"I got kicked awake."

"Kicked! Where did you sleep?"

"With the goats."

"Why'd you sleep there? What's wrong with your tent?"

"It was too dark to try putting it up."

"It's a pop-up tent. It's really easy."

"I've put up a tent in the dark. I don't remember it being easy," he said grumpily.

She dropped a few beetles into her mouth to chew on. She didn't want to aggravate the situation. Swallowing, she broached the silence with a tentative offer. "Well, I'm not interested in sleeping on that cliff again—*ever*—so... if you're not going to use the tent, can I?"

"Oh! Um... oh," he stammered, obviously taken aback.

Belatedly, she realised that her phrasing excluded him from the tent when he was probably interested in using it rather than being kicked awake by animals again.

"Sorry, you're planning to use it tonight. Could I share it?" she asked hopefully.

He took longer than she would have liked to agree but he did, if hesitantly.

"Thank you. We'll have to get our stuff out of that tree first," she reminded him with an awkward little laugh.

As she bit into some fruit, Daeson nodded, looking at the half-finished basket on the ground between them before he picked it up and began weaving again. She watched him work on it, thinking that he didn't look happy. He'd likely agreed to her sharing his tent out of politeness—which would only make things more awkward between them.

With a sigh, she focussed her breakfast. Tagan looked like he still wasn't sure what was going on but he settled into eating as well, watching them both with an occasional frown.

Frankly, she wasn't sure about anything, either. The Mukake were kind to host them but it was an arrangement that couldn't last. Between Daeson's fear of heights and her inability to communicate or travel great distances by sea without getting sick, they weren't well suited to this world. It didn't feel like it could be a home, there were too many barriers. Synjan thought that Daeson was logical enough to draw the same conclusions as her but she decided to introduce the subject gently.

"This world isn't a good fit for us," she observed, nibbling the last bit of mango flesh off the skin she held.

"No. It is not."

Daeson's staccato delivery and his serious expression were noted; his mouth was compressed and he looked disappointed. He seemed to agree with her. She was greatly relieved.

"Hopefully the Portal will move closer."

"It can do that?"

"Yeah, I... did mention that."

"When?" he asked in surprise.

"When I was, uh, overloading you on the drive. In Gredann," she admitted sheepishly.

"Oh," he said. Beside him, the pregnant woman sang something to a person over her shoulder, laughing as they answered back less melodically. Daeson looked bothered by the noise and gave Synjan's breakfast a pointed look. "Are you done with that?"

Thinking he wanted something from her leftovers, she picked the mat up and handed it over. To her surprise, he put it aside and got to his feet. "Let's go somewhere quieter."

Blinking, Synjan followed, walking at Daeson's side. As they headed in the direction of their suspended bags, Tagan joined them. Daeson looked over and frowned darkly.

"Can you send him away?"

"I don't—"

Synjan was saved having to make excuses when a woman called out Tagan's name. All three looked back to see Paki, the long-haired native who'd met them on Exclamation Island. Tagan sang back—it sounded like a refusal but Paki replied more insistently. Tagan threw Synjan a wistful look and trotted away.

"Why'd you bring him to breakfast with you?"

"He brought me. He... was being helpful," she murmured, not wishing to offend Daeson by defending Tagan but also wishing to show that the annoying native had a thoughtful side. The relief she'd felt when Tagan had conveniently left now turned sour inside her.

The quartet of trees was on the western edge of the cliff but the ocean still sparkled beneath a fresh morning sun. Despite the fact that she felt they didn't belong here, it was a beautiful place, the view invigorating.

As Synjan had hoped, the bags were easy to untie and get down. Daeson knelt beside his pack and began opening zips, seemingly at random. The trills of repeated openings and closings caught her attention. It was obvious that he was looking for something specific but couldn't find it. He noticed her observation and gave her a self-conscious look. "Sorry. I wasn't really listening in the shop, either," he admitted with a bashful smile. "Where are my shorts?"

Synjan laughed. He was very handsome and she

thought he was probably aware of the effect he had on women when he smiled at them like that. She was certain he'd managed to get everything he wanted with his big blue eyes, vulnerable aspect and perfectly proportioned body—it was certainly working on her.

"In here," she said, abandoning her own backpack in order to show him where everything was in his bag. At first, she told him why she'd packed it the way she had but they eventually ended up pulling every item out and reorganising it together into a system he liked. His exclamations of surprise when she revealed certain items had her grinning wryly and thinking to herself that he certainly hadn't been lying when he'd admitted he hadn't been paying attention to her—and then she remembered he couldn't lie. She needed to get used to that.

Leaving Daeson to finish with his gear, Synjan turned to her own. She'd realised the day before that she didn't have enough island-appropriate clothing—she planned on climbing down the cliff at some point to swim in her clothes if she couldn't figure out a way to wash them— but she *did* have a large hunting knife in its own scabbard. It didn't seem right to wear guns here (and Daeson would likely stop her if she tried) but a knife had a multitude of uses.

While she worked the scabbard onto a belt and wound it through the loops of her shorts so that the knife would hang at her right hip, Daeson found the pants he'd wanted and started to strip. She didn't see where his shoes and socks went but when he stood up and shucked his pants and shirt, he got her attention. He didn't seem too worried about standing beside her in his soft, body-hugging underwear—he was quite focussed on stepping into his cooler shorts—and she wasn't fazed, either. She *was* impressed, though.

He wasn't particularly hairy, she noted through repeated glances, so his skin had a smooth, bronzed appearance that made her palms itch to rove all over him. Although he wasn't lean enough to display prominent muscle, when he flexed, each movement showed that there was obvious strength and definition beneath that skin. His shoulders were broad and his waist was narrow; she probably looked too long at his chiselled hip bones and the delectable v of muscle that angled beneath the band of his underwear but she learned everything else she might want to know about him at that point also. He was consistently big. All over.

Synjan forced herself to look away, finishing closing her belt and examining her blouse instead. She wasn't sure it was worth salvaging. She took it off, deciding that she'd ask about one of the grass chest plates before she climbed down the cliff again. After an internal debate, she also decided to change her bra to one more suited to the workout she'd get climbing up and down the cliff. She had a navy blue one that was better. It was softer but more supportive, with straps that crossed over at the back. Without checking to see if Daeson was looking at her, she deliberately chose not to hide her naked breasts in the changeover. She wasn't worried about him seeing her and she believed they'd have to get used to such things if they were going to be travelling together and sharing a tent.

Once she'd changed and stowed her torn blouse, Synjan sat against the base of a nearby tree, watching Daeson. He'd decided to remain shirtless and she approved.

"So... we're somewhere quiet now," she said leadingly.

He settled beside her, also leaning against the tree but looking in a slightly different direction. Her left shoulder was pressed against his right and it felt companionable for them to chat this way. She thought it would be easier for each of them to speak from their hearts if they didn't have the added pressure of eye contact.

"You were saying that the Portal moves?"

"Yes. Once it's touched by Wanderers, it moves in a random direction and stops where it wants to."

"What do you mean, 'where it wants to'?"

She twisted her lips, considering her phrasing and not sure why she'd said it that way. It did sound odd, now she thought about it. "Well, hmm..."

"Do you talk to it?"

"No, but... I've watched it my whole life and sometimes it stops far away and sometimes it stops close to where it was originally. It seems to decide. That sounds weird, doesn't it?"

"No. I felt like it talked to me. Both times. Not with words or anything, but it was definitely calling."

"Oh, Gods *yes!*" she enthused, briefly touching her fingertips to his arm. "It practically *drowns* me when it's close. My heart pounds, it fills my senses and it's so bright and colourful, it's blinding!"

"It's not that colourful. It's *bright* but it's just white. Do you see colours?"

She leant forward to peer at him in amazement. "You don't?"

"No. Your one sounds pretty."

Encouraged, Synjan described her version of the Portal. Her words seemed paltry in comparison to reality but she did her best to do it justice. He listened intently and when she was done speaking there was a time of quiet while they both fell into their own thoughts, reflecting on what she'd described while staring off into the distance. Daeson eventually had another question.

"So a Wanderer has to touch it before it will move?"

"I believe so. I've never thought about it moving by itself but maybe it can?"

"Well, let's hope it does and comes to us. Can you call it with your power?"

She smothered a grin, finding his ignorance endearing. She found she was greatly enjoying talking about Wanderer topics with him and she didn't want to dissuade him with a flippant laugh. "No, Navigators can only locate it and travel to it. Which is not good on this world."

"It would've been nice to know this world was next," Daeson mused.

"Would it have stopped you?"

"Probably."

Synjan grunted surprise. He'd intended to stay in Trent, thinking he would be safe from Omerri's reach because he was out of town and on a farm. She felt like he still didn't understand what Omerri would've had in store for him if he'd stayed. Besides, if Synjan *had* had the forethought to mention the next world, she would've unintentionally misled Daeson based on the Authority world list, anyway.

"As far as I know, the world after Trent is called Femme but everything I've heard about it is nothing like this. I don't know if we're maybe on a different continent or just really far away from the populated places but... I don't think this is that world."

"Is Femme better than this world? Do you think it's the kind of world that we could settle down in?"

She wrinkled her nose. "Nah, it's a slave world, I don't think we'd want to live there. Do you... not want to keep Wandering?" she asked hesitantly. Her heart skipped a beat and then did double time as she waited for his answer.

"I only Wandered because Gredann didn't feel like home. I want to live in a place where I feel safe. Where I can start a family."

"So if you don't find that place right away, will you keep Wandering until you find it?"

"Yes."

His answer was reassuring because it was so

perfunctory. "Good, because I'm not ready to stop just yet," she smiled.

"No. I don't want to stay here," he agreed.

Bo approached on quiet feet, bearing an inviting grin and making the familiar gesture that meant he wanted them to come with him. Synjan returned his smile as she got up, dusting off the seat of her shorts. Bo inspected her change of attire with open interest, his gaze lingering on her cleavage before he looked into her eyes. Somehow, after the extended conversation she and Daeson had shared and the preliminary intimacy of changing clothes in front of each other, Bo's obvious attraction to her seemed like an interference. Not that she owed Daeson anything, but she hoped he didn't notice the way Bo looked at her (or how it made her feel), as she didn't want to make their burgeoning relationship awkward.

"What do you need?" Synjan asked the Mukake man, lifting her hands in a nonplussed manner.

Bo grinned and sang something she couldn't decipher, grabbing her hand and Daeson's in order to drag them with him.

"I think that's the word for food," Daeson mused, allowing himself to be pulled a few steps forward.

"Oh! Excellent," Synjan exclaimed, less inclined to fight against Bo's insistent tugging now that she knew food was on offer. It didn't seem all that long since she'd breakfasted but she and Daeson had been mucking about with their gear and chatting for a couple of hours and she knew she could fit more in.

Once they were all headed in the right direction, Bo let go of Daeson's hand but he got a more comfortable hold on Synjan's and held it the rest of the way.

CHAPTER NINE

Lost Child

HEAT waves blurred Daeson's vision as he approached the cooking pit. A woman and man stood either side, using hooked paddles to lift out steaming packages. Close to the pit, a dozen people huddled together, holding out woven trays and baskets. With expert flicks, leaf-wrapped morsels were launched onto their mats or into their baskets to be taken away. Daeson was impressed by the skill and wondered if the paddles were ever used for sport.

Bo led him and Synjan to the back of the group and left them. Daeson remained where he was, not confident enough to leave the small crowd. Bo returned with some woven bowls and handed one each to Synjan and Daeson. Daeson admired the craftwork, knowing the effort that went into them. He hadn't even finished one bowl properly in the same time the others had made four or five. The upcoming feast was probably why they'd been making so many.

As people carrying food worked their way out from the crowd, the group shifted forward and Daeson and Synjan moved with them. Over nearby voices, Daeson thought he could hear a call of distress. He stood straighter and listened. A woman's voice cried again and he clearly heard panic. "Malahu!"

The word was familiar but Daeson didn't know what it meant. He looked in the direction the voice had come from but couldn't see anything until a short-haired woman—Kahu, he thought—walked past the waiting crowd.

"Malahu! Malahu!"

A few people looked her way, including Synjan.

"She sounds upset," Daeson said. "I don't know what she's saying." He was surprised that nobody went to her, asking what was wrong.

"Malahu is her daughter's name. She's always running off so I suppose she's done it again."

Synjan's answer explained why nobody was helping the woman if it was a matter of disobedience rather than someone being hurt or needing help.

"Do you know where she is?" Daeson asked, thinking that Synjan's talent would prove useful here.

He felt a presence overhead, enough to have him looking up, though he saw nothing but the vivid blue of a cloudless sky. It made him feel calm and protected, as though someone was looking after him. It was a warm sensation, though nothing like the discomfort of the weather. After a moment, the presence retreated.

"Yeah, I should probably go and get her."

Synjan handed him her bowl and left the line to collect Malahu. Daeson watched her go, knowing that it must've been her Navigator talent he'd sensed overhead. He wondered if every Wanderer was drawn to a Navigator the way he was. Was that a part of her bloodline... to draw in and help Wanderers to reach the Portal? It also meant she would be quite vulnerable to Wanderers who would want to exploit such a talent. She couldn't keep the sensation a secret.

The wind changed, bringing delicious smells with it. Daeson's stomach gurgled as he stepped forward, now in front of the crowd. Heat washed over him, tightening his skin. He was eager to escape. A paddle hook dove in and flipped some blackened oblongs into his two bowls.

Daeson turned and the natives parted, though the group was a lot smaller now. He followed the others who were carrying food to a long row of knee-high tables. The planks were arranged on logs higher than at breakfast. Daeson shifted some bowls and mats around to make space and stood off to one side, unsure where to go.

A memory surfaced and he closed his eyes to focus on it. With the exception of it being daytime instead of night, he could be having a bonfire feast with the tent people of Kharltae right now. Sounds of laughter and talk—the singing nature of the language was drowned by the multiple conversations—and the smell of cooked food made him feel like he was with Anna and her family. He didn't remember the rest of their names, it had been a long time since he'd thought of them.

When he opened his eyes, he saw that Synjan had returned. Her golden hair was easily spotted in the crowd. Daeson was glad mother and child were together though Malahu looked far from happy. He joined them.

"Where was she?"

"In the cave."

"There's a cave?"

"Yeah, it's just past all the rocks. It's a short climb down. The women go there to, uh, relax for a few days every month, I guess. She was chatting with a few of them."

Synjan's diplomatic answer was enough to let him know what the women were experiencing. How strange that they wouldn't be joining the rest of the natives for the feast. Were they not allowed to? He wondered if Synjan would have to go there while she had her menses.

"Wait. How do you know that's what the cave is for?"

"I can see what's happening with their patterns."

"You can see... *that*?"

"Patterns look different when they're hurting or happy."

He was considering the things she could see with her talent when the bosses—the Shinu—stepped into the centre of the gathered natives and sang a short speech. The word 'Wandruh' was mentioned many times and Daeson had the idea that the feast was somehow in their honour—except the boar had been captured before he and Synjan had been discovered. There was a peculiar sentiment that he picked up from these people; they were welcoming and happy enough to provide for them and he even felt revered at times, but he also felt like a burden. It lent to an odd sensation of detachment.

The Shinu gestured at the low table that held the roasted boar and the crowd took this as a sign to surge forward and feed themselves. Daeson hurried alongside them, grinning when he was handed a mat to pile food onto. He finished collecting his meal the same time as Synjan and they found a place to sit together.

A number of natives began to sing the same two phrases over and over as others stood up to dance. Their dancing was graceful and flowing, as though they were leaves being tossed and turned by the wind. He noticed there was no difference between how the men and women danced, they all performed the same way. There were no set steps that Daeson could see. Many children joined in while other natives watched and sang to one another.

Daeson picked up one of the black crunchy things—a delicacy he'd discovered at breakfast—just as Synjan leant closer to speak with him. "There are four people rowing over in a boat," she mused. It took him a moment to realise she must've used her talent to see them.

"They better hurry up or there won't be any food left," he replied.

Daeson looked at the delicious thing in his hands, wondering if it was a kind of roasted seed. On Trent, he'd developed a taste for a variety of nuts and this thing tasted a bit like cashews.

There was a line down the middle of the black seed. When he flipped it over, he was horrified to see six lines and a smaller, sectioned area. His stomach lurched when he realised it wasn't a seed but a large insect, some sort of beetle by the look. He set it back down on his food mat and looked over at Synjan just as she put one in her mouth. She had three more of them and he didn't know if she'd figured out what they were or not. He debated whether to tell her.

Hiyani approached them with a large bowl of food in her hands that she was passing around. When she got close enough to Daeson, she held up her hand and opened and closed it quickly, singing another praise for him, he thought. Daeson smiled and was thumped on the shoulder again before being offered a bowl of black bugs to eat. He declined and watched Synjan take another handful. He decided not to tell.

When Hiyani left them, Synjan spoke again.

"Why did she open and close her hand like that?"

"This morning before you arrived, I saw that she had the Old Scourge."

"Old Scourge?"

"Something that people get when they age. Their knuckles swell up and they lose movement. So I Healed it away for her."

"You Healed it?"

Daeson heard surprise in her voice. "Looks like I did," he confirmed.

"You're amazing," she complimented.

Daeson looked sideways at Synjan, uncomfortable with her praise. "I thought maybe I would be asked to Heal everyone, but they're not doing that. I mean, I wouldn't blame them but... it's nice not to be used." He struggled to explain how meaningful it was to be asked to weave baskets, to be taught a different skill and to be accepted as normal instead of special. Being special came with a price that he no longer wanted to pay.

"Like you were in Gredann." Her tone was disapproving.

"Yes, but Healing is the only useful talent I really have. The other one just causes problems." He saw Synjan's expression change so he pushed on, wanting to explain. "There was a man called Spier who lived and worked at the Queen. He had a bad leg, did you know him?" He waited for Synjan to nod. "I could've Healed him, I think, but I never tried because Nick told me that my talent wouldn't work on bones that had already mended."

Synjan scoffed. "How would Nick know?"

"It was enough that he believed it so I believed it. Sometimes it's easier for me to be deceived. I relied on my ability and I shouldn't have." Daeson set his food mat upon his lap, having lost his appetite.

"What? Why not? I lived by my talent."

"And it couldn't protect you. I had to save you," he said, thinking of her arriving half dead at the Queen. It was safer for both of them not to rely on their abilities for everything.

Synjan gaped. "That was one time!"

"One time is enough," he pointed out. By the look on her face, he could tell she disagreed.

She made a few false starts before finally replying. "No, I will continue to rely on my talent and so should you."

"I've already relied on that talent and it's brought me nothing but pain. It would be foolish to depend on it further." He glared at her. He didn't want to hear arguments against something that he already knew was truth. It had been proven to him, over and over, that his ability was unreliable.

"What would be foolish is letting one bad experience stop you from being what you really are."

"What am I, then?" he challenged.

"You're an anomaly," she said after a moment of struggle.

"What's that mean?" The word was unfamiliar.

"You're not, um, you're different to other Wanderers. You've got two talents. That's never happened before."

Omerri had said that to him, speaking about things like 'evolution' and 'genetic leaps'. Her praise had always made him feel uncomfortable. It felt like she was talking about a thing instead of him, a person. It wasn't anything he'd earned for himself either, nothing that he could be proud of. The Healing, he enjoyed that, he enjoyed helping others. The knowledge of truth was something that got in the way. He couldn't tell jokes or enjoy the ones he heard, he couldn't encourage people when they needed support, he couldn't even use it to protect himself from liars if they were the kind that deceived themselves. What good was an unreliable talent? Being half an Intuit was worse than being none at all.

"I'm a Healer. That's all I'll rely on."

"But... I don't think you should deny your other one just because Nick—"

"It's not because of Nick," Daeson interrupted.

"Well, Omerri, then. They—"

"Not because of her, either. I've been fooled my whole life, manipulated by everyone I've ever cared about. By people who were supposed to care about *me*, who were supposed to be honest to *me*!"

Daeson realised he was shouting and he looked around to meet the stares of the natives nearby. When he looked back at Synjan, her expression was one of realisation. He couldn't face her understanding. He set his food mat aside and stood.

"Wait, I'm sorry."

"I need to have a walk. Alone." He decided not to spare Synjan after all. "Those things are bugs, by the way."

He stalked off when she looked down.

Synjan found him beneath the sleeping trees. Daeson had noticed one of the stretchy vines on the ground and sat down to play with it, wrapping and unwrapping it around his fists as he thought about why he was angry half the time and scared the other half. He didn't want to be angry or scared anymore—it was exhausting. Fighting with Synjan would do no good either.

"May I join you?"

Daeson thought it was good of her to ask. He wondered if he'd spoiled her appetite.

"Did you eat the bugs?"

She smiled. "Yes, I think they're delicious."

"Sit down, then."

She sat near him but not touching. "So... I have to eat bugs to be allowed to sit with you? You're a funny guy, Daeson."

"Except I'm not laughing."

"And I'm not laughing *at* you, not like that. I don't want to upset you. You and me, all we've got is each other."

Her words were statements that couldn't be interpreted in different ways. He liked that about her; her declarations and bold opinions. Even though he didn't agree with her, he preferred that over duplicitous assurances or charming comments that meant nothing. He sighed, aware that he'd over-reacted.

"I know. I thought I'd worked past what happened in my world. It came back when I got fooled again. You're not who I'm angry at."

There was a long pause before Synjan quietly made her guess. "Omerri?"

Daeson unwound the vine and then tossed it away, his hands motionless in his lap. "Yes. Omerri." Her name seethed past his lips. "I love her. I *loved* her."

How interesting and confusing, that both declarations were true.

Synjan made a breathy sound and then said something astonishing. "I thought I loved Nick."

Nick. The abuser. The arrogant womaniser who would disrespect a woman enough to have sex with her when she was unconscious and the man psychopathic enough to murder his friends to keep a secret. She loved *that* Nick. He stared at her and she must have felt his gaze because she shifted position twice.

"What's there to love about Nick?"

The silence expanded into a lengthy one but Daeson waited her out until she had something to answer with. He thought the delay was more telling than her words.

"He was there at the Bunker when my family died. He helped me and I... I worshipped him." She puffed and looked away. "Gods, that sounds ridiculous, doesn't it?"

Daeson thought her question was more to herself than to him, so he said nothing.

"I was young and he was everything," she added.

Daeson thought he knew what she was trying to say. "So he got to you when you were vulnerable?"

"He was different when he worked for Ellis." She sounded defensive. Daeson glanced over and noted her wary expression. Was she defending Nick? Her words implied that Omerri had changed Nick into the bastard he was now. Was he a bastard with Omerri? He doubted she would put up with his rank behaviour. Daeson remembered that he was the one who'd shunted Nick aside. Nick had continued seeing her, with the knowledge that she was sleeping with someone else.

"I think Nick loves Omerri. Really loves her."

"I agree with you. But *I* don't see the attraction," Synjan said bitterly.

"When I was with her, her world revolved around me. I felt important."

"She made you feel special," Synjan clarified.

She looked after me. She explained how the worlds worked. She protected me from the Authorities. She gave me what I wanted.

He was selfish and shallow. He loved her because of the arrangements she'd made for him. He hadn't even known her properly. Was that her fault or his?

"Maybe that's why I don't like being called that now. Special."

"Do you think she was only with you because of your talents?"

He was shocked by the abrupt, harsh quality of her question. Perhaps it made him cringe because it was the truth. It was time to face it.

"At the start, I think yes. After two years, it developed into something more. When she told me she loved me, it was true. I'll never know if it was a lie she made herself believe."

He thought about her taking him to the world of Mwavey immediately after she'd discovered he was a Healer. She'd already known from his fumbling attempts to romance her that he was interested but hadn't encouraged him until the vacation. Had she decided to take advantage of him? Was it even possible to take advantage of someone who was willing? Synjan interrupted his thoughts before he reached a conclusion.

"That's why you don't trust your other talent. She took that from you."

Synjan seemed to take great delight in blaming Omerri for everything but it didn't feel right to Daeson.

"She wasn't the first."

"How so?"

"On my home world, my parents tried to protect me with a lie and the Cleric tried to save me with deception. They meant well but it only ended up hurting more than helping."

"Ohhh, that's what you were getting at in the vehicle yesterday."

What vehicle? Does she mean the limo? Was that yesterday? Wasn't it days ago?

No, Synjan was right. Only one night had passed after touching the Portal.

"Feels longer than one day," he said. They'd been through a lot.

"It was a very long day considering we left Trent in the afternoon and arrived here in the morning..."

"Imagine leaving in winter and arriving in summer. That's what I did the first time."

He expected Synjan to ask him questions but she burst into laughter instead. It surprised him into joining in and he spoke while chuckling. "Now I don't know if I'm eighteen or eighteen and a half. I ended up switching my winter birthday to a summer one."

Her laughter died down and they looked at one another.

"Huh, I thought you were my age. Which is twenty-four, by the way."

"That's the same age as Jade!" he said. He remembered the delight in her eyes when he'd presented a cupcake to her on her birthday. She'd thrown her arms around him and been ecstatic, over a simple cake. Her reaction had told him how little she expected from others and how a small gesture meant so much.

"Were the two of you good friends?" Synjan asked.

"She was my best friend." He felt a sharp pang in his chest when thinking of her. It was akin to the grief he'd felt when his father had died, which was silly because Jade was still alive. His arms ached to hug her again.

"What did Omerri think about that?"

Synjan shattered the memory and a vision of Omerri's glare surfaced.

"Uh. She knew we were friends. She knew we weren't sleeping together."

"She didn't approve, did she?"

He wanted to defend Omerri but didn't have the words. Her jealousy hadn't been hurtful but fuelled by her insecurity. Omerri thought so little of herself that she believed Daeson would move on to someone else. He had to constantly reassure her. Synjan took advantage of the silence to speak again.

"Hypocrite. The whole time she was with you, she was having Nick on the side. You should've slept with Jade."

The whole time?

Synjan knew about Omerri's indiscretion. Of course she did, she was a Navigator, she could see when people were cheating or sneaking around. He'd not known that Omerri had taken Nick into her bed from the start. He'd thought it was a more recent tryst, that Nick had pleaded with her, that she'd fallen for an old flame. But Synjan, with her Navigator talent, would've been able to see. A slow realisation came to him about what she *had* seen. He didn't ask because he didn't want to know. Unfortunately, Synjan confessed.

"I may have watched the two of them… and the two of you." There was a small pause. "Sorry."

It was getting worse. The less he said, the more she filled in the silence. Daeson leapt to his feet and swiped his hands on his backside to clean them.

"Let's put up the tent," he suggested, unable to meet her gaze. He had the impression that she was peeking up at him with embarrassment. It was a sensation they were sharing, then.

He led the way to where they'd left their belongings.

CHAPTER TEN

The Mission

THE weekend was chaperoned by a soft patter of rain. It was the kind of half-hearted weather that gave pause to outdoor plans yet promised rainbows. Hawke hadn't seen any rainbows but didn't care; he was entertained reacquainting himself with Brita's body. In between coffee breaks and snacks, they'd spent the day in bed. They were seeing in the afternoon when Brita's landline rang. She ignored it and curled against him—the answering machine would do its job. Hawke's own phone was off and still shoved in the pocket of his pants. There was nowhere for either of them to be.

Brita's message chirpily played and was met with dead air. Hawke expected the caller to hang up and leave a dial tone but then a strangled word was spoken, "Hawke."

He sat up in bed, startling Brita. The caller's voice was gravelly and tight. They were either disguising their voice or they'd gone through something violent. Regardless, he was being asked for on *Brita's* landline and very few people knew he stayed here.

"Who's that?" Brita asked, also sitting up. Hawke swung his legs out of bed to go to the phone but it was too late, the caller had already hung up. The dial tone buzzed savagely before the answering machine cut it off.

Hawke spied a wayward leg of his pants on the floor under his shirt. He snatched them out and dug through his pockets for his mobile phone. His thumbprint unlocked a screen that showed many missed calls, all of them labelled 'Kegs'.

Kegan Frederickson would've known where Hawke was. After getting no luck on Hawke's mobile, he would've tried Hawke's apartment next. No answer there and the next logical step was Brita's place.

"What's going on?" Brita asked.

Hawke shrugged and pulled on his underwear and pants before dialling Kegsy's number. He didn't want to reveal who it was because of the strange method used to attract Hawke's attention. Brita had met Kegsy a few times but her ability to identify him by voice was very slim—yet Kegs had taken no chances. It would be wise to respect that since Hawke didn't have any more information to go on.

Brita slid out of bed and went into the bathroom, closing the door behind her. He was grateful that she'd distanced herself from the conversation. Kegsy's mobile barely rang before he picked it up.

"Hawke," he stated. Kegsy's voice still sounded peculiar and raw but Hawke recognised it.

"Yeah." He considered the fact they were talking on mobile phones and understood what such a thing meant; Kegsy was on Othello. Portal phones couldn't connect with mobiles. "Where do you want to meet?"

"I'm downstairs."

Hawke was surprised. Something serious must be going on. "Okay. Two minutes."

He hung up and knocked on the bathroom door to get Brita's attention.

"I'll be back in a bit," he said to the door.

"Sure," Brita's voice floated back to him. "I'll get

ready."

For a moment he didn't know what she meant, thinking that she was getting ready to come along with him before he remembered that they'd made plans to go out. She was not-so-subtly telling him that she didn't want those plans to be changed.

He grabbed his shirt off the floor and smelled it before slipping it on. He couldn't find his loafers but his sneakers were near the front door for the morning run he hadn't taken. He shoved his feet into them before heading out, not bothering to lock the apartment door.

He pressed the button to call the lift and took advantage of his waiting time to adjust his sneakers and finish buttoning up his shirt. He entered the foyer within his two-minute timeframe and spied Kegan positioned in an armchair in the back corner of the lobby. There was nobody else around. Brita's building wasn't a dormitory full of students but an apartment tower for those who worked in Astro City—if eight floors could be considered a 'tower'.

Kegsy stood up to greet him as he approached and then pulled him into a tight embrace. As he entered the hug, Hawke was alarmed to see the Unit Commander's eyes were rimmed red. He patted Kegsy's back and they both sat.

"I need your help," Kegan began.

Obviously. Hawke bit back his sarcastic comment. Something had hit Kegsy hard for him to be in this world, chasing Hawke down the way he had. Hawke would never talk to him disrespectfully; as much of a friend as Kegsy had become, he still felt like a mentor.

"I'm here," Hawke said.

"A friend of mine, a *good* friend, has Wandered. I don't want a Hunter going after her. I don't want her to be..." Kegsy didn't finish his sentence but Hawke didn't need him to. He watched as Kegsy twisted in the chair and fished around in his back pocket for a rumpled card. "*You* have to get her back," he said as he held a photograph out.

Hawke took it from Kegan's unsteady hand and studied the candid, blurry image of a blonde woman. Even with imperfect focus, he recognised her. Synjan N'dia Walker. A known associate of Howard Ellis, Synjan was in her mid-twenties and Trent-born. Synjan held the position that was supposed to have been his, the one he'd unofficially rejected over twenty years ago. Personal curiosity was responsible for Hawke pulling her file one day while on Oceangate. The only connection he had to Ellis' enterprise nowadays was Kegan Frederickson… and that had grown into a separate relationship. Still, he knew enough about Synjan to understand she would be a formidable opponent. Ellis had intended to groom his protégé to accomplish a great many things—all the promises he'd made to Hawke had been bestowed upon her instead. Hawke had no doubt Synjan would be a skilled fighter, intelligent and educated, and likely trained with weaponry. Perhaps even mentored by a skilled Unit Commander.

"Did you train her as well?"

"Yes."

"When was the last time you trained her?"

"Last week."

"Last *week*?" Hawke asked sharply, surprised that Kegan had continued to train her as an adult.

"Ellis is…" Kegan began. Hawke waited for the rest of the sentence but it was left unfinished also. He debated pursuing it but changed the topic to something more important.

"What is she?"

"Somebody I care about," Kegan said, misinterpreting the question. Hawke didn't think it was purposeful but he did find the answer interesting.

"No, I mean what bloodline is she?"

Kegan's expression changed. It was striking to see how shuttered his face became after it had displayed every desperate emotion clearly up 'til now. Hawke was pissed at the implication.

"Fuck you, I'm not going to betray you. I need to know."

"Navigator."

Her Wanderer talent was in high demand. There were whispers of Navigators working with the Authorities in the past but they'd become nothing more than urban legends. If the Authorities didn't find another Shielder to replace him, he might become the same. Only bad things would happen to a Wanderer Navigator if taken alive. He knew that much.

"Your girl has the shittiest timing. I've had my three missions already," Hawke complained, already considering that his last mission had been noted as 'suspended'. If he could somehow swing it as a failed mission, he'd be able to try again with another. That would attract even more attention, though. Hawke rarely failed. It would look doubly peculiar for him to request a failure on record once he was already on leave.

"And a fourth is impossible?" Kegan implored. Hawke stared. The question stank of desperation.

"No, but—" Hawke recalled the conversation he'd had with Evan, Brita's asshole friend. He'd mentioned the Spy Division requiring Hawke's help on Femme. It wasn't the only world they wanted Hawke's help on but the one that they were the most relentless for. The persistent amount of paperwork that hit Cayden's desk from Nakhari Base had led to numerous complaints from his superior. He suspected that was half the reason Cayden had never lent him out.

The thing was, Femme was the next world in line from Trent, which meant Synjan was on it now. It was a bizarre coincidence that the asshole friend had mentioned Femme just before Hawke had to go there and find someone. A handier coincidence would have been Kegan needing Hawke's help just before he'd picked his third and final mission. For fuck's sake, if he went to Nakhari Base and the asshole friend was there (lying about never being on Femme because that's what Spies did best), that would be the worst coincidence of all.

"But?" Kegan pressed.

It wasn't in Hawke's typical behaviour to request work with another division—least of all with Spies. Cayden also knew how much he despised all slave worlds, Femme in particular because they fancied their slave culture was elite. For him to request a Spy-based assignment on Femme would be *exceptionally* strange... unless he was chasing tail.

He would end up looking like a bastard and a deviant, skipping out on his time with Brita to pursue something cheap and thrilling. Cayden would disapprove but he would also believe it. Even though Hawke's indiscretions always happened while on a mission, Cayden knew Hawke had fooled around with enough women that he probably wouldn't question a peculiar request. Not if he thought there was some kind of gratification or conquest involved.

"Hawke!" Kegsy said impatiently, his voice raw.

"I'm thinking," Hawke explained. "I can assign myself to Femme because there's a request for my assistance. While I'm there I can look around for your girl, since I know what she looks like."

"She's not alone."

Hawke set his jaw. "The fuck?"

"There's a guy with her."

"Who?"

"Another Wanderer named Daeson. He...we want him too."

"Who is 'we'?" Hawke asked though he thought he

knew. It was better to be clear than to make assumptions.

"Ellis."

Neither of them said anything immediately after the statement. It wasn't Hawke's business how Kegsy was connected to the man. He'd turned his back on that knowledge decades ago. It didn't matter what Kegsy owed Ellis. It was what Hawke owed Kegsy—which was a lot. He'd unquestioningly provided Hawke with an alibi years ago, saving him from being expelled from Willets Academy. He'd continued to train and mentor him, steering him through the ranks of the Authorities alongside Cayden, supporting and guiding him in countless ways. Ultimately, it had all begun at Willets. Hawke was convinced his life would have turned out shitty if Kegsy hadn't covered for him way back when.

"I don't think I can get two back."

The Unit Commander winced but the grimness in his eyes communicated that he understood. The fact that Kegsy didn't push it told Hawke that the guy was expendable. Until he said: "He's a Healer."

The fact Kegsy knew about a Wanderer Healer and hadn't reported it was astonishing. Hawke's mind fed him multiple scenarios about why Kegan would keep such a thing secret, considering the payoff that came with finding a Healer and delivering them to the Authorities.

If Hawke 'found' a Healer, he would be able to negotiate for Synjan's freedom. He could always sell it that she'd been the tail he was chasing, even though blondes weren't his preference.

"I might have to use the Healer to get Synjan out," Hawke said bluntly. He wanted no surprises or accusations later. "I'll do my best but I don't know how I'm supposed to bring them back through an Authority portal."

"Uh..." An expression that Hawke couldn't recognise

appeared on Kegan's face. He looked like he was trying to decide whether or not to say something. Kegsy wasn't a deliberating man; he was one of action. His indecision was a clue.

"You have access to some other kind of portal?" Hawke pressed.

"Just the Authority ones."

The conviction of his delivery would've sold the lie except Hawke was already suspicious. There were no energy flares on Trent, but the Authority portals weren't designed to monitor their own signatures and frequencies. There were usually two or more portals per world, covering different hemispheres or on opposite sides of the planet. Some worlds had several portals; every Alpha Base world had at least five, and Alpha One boasted fourteen of them.

Were there portals reserved for high-security purposes? It made sense. Kegsy was a Unit Commander of the Interworld Tactical Response division so he might have access to such things. If this was the case, why not tell Hawke about them?

"And when I catch up with her?" he asked.

"Call me from a portal phone."

"Await further instructions? Can you not help me help you?"

"It depends which world you find her in," Kegan said abruptly.

"I'll find her straight away. She's unseasoned."

"So how are you supposed to catch up to her on Femme?" Kegan demanded. Hawke figured he'd want specifics.

"I happen to be a Shielder."

"What?"

Hawke thought that if his friend hadn't been so overwrought, he'd have made the connection more easily. "Being a Shielder is why they want me. Why else do you think the fucking Spy Division on Femme is requesting me?"

"But...*working* with the spies?" Kegan repeated, finally realising what Hawke was getting at. He glanced around the empty foyer. His voice dropped to a barely audible rumble. "An inter-world incident is bound to attract attention," he hissed.

Hawke was well aware of the restrictions of his two-minute plan, but it was the best he could do at short notice. As with all Authority bases, the one in Femme was dedicated to a specific purpose; spying. He couldn't change the placement of the Spy Division headquarters. If Kegs was thinking more clearly, he'd be grateful that Hawke had a standing request—and therefore an excuse—to work there.

"Do you want my help or not?" Hawke said, careful to keep his tone pleasant. Kegan's questions were on point. Hawke was going to have to figure something out and he was going to have to do it on the fly.

"Sorry. Yes, it's just... what if there's another Hunter?" Kegan asked.

"There won't be from a Trent flare. They wouldn't even bother flagging it for a flare report on Femme because there's a constant amount coming out from that world. All their bullshit 'accidental Wanders'."

"Good," Kegsy breathed. "So you'll do it? You'll get her for me?" Kegsy's voice was mostly steady but a mild break in the second sentence gutted Hawke. Other than a stern facade or quiet amusement, he'd not seen his mentor and friend this emotional. He felt obliged to do his best. No... *better* than his best.

"Yes. I will bring Synjan back."

When Hawke returned to the apartment, Brita was already showered and wearing a conservative but stylish navy dress. Her wet hair was bundled into a towel as she searched the drawers of her dresser. She spared Hawke a quizzical look when he entered the bedroom but didn't stop to ask him what his urgent business had been about. She must've assumed it wouldn't affect their time together.

He wasn't looking forward to telling her different.

While Hawke debated how to begin, Brita found what she was looking for and returned to the bathroom. Moments later he heard the breathy whirr of the hair-dryer and he took the opportunity to get a head-start on pulling his things together. The more he got done without her seeing, the more peaceful his exit was going to be.

His messenger bag had been thrown into one corner of the wardrobe, empty except for a few travel-convenient items. He grabbed the bag and unbuckled it, flipping it open and quickly shoving in the few clothes he'd brought straight off the hangers. He travelled light so it took him very little time to gather everything. When he moved to Brita's dresser, opening his assigned drawer, she must've noticed movement because the dryer whirred down and she spoke from the doorway.

"Why are you packing your bag? You only just *got* here. We were going out for dinner."

She spoke as though he'd forgotten their plans when wiling away the day.

"I won't be able to make it."

She disappeared into the bathroom and he heard the clunk of the dryer being set down. Hawke shoved underwear and socks into his bag as quickly as he could, knowing that he wouldn't be able to escape without hearing whatever Brita wanted to say.

He owed her that, even though he couldn't tell her what was going on. She wouldn't ask where he was going because she never asked. This time, he was wrong.

"You've completed your missions so where are you going?" she asked, striding across the room so she could stand close, watching as he shut the drawer and then set his bag on the dresser to do up the buckles.

"Something else came up."

"Something *else*?" she asked. He could hear the terseness in her tone.

"Something else," he repeated. Once he had his bag closed, he turned to face her. She was furious, he could see it. Her cheeks were pink with rage and her glare was intense.

If only she'd looked like that at the dinner last night with her asshole friend. But that wasn't fair, he was coming up with excuses to make leaving her easier. For nine months he'd been looking forward to coming back to Othello, to spending time with her.

Kind of. He enjoyed his job, didn't he? Except for the final part, which never felt the way he wanted it to and the nightmares that haunted him. He'd learnt to deal with it on mission, operating on very little sleep—but he slept so peacefully on Othello, in Brita's arms.

How would he sleep while on Femme?

"It's not the DOME, is it?"

Brita's question was asked haltingly and shocked him into silence. He hadn't suspected she might think such a thing and her compassion for the experiments he continued to endure at their hands (laughably simple now, but he never gave her details), allowed him an easy lie.

It would make things uncomplicated between them if he said yes. If it was the DOME calling, he would be walking away from her doing something he hated but was obligated to do. He would be forgiven for leaving so soon, the Hunter Division wouldn't get the blame and she wouldn't complain to Cayden. Except there was a good chance she would be calling Cayden anyway because this was Brita and that was what she did. She connected with people. She checked in with people. Or was it checked up on people?

"It's not the DOME," he confirmed. Her reaction was volatile.

"What is it, then?" she blurted, smacking his shoulders with the palms of her hands before throwing them out to her sides. The one closest to the dresser flicked against the mirror and she put the knuckle of her littlest finger in her mouth.

He swallowed his instinct to ask her if she was alright. He could imagine her answer. Her knuckle came out of her mouth.

"Stop making sad face and tell me where you're going."

"Brita, you know not to ask me when—"

"Don't give me crap about missions! I don't ask you about missions!" She jabbed her index finger into his chest. It was surprisingly painful. "You said yourself this is not a fucking *mission*."

He blinked at the swearword. She wasn't so prim or prudish that she had a problem with profanity—she certainly didn't care if others swore around her—but he couldn't recall her saying anything stronger than 'shit'.

"Who was that on the phone?"

"A friend."

"You don't have friends," she said. The statement cut him deeper than he wanted to admit. She must have seen something in his expression because she relented. "You tell me that all the time."

"I don't tell you that all the time. Do you know where my shoes are?" he asked.

Brita glanced at his feet momentarily before she placed a hand on Hawke's chest, over his heart.

"How long will you be gone for?" Her question was calm and he was wary. He couldn't believe that the storm had passed.

"Not long," he said.

The pink colour rose in Brita's cheeks again and he knew his answer had been the wrong one. She shoved herself away from him, using his chest. She went to the bed and sat heavily on the edge.

"I hate when you lie to me," she said to the carpet.

"I don't know how long it'll take," he amended. "I hope it won't be long. Then I can be with you."

"Are you sure that's what you want?" she asked, her stare lifting to his face. He didn't like the careful quality of her anger. He would prefer her to be unreasonable and throwing things at his head instead of logically assessing the problem between them.

"Yes, that's what I want."

He couldn't imagine his life without her. He didn't want to. She was his foundation, the only part of his existence he looked forward to. She was perfect for him. He just wasn't perfect for her.

"Why do you do this, then? Why do you leave me? Why do you want to run around those other worlds and be with those other women? Aren't you tired?"

He'd made a single step towards her so that he could kneel at her feet, but her questions—not formed like accusations but like she knew for sure—stopped him. His inability to speak gave her a chance to continue.

"I don't mention them because I'm jealous. I mean, I guess I must be a little bit, to mention them at all, but it doesn't bother me in the way that you think."

"How does it bother you, then?" he asked, sitting beside her instead of on the floor before her. It felt more appropriate.

"It's a symptom, not the problem. You have your life, I have mine and we meet in the middle, pretending that we could have more."

He considered her words. "You don't think what we have is enough? It's more honest than what others have."

Brita breathed a soft laugh as she looked at him, then

twisted around so she could hold his face. It was like she was about to kiss him but he knew that wasn't going to happen.

"Even though it doesn't sound it, I like that you've never promised me more because it will have greater meaning when you do." She puffed a soft laugh and released his face, her hands falling to her lap. "*If* you do," she said to herself.

Her answer was clear enough even though she hadn't said it directly. She was holding out for more. She wasn't sitting at home waiting for him, though.

"I want you in my life, Brita," he said to her. "Every time I come back I wonder if you'll be there to pick me up, or if you've moved on with someone else."

"Hawke…"

"It doesn't bother you that I've been with other women because you've been with other men," he said. The words out loud made it more real, more hurtful. He understood now why they'd never talked about it, why she'd held her tongue. How long had she known? Maybe she'd always known. The possibility horrified him.

"The way I feel about those men is the same way you feel about those women," she said. "They're nothing. Nobodies." She looked at him, searching his face. He wasn't sure what she was looking for until he realised she was seeking affirmation. He nodded and she seemed to relax.

"I'll come back to you when this is done. I don't want to lose you."

"Oh, Hawke, haven't you figured it out by now?" Brita said, leaning against him. "To get rid of me, you'd have to push me away."

CHAPTER ELEVEN

Invisible Threat

DAESON didn't know why Synjan had bought him a two-man tent when they'd shopped for supplies. She'd chosen it on his behalf because he'd been overwhelmed; of Wandering to another world and leaving Trent behind, of breaking up with Omerri, of potentially attracting the Authorities' ire for travelling illegally and being on his own again. If Synjan had mentioned back then that she'd planned to come along, it might have made him feel better.

He detached the tent, which was in its own flat bag. He handed it to Synjan who plotted a clear section of ground near the sleeping trees before unzipping it.

"Why'd you buy me a two-man tent?" he asked.

Synjan gave him a sideways glance and pulled the tent out of its bag.

"You're big. I figured you'd need room," she said while undoing a tie.

The tent exploded open and Daeson flinched, not expecting it to assemble itself. He boggled at it as Synjan staked the four corners. She'd called it a 'pop-up' but he'd had no idea the name was so literal. He watched her unzip the door flap and roll it open. Her answer had been truthful but he was suspicious. Was she omitting information?

"Not for travelling with someone else then? Like you?"

She stood up straight and grinned at him with hands on hips. "Alright, out with it. What do you need to say?"

Daeson stared back. Now that she'd addressed him directly, he felt petty for making the jab.

"Were you hoping I'd take you?"

"I can Wander by myself. I just couldn't... make the break. I was scared."

What could scare *her*? She was the scariest woman he'd ever met. He watched as she gazed at the tent, her eyes faraway. Her body heaved with a drawn out sigh and her posture shifted. She looked unexpectedly vulnerable.

"Of what?" Daeson asked.

"Everything. Letting Ellis down, the work I had to do, getting caught by the Authorities... dying." Synjan looked back at him. "That day, all my fears were realised. But I was still scared of Ellis, I couldn't consciously decide to leave him, even though everything in me knew I had to. Seeing you go triggered something. So I left with you."

Perhaps he would never understand her or the life she'd led but he could understand why she'd taken his hand. He'd done the same thing when his farm was beyond hope—he'd seen what he'd wanted to see until forced to leave. At least she'd made her own decision.

Her words prompted more questions that he didn't think were relevant. Had she been in love with Ellis? Had Ellis used her the same way Omerri had used him? It didn't matter because they'd left both of them behind but he did realise that they'd talked a lot about Omerri and not much about Ellis. He acknowledged her words with a nod but couldn't ask about her past without feeling like he was prying. He looked back at the tent.

"I think I might prefer this over the goats."

Synjan laughed. "And I, over the cliff. We should both fit. Luckily I'm small," she said, eyeing him over.

"You're not that small," he said, glancing at her breasts before diverting back to her face. He hoped she hadn't caught his slip but she snorted laughter.

"You won't be pushed out of the tent."

"I won't try anything," he promised, feeling guilty at being caught looking. She wasn't a girl from the Queen whose living depended on her desirability. He didn't have permission of any kind from her. "You're safe with me."

"Thank you, good to know. I'll keep my hands to myself as well."

Daeson mused on her reply, feeling the familiar tinge of a lie and surprised by it.

"But you don't want to," he challenged, wondering what she would say. Her eyes widened and her cheeks flamed pink. She pressed her lips together like she was holding back and he thought it might be a good idea to wait her out. She liked to talk, he'd noticed.

She was saved by a burst of loud singing, many voices atop one another. They sounded upset.

"Something's wrong. Let's go see," he said. Her response was immediate and they both ran towards the singing.

The Mukake people were gathering at the narrow end of the pillar. Some of them were sing-shouting while climbing up and others climbed down. It was chaos. A trickle of natives peeled away from the main group towards the Shinu, who approached the mob. There was more excited singing before the female Shinu quieted them with a gesture. She pointed to a spokesperson, a man that Daeson didn't know. He listened to the song that followed, hurried and difficult to make sense of. The only word he recognised—because it was repeated—was 'kapu'.

"They're talking about a boat. Something's gone wrong with a boat," Daeson explained to Synjan, not wanting her to feel left out.

"A boat? Could it have something to do with those four people earlier today?"

Daeson thought her guess was a good one and trepidation filled him. Had four people drowned while everybody partied?

He heard a few people say 'piangi'. It hadn't been long beforehand when he'd been asked if he would take a boat and leave. "Now they're saying the boat has left."

He looked at Synjan who appeared on the verge of understanding. She closed her eyes and Daeson felt her presence shift. She was mapping. When her eyes sprang open, her expression was one of surprise.

"They're not from here, they're from that other island! I can see their patterns! They're in three different boats! By the Gods, they've taken *two* of the Mukake's canoes!"

She kept saying 'they' but Daeson thought he knew who she meant. There had been another group of natives hiding in the jungle while he and Synjan had gone with the Mukake.

"Do you mean the invisible people?"

"Yeah, I think they're enemies."

"They must be because friends don't steal other friends' boats."

She snorted a laugh before she grew serious. "We should tell them."

"Because we want them to be angry?" He was surprised by how much Synjan wanted to share information. As much as he didn't like Omerri's deceptive qualities, she'd taught him about keeping things to himself as a matter of survival. He'd kept the secret of his being a Healer, and he knew from experience that he was better off not letting people know he could discern truth from lies. Synjan wasn't much of a secret-keeper.

His words must have affected her because Synjan seemed calmer when next she spoke. "No, we should tell them because they're upset. They should know what's happened, shouldn't they?"

"Wouldn't they already know?"

"Do you think they realise it's their enemy?"

"Who else would steal their boats?"

His logic led to her silence. They both listened to the singing, which sounded angry. One word Daeson heard spat many times registered as significant enough for him to tell Synjan.

"That must be the name of their enemy," he observed.

"What is?"

"Techatachenti."

CHAPTER TWELVE

Old Habits, New Uses

EVEN though Daeson convinced her it was pointless to tell the Mukake about the Techatachenti thieves, Synjan felt bad for their hosts. The contentment after the celebration feast was tainted by the stolen canoes. Everywhere she looked, people were bunched in tight groups, frowning and gesturing angrily, their shoulders stiff and mouths drawn. The Shinu were kept busy, splitting up to accommodate the amount of people that wanted to speak with them about the group's loss. There was obviously more to the theft of the canoes than Synjan understood.

Believing that no work would be undertaken, she and Daeson decided to collect some water to drink and wash in. Before they left, she positioned the solar-powered lantern she'd bought so that it would catch the last of the daylight. She also fished a plastic disc from his pack—it snapped open to become a large bowl—and collected their water flasks, a cake of soap and her tattered blouse so she could freshen up.

As they walked through the golden afternoon light, deliberately avoiding Mukake members so that they didn't get drawn into the drama anew, they chatted about camping technology. It led to a discussion about

Authority inventions. Daeson was interested to hear that the Authorities had only revealed themselves to the world of Trent some sixty years previous and nodded thoughtfully as Synjan told him of the offence taken by the inhabitants at having their world taken over. Importing sophisticated things was only the beginning of a mountain of insults that was crowned by Oceangate Base. The people young enough to have lived the changeover were old timers in Trent now and they were no more forgiving than they had been when everything began.

After Synjan and Daeson filled their flasks at the water tank, they left them behind and took a bowl of water to the rocky outcrop nearby. They found a secluded place to bathe. Synjan went first, stripping once Daeson had returned to the tank. She scrubbed her body before attending to her clothes. While washing her hair, she discovered that she had cut her head on the rock that morning. The way the suds turned pink between her fingers was disturbing and she was glad to rinse it away.

Pulling on wet clothes felt strange but the smell of soap was refreshing and the heat of the dying day was as relentless as it had been in the morning, so she was warm. Synjan returned to Daeson and he headed for the washing spot next, armed with the soap and her ripped blouse to wash with. She found a place to lay her socks and stretch out to dry in the sun while she waited, closing her eyes and finger-combing the long strands of her hair. The Mukake were still upset so she amused herself by watching Daeson's pattern as he washed. Her imagination filled in the details she was unable to actually see.

When Daeson returned, she smiled at him as he filled the bowl to take to the tent with them, hoping she wasn't blushing. She ducked her head while she gathered the rest of their things and did her best to look serene as they strolled back to their campsite.

Eventually, they ventured back to participate in the evening's meal but it only involved a small selection of food and continued debate about canoes. They kept to themselves, mostly unnoticed bar a smile from Bo and a cackling interaction with Hiyani who seemed greatly amused by everyone's agitation. It was a relief to withdraw to Daeson's tent when the sun began to fade in earnest, leaving the rest of the group still debating.

Synjan collected the lantern and clicked it on, crawling into the tent before Daeson. She zipped the screen door closed behind him and held the lantern up while she inspected the air, wanting to be sure nothing had flown in after them. Satisfied, she turned off the light, wriggled out of her shorts, wiped off her feet and relaxed back onto her pillow of folded clothes. It felt odd to be in her underwear when she was used to sleeping naked but she would have to get used to it. It was impractical to be completely vulnerable when they were already in unknown territory.

"This is a thousand times better than where I slept last night," she sighed, revelling in her horizontal position. The first soft taps of rain pattered on the tent's roof, adding to the cosy atmosphere and reinforcing the wisdom of her decision to invite herself into the shelter. There'd been no clouds all day but these drops augured a more substantial shower than they'd previously experienced.

"Agreed," Daeson murmured. She was sure of the smile in his voice.

"And now that I've had a wash, I smell better than the goats, too."

His laughter was companionable and filled her with a profound sense of satisfaction. It was far preferable to irritating him and having him need time away from her to calm down.

"Thanks for letting me share with you," she told him

intently. "I really appreciate it."

"You're welcome." The rain began in earnest now, isolating them and sending cooler air through the mesh door. The scent of the rain filtering into the grassy soil nearby was fresh and lovely.

"Hopefully we'll be able to find some better supplies in Femme and I can get my own tent," she mused.

"If we make it to the Portal."

"We'll figure it out," she assured him through a yawn. "Wanderers have been doing this for years uncountable before us and I'm sure they'll continue long after we're done. The situation could be worse. I vaguely recall my father talking about how tough Wandering was. We're not giving up."

"Your father Wandered?"

"And my mother. They met Wandering, fell in love while Wandering, got married while Wandering. They only stopped because Mum was pregnant with my sister, Chandler."

"They *chose* Gredann?"

His tone made her giggle. "Yeah. It was not so bad, compared to where they'd been, I guess." Her head lolled towards her shoulder and she could make out his profile in the darkness. Her blinks were slowing and she could feel her muscles loosening.

Daeson was quiet for a moment. "I didn't even know that Wanderers existed and you grew up knowing everything about them."

"Well, not *everything*. I remember being told about the twelve powers and I know their names but I couldn't give you details about what they do. My parents told me some stuff but mostly it was my dad teaching me about Navigating. The rest... I've forgotten. I was little when they died."

"There are twelve powers?"

"Definitely," she nodded, even though he likely wouldn't see the movement in the dark. It prompted another yawn and she realised that lack of restful sleep was catching up with her. Fast. Her words were slurred with exhaustion. "But the Authorities don't know about... about—I think it's two of 'em? Mmm, I can't remember that, either. It's in the folder Ellis gave me. We can look'it in the morning if y'want."

"Okay," he agreed and she thought she heard him mention Ellis' name but she wasn't sure because her conscious mind flew into slumber, leaving any chance of more discussion far behind.

When Synjan's eyes opened, she was lying on her side and the tent was bright enough that she could tell the sun had crested the horizon. Daeson's arms were wrapped around her and he was pressed against her back, his body spooning hers from her head to her heels. Blinking away the last vestiges of sleep, her eyes focussed on his arm extending from beneath her head to where her hand was entwined with his. His other arm curved over her hip and along her stomach, his hand curled upon her breast. His breathing was slow and steady, telling her he was still asleep.

It occurred to her that she should feel embarrassed... but she wasn't. At the very least, she should try to get away from him... but she didn't. The puff of Daeson's breath across her cheek was soothing. He smelled of masculine sweat and a long, deep sleep. She could feel the thud of his heart and the smooth quality of his skin. He made her feel tiny and protected in the most complimentary way she'd ever experienced—because it was subconscious and innate.

She smiled as she remembered his solemn promise the day before, telling her he'd keep his hands to himself. It was tantalising, lying against him, very little between her and his morning salute. But he was her travelling partner, a man she wanted to befriend more than she wanted to bed. She yearned for them to like each other. He was younger than her and bruised where she was broken but he was so *good* and kind and thoughtful. He'd never killed, never even harmed another and all he'd had to give when he got to Gredann was his heart. She hated that Omerri had ruined that.

Right now, she had to protect him from herself. By following his example, she might come to be as good a person as he was. Daeson would be the light that would guide her, she was sure of it.

Daeson's breathing changed as he shifted closer to wakefulness and Synjan did her best to relax, wondering how he would react when he woke to find himself entwined with her. She didn't want to influence him and she believed she didn't because he flinched back in surprise. He carefully extracted his arm from under her head and shuffled away.

Synjan was still debating whether she was being dishonest by not greeting him when he slid into his shorts, unzipped the tent door and crawled out. She rolled onto her back, mapping him heading for the toilet area, and sighed. She supposed she ought to follow him but what was she supposed to say? The time for talking had passed and anything she said now would be awkward. She pulled on her shorts and got a clean pair of socks out of her bag, cursing herself for not speaking sooner.

Just as she pulled on her second boot, Tagan stuck his head into the tent, singing her name as brightly as he had the day before. She almost kicked him in reflex.

"Synjan?" Tagan queried.

"Give me a second," she told him apologetically, gesturing at him to wait so she could finish tying her lace.

When she got out of the tent, Tagan snatched her

hand and led her towards the climbing edge of the cliff, rather than the area she associated with meals. This surprised her enough that she resisted his hold, insisting that she needed to relieve herself before she started her morning with a perilous climb. When she returned, Tagan took her to the place she'd climbed up two days before, where there were lots of posts with vine lassos tied to them. She knew this was the beginner's climbing wall—for whatever good such a label did—but it was just as intimidating as it had been the day she arrived.

"You want to go down?" she asked Tagan.

He sang something as he put a lasso over her head and manoeuvred her close to the edge.

"I guess we're going down," she muttered to herself, wondering why it was necessary but trusting her green-eyed companion's judgement. After a few warm-up stretches, she allowed him to direct her over the edge of the cliff and guide her. She found it much more difficult than going up and relied heavily on his direction to find foot and hand holds.

When they were halfway down, Synjan heard another climber approaching. She looked up to see Bo descending on her other side. Her jaw dropped at his speed and assuredness and he reached her in a dizzyingly short amount of time. Instead of saying anything to her, he only had eyes for Tagan.

Once they were level, the two men sang angrily at one another. Not knowing what to do otherwise, Synjan clung to the rock, pressing her body in as close as she could. It was just as well she did because the singing deteriorated into grunting spits and then they started pushing and shoving one another—over the top of her!

She mewled, closing her eyes and trying not to look. The two men were jostling closer to her and the sound of flesh striking flesh was as loud as gun shots in the morning air. They were trying to slap each others' hands free of the cliff!

When Tagan finally collected her in one of his swipes—no doubt because Bo had hit him mid-swing—Synjan had had enough. She opened her eyes, pulled her head back from the cliff and glared at them both in terror. "Fuck this!" she screamed. "Fuck you *and* you, you're both crazy and if you think I'm going to hang here until one of you goes splat, think again!" She started climbing upward, willing her shaky limbs to obey.

Her fury united them and she was apologetically stopped and directed to continue downwards. She wasn't sure she wanted to but also wasn't sure she had the strength to complete an immediate up-climb after hanging around so long in the middle.

Once she reached the broad shelf of rock at the bottom of the cliff, Synjan was only allowed a brief respite before Tagan took her hand again. She didn't understand his urgency until he led her past the pulley area and around to the farthest end of the rocky platform. The island was broadest here, but the jetty came to a tapering end far below where the women's cave was.

The tide was low enough to reveal another smooth, flat section of rock jutting out of the cliff but it was at least a metre below the main one and didn't go very far. Tagan helped her down onto the lower shelf, leading her towards an opening in the cliff that she had to duck slightly to get under. Beyond the lintel, it opened out into a small cave and she could stand freely.

"Oh, wow," Synjan breathed her appreciation as she walked up a floor covered in soft sand, weaving between stumps of rock towards the rounded conclave at the back. There was a salty smell and the walls were darker at their bases, indicating that the tide hadn't retreated that long ago. The morning light was creeping up the sloped floor and casting minimal light elsewhere but that gave the little space an even more intimate feeling. "It's beautiful." She smiled at Tagan, understanding that he'd needed her to follow him before the tide blocked their access to this little gem.

Tagan looked very pleased with himself as he sang at her and pointed out some of the cave's less obvious features; a midden of lost shells gathered at the back wall, a strip of glinting, glass-like rock streaking down one of the rocky stumps and a huge fish skeleton from so long ago it was now part of the rock itself, framed in the eastern wall. She followed him everywhere he led, amazed by it all and responding appropriately.

Bo stood apart from the pair of them, watching with an unhappy expression that Tagan seemed to delight in worsening. At first, Synjan noted Tagan singing little songs that compressed Bo's lips or had him shake his head in negation, but then he progressed to making longer comments and sounding like he was asking the taller man questions. Synjan knew they were about her because of the sly way Tagan looked at her before he sang at Bo and then laughed in a superior manner when the larger man glowered at him.

She was about to step in and say something when Tagan must have told Bo something truly controversial, considering the way he looked at her.

"What?" she asked, equally as startled by his expression.

Bo spared her a tight smile and then sang something at Tagan, who merely laughed and seemed to ask another probing question.

Whatever it was, Bo's folded arms and distant stare told her he refused to discuss it. Tagan seemed to have no such qualms and he finally included her in his games.

"Synjan," he sang, holding up a hand she took to represent her, "Daeson." His other hand came up, palm facing palm. He gave her a questioning look as he pressed his fingertips together gently then rolled the rest of his hands together. After a bit of up and down rubbing, he started slapping the heels of his hands together and making moaning and sighing noises. His role-play was very obvious. His hands finished mimicking sex and dropped.

Synjan blushed and broke eye contact, looking at Bo instead. He was still standing with his arms folded but he was also looking at her curiously. He wanted to know the answer as well, even if he'd been too dignified to do the asking. It occurred to her that she'd got herself into not just an awkward situation but a potentially dangerous one. She was alone in a cave with two men that were both so interested in competing for her attention that they were willing to fling the other off a cliff for the privilege. No-one knew she was here and now they wanted to know what her relationship with her travelling partner was like. A frisson of realisation ran down her spine.

"No," she answered, shaking her head. She took a step away from the two of them, assessing the distance between them and her, their body positions and contemplating how she'd disable them if they made a move she didn't like. As much as she wanted to escape the negatives of Gredann and her work, the comfortable skin of suspicion and readiness was welcome. Some things she needed to leave behind; her training and ability to look after herself should not be one of them. Daeson wasn't the only one that needed protection. "Daeson and I don't have sex," she added, lifting her hands with the palms pressed together before she very obviously pulled them apart.

Tagan's eyes lit up and he turned to crow delightedly at his companion, however Bo was more observant. He was no longer interested in her answer. He took a step back, glanced around and found a rock to sit on. He loosely clasped his hands between his knees and looked up at her, seeking approval.

She smiled at him gratefully, ignoring Tagan until he hooked an arm through hers and dragged her over to sit on a rock not quite opposite Bo. He was gabbling something she couldn't understand, looking pleased that he'd got the answer he wanted *and* she was now sitting beside him, but she didn't pay him any attention. Bo's expression had changed and the look he was giving her now was heated. A flighty, needy part of her responded brazenly to it. It was very hard to concentrate on the conversation, though it seemed Tagan was content to talk for all of them—until he finally realised that the other two in his party were simply staring at each other.

"Synjan?   Bo?"   he   sang,   waiting   for acknowledgement.

When Bo looked away, Synjan swayed forward slightly, feeling the break in their silent communication like a physical wrench. Her heart did a flip that echoed all the way down to where she was quivering and she managed a rueful smile as she looked at Tagan. "Yes?"

Bo sang something and waved his hand. Tagan frowned and sang back, waving his hand in much the same way. Bo sang again and suddenly the two of them were sing-arguing. Over her. Again.

Synjan cleared her throat. "So, how about those Techatachenti assholes taking your boats yesterday, huh?" she asked with false cheer. It had the desired effect; both men stopped arguing and looked at her like she'd just sprouted another head.

"Techatachenti?" Bo asked in his deep voice.

"Yes, four of them took your boats yesterday," Synjan agreed, holding up four fingers. She wished she could remember the word for 'boat'.

Tagan reached over and touched each of her fingers, before singing a question at her that she didn't understand.

"Four Techatachenti men," she explained, adding to

her acting repertoire by getting up and miming four men as large and barrel-chested as Bo, with dour faces and stomping feet. She made a point of showing how the four had rowed over to the Mukake's island squashed into one canoe and then two had snuck out of their boat into the Mukake boats, whereupon all four had made a getaway. She improvised at the end by drawing the final, retreating formation of the thieves in the sand.

Her captive audience was quiet for a few moments, then Tagan asked Bo a question, pointing to her sand drawings. Bo's forehead was creased as he put thought into the answer, glancing at Synjan like she might be able to clarify before he also pointed at the diagrams, telling a different story. From what Synjan could tell, there seemed to be a discrepancy between the number of rowers and the number of boats taken, so she got up on her knees to clarify. She wiped the sand clean to start her story again, drawing the exact positioning of the Techatachenti's island, the Mukake's island and the exclamation islands she and Daeson had woken up on between the two.

"Techatachenti," she said, pointing at their island and drawing a boat shape with four stick figures in it. "Four," she repeated, holding up her fingers. "Sailed here..." she drew a line in the sand to the Mukake's island, "took two—*two*—Mukake canoes," she said, changing fingers and then drawing two canoes either side of her newly-arrived one. "Then, go," she finished, employing the use of several arrows, flying stick figures and some half circles to represent the theft of the two Mukake boats.

Tagan and Bo shot to their feet when she was done and stood either side of her map, conferring about what was going on. They said the two tribal names she knew and the word for boat that she'd forgotten many times and just as Synjan was beginning to despair that her story had gone awry, Bo knelt down beside her and pointed at something unexpected.

"Techatachenti?" he sang, pointing at the island she'd drawn to represent their home.

"Yes, that's where they all live," she nodded.

Bo and Tagan exchanged stupefied looks and then gaped at her. She couldn't understand why they were so amazed that she knew where the Techatachenti lived... and then it hit her.

"Oh! *Oh!* You're wondering how I know!" she cried. "I'm a Wanderer," she explained, using a word they would recognise. "I can *see* in my mind," she told them, exaggerating her movements as she closed her eyes, used her hands to mimic the top of her head flying off and hovering over the top of the drawings in the sand. "I can see with my mind. Navigator," she told them, moving her hand from her head to her chest to indicate she was talking about herself and her talent.

Bo looked up at Tagan and then the two of them exploded into excited conversation, singing with such long notes she was awed. It was her turn to gape at *them*. Her admiration was cut short when Bo grabbed her hand and pulled her to her feet. He dragged her out of the cave after him, with only one word making sense in amongst his rapid singing: "Shinu!" He wanted her to tell the Shinu what she'd seen or he wanted her to be with him when *he* told the Shinu.

She'd never got into a lasso so fast. As soon as it was on, she was climbing. As considerate as Bo was towards her, he wasn't giving her a chance to refuse and no time to think about whether she wanted to go back up the cliff so soon after making it down. As the three of them climbed, she frequently found herself getting a boost to help her move faster. The first time she wasn't prepared for it and stiffened when her rear end was cupped by Bo's large hand. When he exerted enough pressure to move her up half a metre, she relaxed, realising what he was doing. She was more prepared for it the next time it came, though he became more confident once she expected it and she found herself squawking more than once as he propelled her upward much farther than she anticipated.

They made it up the cliff quickly but Synjan didn't get a chance to catch her breath because this time Tagan snatched her hand and ran her to where the Shinu were. Synjan left the storytelling to her two companions, watching the singing exchange avidly. At first the Shinu were startled to be approached but soon were intrigued. Finally, they looked past Bo to where she was standing at the rear and gestured her forward. Bo positioned himself between her and Tagan, a comforting hand in the small of her back.

The Shinu sang something incomprehensible to her, finishing with 'Techatachenti'.

"I know where the Techatachenti live, yes," she nodded, at a loss about what she was being asked.

More singing was exchanged. Synjan considered getting down on her knees and repeating her performance in the dirt... and then she had a better idea.

"I'll be right back, stay here," she told Bo, swivelling and resting one hand on his arm and making a waiting motion with the other before running off. She ignored the calls of disappointment at her back and concentrated on getting to her backpack as quickly as possible. The zip on the tent opened with a speedy *zweee*, startling Daeson, who was reclining on his bedding.

"Synjan," he cried, sitting up as she lunged for her backpack. "Where have you been?"

"With Bo and... Tagan... in a cave down... the bottom," she panted as she dug around inside her pack for the pencil case and Wanderer file she'd talked about pulling out for Daeson. She ripped a page she deemed unimportant from the binder and tucked the pencil case under her arm to run with, glad she'd included the folder at the last minute. "I'll be back!" she told Daeson but the statement wasn't necessary because he zipped up the tent and jogged after her.

She pushed her way through the gathering crowd until she was sitting before the Shinu. Again, Bo inserted himself between her and everyone else, shielding her silently—she thought she heard Daeson raise an objection to being held at a distance but was too intent on not holding the Shinu up any longer to worry about it. She grabbed a nearby mat and placed the piece of paper on it, blank side up, before she withdrew a pencil from her case.

"Mukake," she began, representing their island with its characteristic shape first. She then drew the islands she and Daeson woke up on, before she drew the fourth island in her archipelago puzzle. "Techatachenti," she said proudly. She took an extra moment, closed her eyes and mapped the exclamation islands again, noting that there were five patterns on it that she knew weren't Mukake patterns. "Techatachenti," she added, drawing five dots to represent where they were currently positioned.

An eerie moment of silence followed her statement. It was like every person surrounding her collectively decided to hold their breath, though many important looks were exchanged. It was the male Shinu that broke the silence, leaning forward to point to those five tiny dots.

"Techatachenti?" he queried, then made a gesture she interpreted as, *'That's where they are right now?'*

"Yes," she confirmed, nodding. "There are five Techatachenti there," she held up a hand with fingers splayed before pointing to their home island, "and about two hundred there." She hadn't counted because the island was so crowded with patterns that it was almost impossible to get an accurate number.

The reaction to this news was opposite to last time; noise exploded around her. People were singing at those beside them, across from them and nowhere near them. Synjan winced, drawing her head down between her hunched shoulders as sing-shouts fired over and around her, obnoxious and abrasive in their excitement.

The female Shinu must have noticed her discomfort because she sang louder than everyone else, quelling the noise. When it was down to a whisper or two, she smiled at Synjan and pointed at the dot of the exclamation islands. "Synjan." She tapped her finger on the paper. "Wandruh?"

The implication shocked Synjan. The Shinu was asking if there were any Wanderers on the island, meaning that not only had the Portal dropped previous travellers such as Daeson and herself off in this area, but apparently it had dropped them in *exactly the same place*. Every time? Is *that* what Bo, Tagan and Paki had been doing when they'd found them? Had they been checking for Wanderers to be sure that their enemies—the Techatachenti—didn't find them first?

Shinu repeated her question, growing impatient because Synjan was just looking at her with an open mouth. "Bin," she shook her head, "no Wanderers there at the moment." There were no patterns on the tiny lagoon island, even the Techatachenti were on the other end of the larger island.

Using the very obvious tactic of taking the paper and pulling it towards her with a questioning look, Shinu asked if she could keep the map and Synjan nodded mutely. She got to her feet and left the group to discuss what they'd learned. With a look, she collected Daeson and headed back towards their tent for some privacy. She had some very interesting news to share with him about Portal behaviour.

CHAPTER THIRTEEN

Nakhari Base

T O get rid of me, you'd have to push me away.

As Hawke waited for the portal medical team to assess his health, he considered what Brita had said to him. Initially, he'd been comforted by the words, understanding them as a lighthearted heckle of commitment. It wasn't until afterwards, while seated in the portal chair and breathing in sleeping gas for his trip out, that his muddled mind latched onto an alternative meaning.

The thought stayed with him upon waking, nagging at him and causing him to wonder if he'd finally lost her after all. It would be so easy for Brita to accuse him of pushing her away, to claim that even after she'd addressed their relationship as a kind of intermission from their normal routine, he'd promised nothing. She said that

to get rid of me

she preferred no commitment to one that wasn't heartfelt. Of course she did, wouldn't everyone share this opinion? Considering that half the marriages in the Authority worlds ended in divorce, he supposed not. But nobody went into a marriage believing it wouldn't last... did they?

you'd have to push me away

It was an aggressive statement. Brita wasn't meek but she wasn't a bully, either. He was over-thinking this. He'd never focussed on her individual words before so why was he pining over this particular sentence like a forlorn teenager?

After his blood pressure was checked and his temperature taken, Hawke was offered a cup of goop that was supposed to be a travel-sickness cure but he declined it. By habit, he rubbed the pads of his fingers across his thumbs until he found the one with a new imperfection—where he'd been pricked for a blood sample.

Exiting the portal took him into a waiting room that he chose not to linger in. His messenger bag sat upon the bright yellow floor strip reserved for collections and he grabbed it, slinging the strap over his head and shoulder. There was an oily taste in the back of his throat that he was keen to get rid of. Nothing took out the taste of portal travel except hard alcohol but he wasn't going to find that on base. Toothpaste was the next best thing.

He was on Femme now; a world he knew only by reputation. None of the Hunters came here, not even the few women who cared to hold his rank. There were no operations, no missions on Femme except the diplomatic. Even those were carried out on base. Only well-paying female tourists were welcome to arrive directly into Femme, at a portal terminal that was specifically designed to impress. Authorities operated the Portal but weren't allowed to interact with Femme citizens or leave the terminal. He'd heard the place was crawling with Intuits (mind-readers) who acted as guides (wardens) to the tourists, helping (policing) them until they received their specs (handcuffs), a wearable technology that 'assisted tourist navigation' of the city they were in (kept tabs on them at all times).

"Hunter Hawke Donovan."

A female voice caught his attention just as he reached the waiting room's exit. He looked to his left, seeing a pair of Authority-uniformed women in deep conversation before his gaze shifted to the one standing by herself nearby. She was dressed in the garb Hawke had seen in documentaries—a shimmering light green evening gown that was more suitable for visiting the opera than for loitering about on an Authority base. She looked to be around his age but held herself in a way that made him think she might be older.

He did his best not to reveal that he was bothered by her personal address. He hadn't sent word ahead, intending to check in when he got here and then report back to Cayden by portal-phone after the process was already underway. Once the wheels of bureaucracy began to lumber along it would be a difficult thing to stop, even with the influence Division General Cayden had.

Who was this woman that could identify him by both name and rank?

"And you are?" he requested brashly. He could hear his own hostility—caused either by the tension of his secret (and secretive) mission or because he'd arrived on Femme with intense bias.

"Ambassador Jinwa Woy," she replied. "We will be working together."

"Is that so?" he asked, glancing at the door that led out of the waiting area and away from this lunatic. He was only humouring her because she knew his fucking name. He wondered where they might have met.

"There is no need for you to Shield yourself," she said. The way she was speaking reminded him of GPS navigation systems and their impersonal inflexions. Right now he was considering making a U-turn. "I have already seen us working together."

She'd *seen* them working together? It took him a moment to realise what that meant.

"Fuck me," he breathed. It wasn't eloquent but it did convey his surprise accurately. He'd never met a Clairvoyant before.

"I want to do you the courtesy of having known me in return," Ambassador Woy continued. Her strange mixture of past, present and future tense was striking and difficult to negotiate but he understood her meaning. Did all Clairvoyants speak in such a way or did the Ambassador have a poor grasp of the Authoritan language? Unless he met a second Clairvoyant, he was unlikely to find out. She looked at him like she expected a response.

"Okay."

Her gaze dropped to assess him, lingering in places that most women would be too embarrassed to reveal an interest in. In retaliation, he took note of her svelte figure; long legs, narrow waist, short torso, unhindered breasts that he guessed would be able to fit in the palm of his hand. He doubted she would let him, judging by the expression on her face when his stare returned to it.

"I will find you again," Ambassador Woy said, her tone sounding as though she faced an unpleasant task ahead.

"Did you tell anyone I was coming?" he asked her, not ready to be dismissed just yet.

"There is no need when you are already here."

"*Before* I was already here. Did you tell anyone I was coming?" he asked again, hoping she would understand this time.

"Of course," she said. "This is why you were requested."

Her answer was difficult to understand. The last time his presence had been requested on Nakhari Base had been a year ago when the paperwork had crossed Cayden's desk. It seemed a long time in the past to tell someone that he would be dropping in today.

"Alright," Hawke gestured to the Ambassador,

indicating that she should lead the way but she only stared blankly at him. "Aren't you here to check me in?"

"Why would I be doing that?" she asked, offended.

He puffed his annoyance and exited the waiting room. Like most first impressions, he'd been right about her. She *was* a fucking lunatic.

Nakhari was a much smaller Authority Base than Hawke was used to. He was more familiar with the sprawling indulgence of bases like Oceangate on Trent or Redrock on Varrell, where the Hunter Division was headquartered. Land was easy to come by on those worlds, where the Authorities could assign themselves whatever they wanted. Here, the High Priestesses assigned land for Authority bases and they weren't generous. The engine that worked a portal took up a lot of space, leaving little for Authorities to move around in. A single building filled the rest of the available land, with a narrow patrol area and a laughable chain-link fence around the outside. Considering how primitive Authority technology was in relation to Femme's, even a two-metre thick, electrified and explosive-implanted fence wouldn't hold the locals back if they saw fit to over-run the base.

His trip from the waiting room took him down a corridor with a series of black and white photographs lining the windowless side of the wall. The pictures weren't of important officers or historical figures, they were stark and abstract, of lines and curves. There was fine print beneath each photo and he angled closer to read them. The lines and curves ended up being extreme close-ups of the Nakhari Authority Base like it was some kind of famous art gallery. Hawke had never seen anything like it. Artwork in the waiting area, sure, but in the corridors? And why would the Authorities take photos of a base and then hang them up *inside* the same base? It would make more sense to take photos of all the well-recognised bases and hang them up on the walls of a Superior General's office.

The photographs didn't prepare him for the main building. He exited the corridor into a grand space that had a large white funnel curling down from the ceiling. The only time he'd seen anything similar was during his two-year training period, between the ages of fourteen and sixteen, where an inflatable deployment funnel had been set up for him and the other recruits to use. It had been much like bouncing around in a funhouse, or the kind of slide that was attached to every aircraft on Authority worlds, to get passengers quickly to safety. He'd never seen a permanent one before, made out of plastic. When he walked towards the funnel to check it out, an Authority Officer approached him, a clipboard held loosely at her side. She offered him a polite smile.

"Sir? Do you require assistance?"

"Is this a deployment funnel?" he asked while reaching out to touch the side of it. He'd expected the warmth of plastic but got the cool of metal instead.

"It is, sir."

Hawke moved closer to the funnel's spout, past large red stickers warning him not to approach.

"Sir? If you could step back, please. Sir?"

Hawke didn't step back but he didn't move all the way to the spout either, seeing that it ended a little way above his head.

"Have you used this?" he asked, fascinated that Nakhari Base had something experimental in its foyer. He supposed deployment funnels must not have been high on anyone's 'topics of interest' list.

"Yes, sir. During training exercises, the base assembles at their designated areas."

She said it without the kind of excitement he would

expect from anybody who'd slid down this thing. He remembered the deployment funnels as an exercise in extreme fun. If stationed on Nakhari, he would use it all the damn time.

He *was* stationed on Nakhari! Well, he was *going* to be.

"How many times have you been down this?" he asked the Authority Officer who was following him around the funnel as he investigated it.

"There have been three practise drills since I've been here, requiring my use of it three times, sir."

"Aren't you allowed to use it otherwise?"

"Yes, sir, but most don't. It impacts your legs and lower back. There have been injuries." She gave him a sideways look. "Did you... want to try it out, sir?"

"Doesn't everybody?"

She grinned at him but it was an unusual smile. Smug, perhaps.

"Yes, sir. But most only try it out the once."

"Can we do it now?"

"Did you not need to check in first, sir?"

"Nobody's expecting me for the moment."

She nodded and then signalled a group of six men that she must've been in charge of. One of them came over and Hawke identified the triangle ranking on his shoulder as Sergeant. The Officer gave him her clipboard and outlined the tasks he had to perform in her absence, then ordered him to look after Hawke's bag. He handed it over before he was led to the stairs.

"No lift?" Hawke asked.

"No, sir."

"What's the highest floor?"

"Tenth floor. Barracks."

"Is that where we're headed?"

"You can deploy from third, sixth or tenth floor, sir."

"Barracks it is."

The Officer smiled at him in a way that made Hawke

feel as though he might regret this decision, but fuck it, if he was going to be helping the Spy Division on Femme, he might as well have some fun with it.

The stairs were doubly wide, quite loud and extremely busy. A lot of soldiers were moving around on the floors above them and the noise swelled as Hawke and the young Officer moved upward. Many times the noise was punctuated by echoing bangs as doors above or below them were shut before the next wave of people passed through.

The crowd thinned out as they reached the uppermost floors. The young officer was breathing a little harder as she held the door open for Hawke. He nodded acknowledgement before passing through.

They entered a wide corridor. All of the doors along it were open. Hawke glanced inside to see long rooms with cots lined up in rows. Typical sleeping quarters for grunts but unusual for them to be on the highest floor.

"Who's on the third and sixth floors?"

"Ranking officers. The higher the rank, the lower the floor."

"With the D.G. on the third floor?"

"The Division General's quarters are on the ground floor, sir. She's not on base currently but we do have the Division Overseer taking up duties in her absence."

"The D.O.'s office is on the ground floor also?"

"Yes, sir. Here's the funnel entrance."

Hawke looked at the small hole in the floor that had cautionary tape stuck around it. A set of footprints were outlined on one side. As he stared uncomprehendingly at the hole, the Officer asked, "Do you know how to fall, sir?"

"What?"

"On impact, bend your legs and allow—"

"Oh yeah, I know all that."

"Very good, sir. Keep your arms contained at all times, hands on your opposite shoulders and clench your buttocks as you slide or you'll slip to the next rotation."

"Clench my buttocks?" Hawke repeated, making sure he'd heard correctly. The Officer looked back at him seriously, not as though she was making a joke.

"Trust me, sir, you don't want to slip a rotation. It hurts."

He had no idea what she meant but he nodded.

"Consider my buttocks clenched."

"Very good, sir," she said with a tiny smile flitting about her lips. "You'll get a countdown before you reach the edge. Don't hit fully braced."

"Thanks for your help, Officer..." he looked for the ID that should've been clipped to her front pocket or belt loop but she had neither.

"Gaulther."

He looked at the hole again, realising that now he was leaping into the unknown. For a moment he was filled with doubt. He should've started with the third floor and seen what it was like there. He doubted the officers would be jumping into a hole in the floor—they probably had a proper delivery chute like the inflatable ones, where a civilised person could sit first before sliding down. He'd almost twisted his ankle jumping out of a tree not long ago, he didn't have the bounce-back of youth.

It was the final thought that drove him to cross his arms over his chest and step off the edge. He was not an old man. He was not a coward. Fear would never be a thing that controlled him.

The hole hadn't looked very wide but he didn't even rub the edges with his shoulders. The free fall was short and exhilarating before the tube angled and forced him into a slightly diagonal fall, like water gurgling down a drain. He could see a guiding ridge that he was sliding along and wondered if that was the thing a person slipped when their buttocks weren't suitably clenched.

He wasn't in any danger of finding out.

Inside the funnel he could smell a mild tinge of disinfectant. He passed underneath a chute which he figured was for the sixth floor evacuees. While looking around for it, he passed another one of the same. Must be on the third floor now. His heart was hammering, his adrenaline was up and he could feel the breeze of speed on his face. While looking down past his feet, he saw a large numeral five rushing up at him. Then a four. Three... and he'd slowed down quite a lot. The funnel had expanded to quite a wide area. Two, and he was sliding at a pace that even a child would be able to contend with. The number one led him to the spot where the chute ended; he could see light coming up from the bottom. He dropped out of the chute at a speed that he had to bend his legs only slightly for.

Applause met him at the bottom. Officer Gaulther's group had decided not to perform their tasks and had hung around to watch his results instead. He could hear the rumble of another person coming down the funnel and he stepped away before Gaulther appeared.

He looked at her with surprise and she shrugged. "Beats the stairs," she said. She found her crew—who were now whooping and applauding—and abandoned Hawke in order to shout angry orders at them. He got his messenger bag back from the soldier catching most of the abuse and Hawke decided he quite liked Officer Gaulther.

The Division Overseer had his full name etched on the window of his closed office door. He also had a secretary seated outside. Hawke had intended on walking straight past the uniformed fellow but he stood up and blocked the way through, as though he'd known

Hawke's intentions. Was he an Intuit? It was possible... there were a lot of them around, happy to wear the Authority uniform and be assigned pleb duties.

Hawke felt himself growing defensive and the familiar sensation of his Shield settled around him, coating his skin like wax. Nobody would sense that he was a Shielder except a Wanderer. The secretary's eyes widened minutely before he scowled, confirming Hawke's assumption that he was an Intuit.

"I'm here to see D.O. Palua'a."

"The D.O. doesn't have an appointment scheduled," came the reply.

"He'll want to see me regardless."

"You may make an appointment to see him. I have his calendar right here—if you could take a step back." The assistant gestured down at a large diary closed on the edge of his desk. Hawke could see it in his peripheral but he pointedly didn't look down at it. He also didn't move away.

"The D.G. has been requesting my presence here for years. Since she's not available, the D.O. will have to do."

"You can't have been on the D.G.'s schedule or you would've known she wasn't going to be here for the next month. Nice try, but we don't accept walk-ins. You *need* an appointment."

Hawke already disliked the secretary but he didn't want to use physical force. As much leniency as he was afforded as a Hunter, assaulting an Authority without cause wouldn't travel well. Pressing his lips firmly together, he stepped back, unable to miss the triumph in the other man's eyes as he scurried over to his desk. The assistant made a show of opening the diary and scrutinising it but Hawke immediately saw an empty block of time.

"The D.O. isn't meeting with anyone at the moment. Just announce me and let me in," he demanded, prodding at the page with a finger. The secretary glared up at him.

"I can't give the D.O. two seconds of notice. I'm instructed not to disturb him unless it's a state of emergency. You can see him in the afternoon."

Hawke looked at where the assistant had marked.

"You're making me wait three fucking hours?"

"You're the one who arrived without notice. It's the best I can do. What's your name?" The secretary sat down, picked up an elegant gold pen and waited, poised.

"Hunter Hawke Donovan."

There was a lingering moment when the assistant did nothing except look at him. Hawke didn't prompt, figuring his name might not be written in the book after all.

"Excuse me for a moment," the secretary said quietly before returning his pen to its stand and leaving his desk to softly knock on the D.O.'s door. He entered without being called and snicked it shut behind him. Hawke watched the closed door and listened to soft voices on the other side. After a few muted comments back and forth, Hawke clearly heard, "Here? Now?"

The secretary opened the door and gestured for Hawke to enter. Once Hawke stepped inside the office, the assistant showed himself out and closed the door to offer Hawke and the D.O. some privacy.

Division Overseer Palua'a stood behind a cherrywood desk. He was tall and broad-shouldered, though his intimidating size was softened by a warm, broad smile of impossibly white, even teeth.

"Hunter Donovan. I apologise for the breakdown in communication. I wasn't informed you were coming."

Without giving Hawke time to salute, Palua'a held out a large hand for the shaking. Hawke took it and the handshake was firm but reserved, as though the D.O. knew he could easily crush Hawke's fingers.

"It was a spontaneous decision, sir," he admitted as

they both sat across the desk from one another.

"I'm glad for it. My predecessor requested your assistance for a decade without luck and now I reap the spoils." Palua'a roared laughter while Hawke smiled along. "She'd even asked a Clairvoyant about you and was cursing her name when she transferred out."

Division Overseers rarely 'transferred out' from anywhere. Hawke remembered Cayden mentioning a reshuffling of leadership in the Spy Division. Only the Division General kept her rank. Cayden had laughed about it as well.

"What did the Clairvoyant say?" he asked.

"That you would show up, of course! She neglected to mention your age."

Hawke considered why his age would be important. He'd signed up to the Hunter Division as soon as he'd finished his four years of Authority training. The first request for his assistance on Femme had been during his first year as a Hunter. Woy didn't look old enough to be predicting for the Authorities for that long, unless she was one of those people who looked ten years younger than what they were.

Hawke's silence prompted Palua'a to return to business.

"You've looked over the latest request?"

"Is it any different to the previous dozen, sir?"

"Not terribly."

Hawke shrugged. None of the requests had been overly informative, focussing predominantly on the fact that he, specifically, was required because of his 'unique abilities'. They could somehow help the Authorities glean important information.

There was a knock on the door. Palua'a looked up but Hawke didn't turn around. Out of his peripheral vision, Hawke saw Palua'a's secretary enter with a bundle of papers in one hand. He placed the documents on one corner of the desk before leaving. Other than the knock and his footfalls, the secretary made no noise. Palua'a pulled the documents over and turned them before he dropped them in front of Hawke.

They were inter-divisionary forms. This paperwork was the kind of paperwork that he heard Kegsy complain about every now and then. He'd described the stack of papers in such a way that Hawke had thought it an exaggeration. He could see now there had been no embellishment. Bureaucracy flexed its muscles when different departments worked together. Hawke had thought his two- or three-page reports that he had to read over and sign (once a low-level clerk in the Hunter Division typed it up) were a hassle. He'd been spared this kind of novel-writing insanity.

"I don't have to read through all this shit, do I?" Hawke asked. Palua'a was watching him closely, he thought, like a curious child studies a bug.

He doesn't know what I'm going to do, Hawke guessed. *I could walk out of here and he won't be able to stop me. I could demand the fucking world.*

"Of course not!" Palua'a said agreeably. "But you do have to sign it."

Hawke could read it all through but it would take him a day to be able to read it and comprehend it. Authority language on documents was fairly straightforward but sometimes the meaning could be ambiguous when interpreted from different perspectives. Hawke hadn't worked with other departments before so he didn't know what was standard. He wished he'd paid the Femme documents more attention in the past. He'd never bothered because Cayden said he'd handle it, and he had.

Hawke had left for Femme straight after Kegsy's request. Would Cayden find out where he was in a single day? It depended solely on Brita, if she would call him. She *wouldn't* call him. Would she?

"Are you taking the pen, soldier?"

Hawke blinked at the object being held out to him. He glanced past it at Palua'a, whose studious expression had turned into something distinctly sharper. He looked like a man who believed he could make people obey him by will alone; perhaps he was willing Hawke to take the pen and start signing.

Because it suited him, Hawke took the pen and started signing.

The phone call back to Hunter Headquarters on Varrell was made at the end of the working day. Hawke listened to open air while Cayden processed the information he'd just received. He imagined he could hear his Division General drawing breath to speak but he knew the portal phones weren't sensitive enough to transmit subtle sounds. Still, a question came to him over the line.

"Did you not think to offer me advance notice of this?"

"I didn't think you'd approve."

"For fuck's sake, are you twelve years old? Do you not realise how this makes me look? I've been halting this goddamn Femme project for as long as you've been a Hunter!"

Cayden usually swore when he'd had too much to drink or when he was seriously irate. Hawke took a moment to recover before answering. Only Cayden could speak to him this way and make him feel guilty instead of angry.

"I filled out the forms as though this was your idea."

"But why, Hawke?" Cayden pleaded. Even though the question was a difficult one to answer, Hawke could hear that a lot of the tension had left Cayden's voice. This part of the mission had become the most difficult, keeping a secret from Cayden. He'd intended to lie about his reason for being here, to speak about a fictional woman he was wanting to bed, but he couldn't do it. Lying was too far. Keeping a secret was... far enough.

"I've got something else going on," he admitted.

"Not trouble between you and Brita? How's *she* taking this?"

"Better than you," Hawke said with a lightness he didn't feel. "She and I are the same as always."

"So what's this something else, then?" Cayden demanded.

"I..." Hawke struggled. "It's something I have to do. Do you trust me?"

There was a long pause and Hawke felt the weight of the silence on the phone line. He felt hurt that the answer didn't come straight away, even though he knew he was asking a lot. He showed blind faith in Cayden—could he not have the same in return?

"Yes," Cayden said finally, in a sigh. "I trust your judgment if not your motives."

Not my motives? What does that mean?

"Okay," he said into the receiver, even though he didn't feel like it was okay. He'd got the answer he wanted but it was tainted.

There was a silence, pregnant with anticipation. Hawke didn't know what else to say even though he wanted to slice through the quiet, to make it less uncomfortable. Eventually, Cayden sighed into it.

"Alright, is there anything you need from me to make this smooth?"

"You'll get paperwork to sign and you'll be informed of my progress, I expect."

"Any more surprises?"

"I'm sure the Spy Division will be indebted to you," Hawke said carefully, knowing Cayden liked to collect favours.

"Don't be slippery."

"I'm not, I'm just..." Hawke huffed and gave up on his sentence. Denial would make him sound like he really *was* twelve years old. He thought about the absurdly long delay that usually took place between a Trent flare and picking up a Wanderer on Earth. "I might be here a while."

"Goddamnit," Cayden said softly but without venom.

Hawke held back the apology that settled on his lips. He licked them but it didn't take away the desire to say sorry.

"I'll report again when I'm able," Hawke said.

"You'll report every day," Cayden ordered gruffly.

"Yes, sir."

A click and dial tone sounded in his ear as Cayden hung up. Hawke blinked his surprise and lowered the receiver back into its cradle. The phone call had gone better than expected as far as achieving his objective; permission to remain on Femme. It had made a bigger dent in his relationship with Cayden than he'd anticipated; a man who'd selflessly nurtured him through childhood. Thing was, Kegsy had begged and Hawke knew he was the only one who could help.

He couldn't turn his back on that.

CHAPTER FOURTEEN

Nautilus

ONCE, Synjan had enjoyed writing. Her young life had been turbulent and, even though Ellis had given her shelter and protection, he hadn't been able to provide stability. Isolated by her age and talent, she'd been something of a curiosity to her housemates at the Bunker and they hadn't known what to do with her.

What she'd craved was love and compassion but Kate and Nick had had their limits. Synjan had comforted herself by drawing pictures of the family she'd lost and daydreaming about the ways her life could have been different. Slowly, she'd progressed from pictures to sentences and then stories written in books she pilfered from the locked room.

When she started earning money for herself, she invested in nicer books with pretty covers and pencils that had fancy erasers on their tips. Eventually, her writing became a journal. She wrote to her mother, telling her the things she learned in school. Sometimes she wrote for her father, telling him the things she learned from Ellis and Nick that she wasn't willing to confess to her mother. Occasionally she wrote to her big sister, apologising for all the times she'd been annoying or had done the wrong thing, admitting that she missed her.

Most of those early entries were about taking blame for the tragedy of losing her family, detailing all the pieces her lonely heart had broken into when they'd been ripped out of her life. It was how she'd come to terms with her loss and become her own ballast.

Sitting on a rock in the middle of an ocean she couldn't name, with one of her legs dangling in the lapping water and the other bent at the knee, Synjan thought about that habit. She knew exactly when she'd stopped writing—Ellis had found her detailing something she'd witnessed that he didn't want recorded and had flown into a fury, gathering every one of her books and stalking away with them. She had the urge now to start again, to chronicle her new knowledge and travels. It was fanciful and she didn't see how she could make it happen, but that didn't stop her wanting it.

"Synjan!" Tagan yelled and squeezed his hands together in some sort of formation that allowed him to project a stream of water at her.

It was cold on her bare stomach and she gasped, swiping the droplets away. She kicked out at him, cackling when he caught a good portion of water in his open mouth.

"Tagan!" she mocked, unexpectedly accompanied by a voice much more melodious than hers.

"Tagan," Kahu clucked disapprovingly from beside Synjan. She and Bo were crouched on the rocky island beside Synjan, working together on one of the grass bags they'd brought with them from Mukake Island.

In truth, Synjan knew very little about what was going on, despite it being her seventh day with the island dwellers.

She'd woken up with Daeson cuddling her, as usual, and mapped to see that there were no new Wanderer visitors or Techatachenti invaders on the Exclamation

Islands—it had become her job to deliver daily updates to Hiyani or the Shinu. Mukake workers rowed over there every second day to get supplies that their tiny pillar couldn't provide so she supposed she was saving them the extra trip to the dot island to check for Wanderers. She and Daeson had talked about the Portal's propensity for depositing visitors in the same spot multiple times and still couldn't decide whether to be amazed or appalled.

During her breakfast with Bo, Kahu and Tagan had approached and the three natives had sung about what their plans for the day would involve. Synjan generally spent her days with the trio because Daeson wouldn't climb down the cliff. It was the main exercise Synjan got, though she'd completed a short run a couple of evenings and used one of the trees to keep up her fighting regimen with, much to Bo and Tagan's interest. Because of her daily climb, she had got better at descending. Her new challenge was doing it without her shoes... though she didn't think she'd ever be courageous enough to go without a vine lasso.

Today's after-breakfast itinerary involved climbing down the cliff in her usual outfit—which included a grass armour panel of her own—and swimming north-west for just over two hours. The highlight of the journey had been trying to drink from the flash downpour of tropical rain that had lasted about ten minutes before dispersing.

Her three companions had brought sharp knives carved out of rock with them. They were carried inside large woven drawstring bags. They'd worn the bags slung over their heads so it dragged behind them on the swim, but Synjan hadn't been asked to tow anything extra. She was glad for that, as the swim had tired her out and she was already thinking about what sort of food she could get for her growling belly.

There wasn't a lot around. Despite a small island

covered with trees about a hundred metres away, Synjan had been directed to stop at this small, rocky outcrop. It was barely above water level and couldn't hold all of them plus the equipment Bo and Kahu were fussing over. Tagan didn't seem to mind. He was obviously some sort of strange fish hybrid person that could swim for two hours and continue to stay buoyant for an infinite time beyond. Not Synjan. She'd needed to stretch her tired body out after that exertion, even if the cost was being squirted by said immature fish-boy.

Kahu and Bo made exultant sounds and, at the same moment, pulled away from what they'd been leaning over. Kahu turned and looped the bag over her head again, a grin on her lovely face as she stood, tugging on Synjan's paler arm. Synjan glanced down at where they made contact, admiring the colour she was taking on. She was no match for the natives but all the time she was spending in the sun was having an effect. Generally, she returned to the tent sore and sunburt but Daeson's nightly Heals fixed that *and* wrought her skin a browner shade than she'd ever been before. Her hair was going the opposite direction.

She was broken from her momentary contemplation as Kahu yanked her to her feet, making some obvious gestures; she wanted Synjan to dive down into the water with her.

"Here?" Synjan queried, figuring that Kahu had been to this little rock island numerous times and knew the best place to dive from safely.

Kahu only pointed, repeating her instructions.

"You guys need to learn to nod," Synjan muttered irritably, having had it confirmed by Daeson that the Mukake didn't have a word or action for 'yes'. What sort of pessimists only included a word for 'no' in their language? "Okay, I'm ready," she assured Kahu and took a loud, obvious breath to prove it.

With a brush of arms, the two women dived into the

ocean together.

A shiver ran from Synjan's head to her toes as she slipped from enveloping heat into biting cold, her skin prickling as she sliced through the water. She'd learned that the only way to swim with the Mukake was to have her eyes open underwater but she was positive they could see more clearly than her. She turned her head to find Kahu casually using the rock island to help her descend and tried belatedly to do the same. She ended up ruining her smooth trajectory and falling behind but their destination was only a few metres down.

Kahu made sure Synjan was watching as she scooped up a shelled animal from the ocean floor—it was the largest nestled amongst countless others, almost as big as her hand. In Gredann, they'd been called oysters but Synjan had never seen any as large as the ones she was hovering above. She watched as Kahu dropped her bounty into her woven bag before reaching for another. Bo and Tagan were doing the same nearby.

Synjan had to go up for air more frequently than her companions but she managed a respectable contribution to the final tally. Since she didn't have a bag of her own, she pooled hers in Kahu's.

On her last swim towards the surface, Synjan spied a familiar, spiralled shell with brown stripes bobbing inside a small grotto. Her lungs were cringing so she was forced to go up and take a breath before she dove back to retrieve it. As she climbed onto the rock island with her prize, Tagan moved in for a closer look, snatching it out of her grasp while she was still wiping water out of her eyes.

"Hey!" she cried.

Bo sang something in her defence but Tagan only tossed it back to Synjan when he realised there was nothing living in the shell.

"Thank you," she told him sarcastically before

smiling at Bo with genuine gratitude. He took her expression as an invitation and sat beside her, looking at the shell with interest. "Nautilus," she told him, using her name for it.

He sang something she could never mimic so she just smiled.

The shell, not quite the size of her palm, was smaller than one she'd left behind in Gredann—a gift from a sailor she'd bedded. She turned it over with interest, admiring the nacreous inner surface as the sun bounced a rainbow across it. The true treasure, she knew, was inside. The one she'd been given in Trent had been a hemishell, cut open to show the spiral of iridescent chambers that had once been home to a many-tentacled creature.

Despite being in the warmth of the sun once more, a cold wave puckered the skin of her arms as she recalled the story she'd been told by the sailor. Striving to give their relationship some purpose, he'd told her how the nautilus animal spent its life building chambers that expanded in size to accommodate the growth of the creature. He'd sought to relate the shell's strength and ever-increasing size to what they could have together. They hadn't lasted beyond a week.

What struck Synjan in that moment was the way this shell represented her journey with Daeson. Rolling it around on her palm, she wanted desperately to share it with him, but what if he felt the same way she had when the sailor had given her his gift and professed his hopes for their future back in Gredann? Would he think it trite and smile kindly because he was really wishing for less of a connection with her? Deciding it was important enough to take the risk, she tucked it carefully into the pocket of her shorts, not wishing to chance it in anyone's woven bag.

Kahu started singing, causing everyone to look at her. Synjan didn't understand what was happening until her friend dived into the water and started swimming towards the tree-populated island a little farther on.

Bo sang something to Tagan which impacted negatively. Tagan was doing a lazy backstroke and gave a snort of derision before he sang his return. His reply included the words 'Synjan' and 'Wandruh', which captured her attention. Bo sang-argued and the two had a quick back and forth that resulted in Tagan sneering, rolling over and striking for Mukake Island.

Synjan looked at Bo in startlement. They were in the middle of two of their party swimming in opposite directions but it only took a few heartbeats before she decided to follow Kahu. Bo swam after her.

The other woman was waiting for them on the shore of the small island and led them inland until the sand became soil covered by leaf litter. She came to a stop before a grey stone formation and grinned triumphantly at her companions. On close inspection, Synjan saw a natural depression in the stone slab filled with what she could only describe as the remnants of Wanderers past.

"Wandruh," Kahu declared.

Synjan nodded solemnly at the aged collection of junk. Pens, pencils, a broken cup, a dog-eared novel and a plastic lighter stood out amongst the deteriorating rabble. She reached over and picked up the lighter, surprised to find it still worked when she rolled the striker. Kahu and Bo flinched when a small flame appeared, proving they hadn't understood the item's purpose. Synjan offered it to Kahu, thinking she'd keep it now that she saw it was useful but it was only placed back in the hollow with the rest of the collection.

"Should I... give something?" Synjan asked her companions, gesturing to the shrine.

"Bin," she was told by both of them.

Synjan frowned, confused about what she was supposed to do. Be impressed that Wanderers had been visiting the Mukake and leaving their crap behind for many years? She didn't understand why this remote island, removed from the place Wanderers reportedly entered this world, was the deposit for things they left behind. The feeling of awkwardness only grew as they all stood there staring at the detritus, like worshippers at a temple. It was very strange.

Kahu broke the respectful silence with a message that included shifting the bag on her shoulder. Synjan took it as an indication that she was ready to swim back home. Bo replied before Synjan could and whatever he said made the native woman's eyes twinkle above her smile. The tone of her rejoinder was teasing and then she turned and left them at a run.

Synjan looked up at Bo, her pulse leaping as she realised he'd manipulated circumstances so that the two of them would be alone.

"Sneaky," she told him, grinning as he removed his bag of oysters and placed it on the stone shelf. It was quickly followed by their chest panels and then he moved to a place where the stone was at a comfortable height for him to sit. He grasped her hand and pulled her gently into the lee between his muscular legs, wrapping his huge, strong hands around her slim waist.

"Synjan," he sang in the sexiest voice she'd ever heard, kneading her rear and pulling her close to his chest.

Initially, she resisted, smiling down into his black eyes and cupping his face firmly in her hands. Bo was very handsome and he seemed to have a knack for heated looks that made her imagine exactly how he would feel sliding into her body. He whispered her name again, pressing on the backs of her thighs and running his fingers across the small of her back, beckoning her with his eyes, his sensual mouth, his firm body.

Knowing it was a bad idea, her lids drooped closed

and she leaned into him, liking that they were the same height with her standing and him sitting. Every deep, dark noise he made echoed into her chest and travelled through her, making her nerves quiver with awareness. When his lips found the sensitive skin of her throat, she wrapped her arms around his shoulders and groaned, unable to fight the way it tore through her, casting shivers upon shivers across her skin.

Part of her was dismayed by her near-instant arousal because she didn't want to seem desperate... but she was. It'd been more than a week since she'd farewelled Nick in a Heal-infused ravaging and she'd rarely gone that long without some sort of release in her old life. Restraining herself for Daeson's sake as well as receiving regular, delicious Heals that lit up her libido in a manner that she was loathe to admit to had taken its toll. Spending her waking hours with two handsome men fighting over her and her sleeping hours entwined with an even *more* handsome man had not helped, either.

"By the Gods," she stammered on shaky breath, finding it difficult to remain standing when he began to draw gently against her skin. Her blood was on fire and his hands were everywhere, squeezing, testing, stroking. Realising she didn't want to return to Mukake Island with a mark on her throat, she reluctantly pulled away from his mouth, only to have her lips captured instead.

Kissing him was a hunger stoked even while her thirst was slaked. She wasn't certain she could ever get enough. After a fleeting press of lips, his tongue moved boldly into the cavity of her mouth, exploring brazenly and encouraging hers into a duel. His lips were sinfully weather-roughened and the whiskers around them tickled; her head spun with the firebarrels of sensation exploding inside her.

It wasn't until his fingers slid up inside her shorts

and pressed between her legs that reason began to clear the fog of lust swelling her brain. His other hand was in her bra massaging her breast so it took some effort to disengage. She had to force his hands away and press them to his chest while she took steps back, getting her lower half as far away from him as she was able.

"We have to stop," she panted, knowing she looked ridiculous in her current position but too afraid of what would happen if she got close to him again. Slowly, she released his hands and straightened, feeling the flush in her cheeks and knowing she looked every bit as ruffled as he did. In an attempt to regain her dignity, she adjusted her bra so that it covered everything again.

Bo just looked confused.

Truthfully, she wasn't entirely sure what had stopped her straddling him right there on the rock but something in his reverent touch had told her it would be wrong. As she got her breathing under control and watched the shift of emotion in his eyes, she began to figure it out. Bo wasn't just interested in her casually. He focussed on her with a doggedness she found flattering but knew was dangerous when she wasn't planning to stay in his world. He struck her as the relationship type and she couldn't give him that—she doubted he'd be able to accept her body and then wave her on when it was time for her to leave.

Living with Daeson had taught her another crucial thing about herself; she wasn't interested in breaking anyone's heart. She was aware she'd done it in her past and it had never really bothered her until she'd watched her travelling partner deal with his loss.

"I'm sorry," she told Bo sincerely, her overwhelming emotions rousing tears of regret to shine in her eyes.

Bo's expression had become something wounded but she knew she'd made the right choice, despite the difficulty they were both having in getting their bodies under control.

Taking a breath, Synjan walked over to regather their equipment, finding the mundane task of putting on her grass shield calming. She was surprised to find Bo right behind her when she turned. She blinked up at him, mutely holding out his grass armour.

"Synjan?" he queried, cupping her face much as she had his earlier. The plea in his eyes was plain.

"We're still friends," she told him with a heartfelt smile, covering his hand with her own.

Though it lacked its usual power, he returned her smile and she sighed, pleased that she hadn't ruined everything with her hasty retreat. "Come on," she told him, pulling his hand off her face and shaking his bag and shield at him. "We should get back before everybody thinks we're over here doing... what we almost did."

CHAPTER FIFTEEN

Man Of Choice

AFTER time spent with the natives, Daeson had a fair grasp of the language. It was a lot easier to learn the vocabulary than he'd expected because he'd made time to sit with Hiyani every day to practise. They'd done some weaving work that morning and were now wiling away the afternoon in conversation, sitting in a patch of shade thrown by the rock barrier and watching everyone else as they moved about.

Even though Daeson sang the wrong note occasionally, using the correct base word meant his intentions were usually understood. Hiyani's few words in Authoritan helped a great deal. Daeson knew that Synjan's progress had been frustratingly slow—she didn't have an ear for singing and mixed up similar sounding words. She was more skilled with gestures and she'd found a close ally in Bo. Daeson would often find the two of them signalling with one another, laughing over misinterpretations and sometimes going quiet in what Daeson presumed to be companionable silence.

From his shaded spot, Daeson could see the pair sitting together now. Bo was teaching Synjan how to strip a *tanga* vine into strings. It was unusual for the large native to be at the top of the cliff weaving when he was usually a fisherman.

Hiyani elbowed Daeson in the ribs sharply enough to make him hiss in breath. The old woman was skinny and had pointy elbows. Coupled with her wiry strength, her nudges were formidable.

"What?" he asked in her language. She replied in his.

"Synjan choose. Tagan. Bo," she sang, using one of the new words he'd taught her.

"Synjan... what?"

"Choose. Tagan. Bo."

"Choose what?"

Hiyani switched back to her own language.

"Husband."

The base word was marriage and wedding, wife and husband were part of that. Daeson didn't know which specific word it was, only that it was sung at too high a note to be the base word, but it was obvious what Hiyani meant. He struggled to respond, unsure if he wanted to tell Hiyani that they weren't staying forever, it was just that the Portal was so far away. Would she expect a marriage sooner than they were ready to travel?

Hiyani looked at him expectantly and he thought about what she'd said. Synjan had two men interested in her, but none of the women had indicated an interest in him. Was this why Hiyani was pressing a husband for Synjan? It made more sense to pair Daeson off with one of their women, since they had more single women to go around.

"Must I choose woman?" Daeson asked.

Hiyani shook her head.

"Choose neh-neh," she said, then cackled.

Daeson blinked, unsure about this new declaration. Didn't *neh-neh* just mean calm or quiet? Perhaps that was the joke. No partner meant no arguing... had they witnessed the tense interactions between him and

Synjan and decided that they weren't a good match?

"What neh-neh?" he asked, wanting to be sure. He considered what they'd been calling him since the first morning. *Neh-neh-ma*. It often brought forth smiles from everyone who heard it.

"Neh-neh!" Hiyani shouted, pointing. "Neh-neh!"

He followed the direction of her skinny arm to see two goats feeding on grass.

Goat Man. They'd been calling him Goat Man. No wonder everyone had laughed, especially when he'd gestured and introduced himself as such. He imagined what it had looked like to them as he'd proudly announced his title and couldn't help but laugh along with Hiyani. Her humour was contagious and it *was* pretty funny. He wouldn't be calling himself Goat Man anymore, however.

"Canoe tomorrow." Hiyani made some gestures along with her words. She sang a line while mimicking chopping and another handful of words as she pretended to sew. No... not sewing, she was *carving*. Hollowing out a tree trunk, maybe. Making canoes. When she held up three fingers and sang the word that he knew meant three, he thought that they would be making three canoes. Or perhaps three people were making one canoe. Hiyani's grasp of 'tomorrow' was fairly loose so it could even mean in three days' time there would be a canoe-building event. Hiyani attracted his attention by kneading the muscles in his arm. "Neh-nah-ma strong. You canoe."

Daeson's stomach clenched at the idea of having to go over the cliff but he would have to face it when he and Synjan finally left. He had to practise paddling while Healing, since she would be in a terrible state. It was probable that he wouldn't be able to fix Synjan's sea-sickness, that his Healing would only give her some respite before the waves unsettled her stomach again. They already knew he couldn't Heal muscle soreness.

"Synjan canoe. Synjan strong," Daeson said.

Hiyani switched to her own language. "Tell Synjan," she sang, and pushed and thumped Daeson until he got to his feet. "Tell Synjan choose."

Daeson didn't reply. He was going to keep that piece of information to himself. This was the first time he'd understood Hiyani's instruction for Synjan but he suspected that the old woman had broached the idea with him already. It was a phrase he'd heard before but hadn't understood at the time. He wondered if Tagan and Bo were getting pressured about Synjan and considered that might be why they were spending so much time with her.

He was almost all the way up to Synjan when he realised how closely she and Bo were sitting. Their knees were touching. Their fingers brushed together and they exchanged a glance and smile. Daeson's step faltered and he stopped as a hard realisation came to him of what a love connection for Synjan could mean.

She couldn't sing but Bo could communicate for her. She could climb and hunt and swim. She wasn't scared of heights. She couldn't go out on boats much but there were many other things that she could do here. For Hiyani to request Synjan choose herself a husband meant that she was accepted. Daeson had been instructed that only the goats were good enough for him. He no longer saw it as funny... the joke had more of an edge now.

Synjan had said she wanted to leave but that had been at the beginning, before she'd started flirting with Bo and spending a lot of time with him. Daeson had lived at the Queen of Hearts for much longer than was reasonable, putting up with Nick and his abuses, tolerating a world he didn't care for... all because of his love for Omerri.

What if Synjan was in love with Bo?

Daeson wanted her to leave with him but not

because he was romantically interested in her. He didn't even care about her relationship with Bo, beyond its potential interference with their plans. If this world was bad for him and the next world was a slave world, he needed Synjan with him to find the Portal. Ultimately, he wanted her to come with him because he needed her for her talent.

He felt sick. He intended on using her. It was despicable, yet he couldn't see any other way. He was aware enough to know that his desire was wrong but selfish enough to try and break up this romance before it got started. She couldn't miss what she didn't have.

Synjan noticed him hovering and he was further troubled by her flushed, embarrassed look. He'd interrupted something intimate. He was both pleased to interfere and horrified by his own emotions. What kind of person was he?

"Daeson! What's up?" she asked, looking between him and Bo and not meeting either of their stares for longer than a second.

"That's not a question I can answer," he said.

"Oh! Okay. Is something wrong? We were just... chatting. Did you need something?"

Daeson felt his jaw tighten with the inability to lie and he looked away. A general answer came to him.

"Just clogged up with thoughts."

Synjan fortunately took that as her cue to leave Bo and stood. Daeson glanced at the large native who shot a resentful stare his way. Bo wasn't oblivious to what was going on. His glare made Daeson feel as though his desire to keep Synjan to himself was transparent. He left hurriedly, relieved when Synjan trotted after him, walking fast to match his pace.

"Did you want to sit somewhere and talk?" she suggested.

"The tent."

They made the rest of the walk in silence and when

they reached the tent, Daeson gestured for Synjan to enter first. He zipped the door flap closed after joining her, wanting privacy. Even though the Mukake people wouldn't have understood the conversation, he wanted to feel like he was speaking with her alone... that it was just the two of them. It felt symbolic.

For a long moment he stared at Synjan, not knowing how to begin the conversation. Perhaps she would fill in the silence as she usually did. After a little while longer, she spoke.

"About me and Bo... I—"

She stopped talking when his eyebrows rose. Daeson wished he hadn't reacted. He wanted to hear what she thought about Bo.

"Didn't you have something you wanted to talk about?" she asked, her voice lifting in pitch.

"You're on the right subject," he said. He saw her discomfort but didn't feel bad about causing it. He wanted to know how she felt. He hoped the pair of them weren't in love.

"We kissed." It was close to the worst thing she could've said. He felt his eyes widen and she gushed more vital information at him. "Only for the first time, today." Her face scrunched. "Actually, we almost did the other day, but today... was full on."

She laughed nervously but Daeson couldn't bring himself to join in. There was an awkward silence after her laughter wound down.

"You're mad, aren't you?" she guessed.

"Do you love him?"

"Of course not. I just..." she muttered the rest under her breath, "...want to have sex with him."

He was surprised that she hadn't hidden her voice better. Perhaps she wanted to discuss it and that's why she'd said it just loudly enough that he would hear. He could always pretend he hadn't but there was a problem attached to her wishes. She didn't understand the custom because she hadn't been able to understand the explanations. It was up to Daeson to tell her what Hiyani wanted, after all.

"That won't work."

"You think I shouldn't?"

"Having sex with him marries you to him. I've been told you have to choose between Bo and Tagan, so that would mean you chose Bo and have to stay here with him." Synjan gaped at him. "As his wife," Daeson clarified, just in case she'd missed it. "Forever," he added.

He watched the shock on her face throughout his explanation. She looked more alarmed with each of his additions.

"Are you serious? Of course you're serious. But that's insane! I've seen the teenagers having sex, *they're* not married."

"Maybe they're too young. I was told and partly shown that being with someone ties you to them. They want you to stay." There'd been a marriage ceremony a few days ago that Daeson hadn't watched all the way to its thrilling conclusion. He'd seen enough to understand.

"But we don't want to stay," Synjan said. Her words unlocked the tension in his body and he could feel the muscles in his back and shoulders loosen.

"*We* are not wanted. Just you."

There was a pause as Synjan digested this information. "Hiyani said that to you?" she asked, her voice soft and cautious.

Daeson bristled. "I've been partnered with the goats."

"Wha-at?"

He could tell by Synjan's expression that she had the wrong idea. He pulled a face at her. "Stop it."

She looked away for a moment then came back with, "Should I stay away from Bo, then?"

Here was his opportunity to deny her potential romance. He was horrified that he was meddling with her life, that he was devising a path for her that she wouldn't have taken on her own. Without him, she might have touched the Portal on her own, ended up here and fallen in love. That might happen anyway. He couldn't let it.

"I want you to stay away."

Her expression changed and he was wary. He didn't know her face that well but he'd seen that look before.

"Does my spending time with Bo upset *you*?"

He stared at her expectantly, saying nothing, hoping she would answer her own question so he wouldn't have to. Synjan leaned forward, her gaze dropping before meeting his eyes again. Her face was unreadable and he felt the control of the conversation shift in her direction.

Synjan gestured between them. "Do you want... you and I to...?"

Realisation swamped him. She thought he wanted her for himself! He didn't know how to reply. If he denied her and said he only wanted to travel with her, it would lead to questions as to why he wanted her to stop seeing Bo. But he couldn't feed her interest in him just to keep her around, that was Omerri's way.

"No, Synjan," he said, looking away. He thought she would be angry with him, that she would accuse him of bossing her. She could do whatever she wanted, she was older than him, she was her own person and he had no say in the matter. Instead;

"Okay, so I'll spend less time with Bo."

He was surprised that he held that much sway over her. He was relieved that she was putting him first in their partnership. It didn't feel good but he didn't want the alternative.

"You'll tell them that I'm not interested in being anyone's wife?" she prompted.

"I wanted to already but I don't know the words." Daeson shrugged.

"Then I'll let Bo know."

Talking about rejecting Bo made Daeson think of the reason why he'd asked her to. "Has the Portal moved?"

She Navigated and the familiar calm hovered over him, making him feel warm and protected.

"Does that happen with everyone?" he slurred.

Her eyes sprang open and she gave him a perplexed look. "Does what happen?"

"That thing you do. When you look for the Portal, or for anything else. It's," he smiled crookedly, "nice."

"I have no idea. I've never been with another Wanderer."

Her words might have been innocent but Daeson felt that the air between them had charged when she'd read into his intentions. He reached to unzip the tent but her hand met his before he got there.

"Don't go," she begged. "I don't want things to be awkward between us."

He looked at her, sensing she had more to say.

"We're adults and we're travelling in close quarters. We need to be honest with each other and open about what we want."

He was stricken with guilt, wanting to confess that he was deceiving her by omission. Her hand was warm on his, making him very aware of her proximity and the fact he'd told her she shouldn't go elsewhere for sex.

"I know what you're thinking," she said. Daeson was astonished and horrified. "I wake up every morning and we're wound around each other. You've just come out of a relationship. You're not ready to move on and I'm used to having lots of different partners."

Her frankness surprised him. "What?"

"We're adults," she said again, like that somehow gave him the answer to everything. He didn't feel like an adult around her. "We have needs. We're not together but we're together, if you know what I mean?" Her hand moved away so she could gesture.

"I do," he nodded.

"So we can talk about sex then?"

"Sure, okay."

"You don't want it and I do. This is how it is, right?"

He felt an odd sort of smile on his face and she blushed. "Right," he relented.

"Okay. I just wanted to be clear. That's enough on that subject for now," she announced decisively and pulled something out of her pocket. "I wanted to show you this shell I found. It's... have you ever seen one of these before?" she queried, holding her cupped palm towards him.

Daeson leaned forward for a closer look. "No," he answered, finding the spiralling shell unfamiliar.

Synjan licked her lips and looked into his eyes. The weight of her stare communicated the seriousness of her message. She was nervous, which worried him also. "It's called a nautilus in Gredann. I was given one once, though it wasn't whole, like this one. I think it symbolises our travelling together."

"Okay?" Daeson frowned, hoping she'd elaborate.

Watching him carefully—he kept his face neutral to not influence her—she began speaking.

"This shell was once the home of a funny-looking creature, a bit like a crab but with tentacles. A nautilus. It's born in this shell and it's *really* tiny but as it grows, it expands its shell. Each time it outgrows a chamber, it closes the smaller space behind it so it can then live in surroundings that better fit its dimensions. The thing is, those chambers are always carried with it, sealed off and unable to be returned to because the nautilus has outgrown them, but still always part of its structure. Its past is always present."

She paused to lick her lips again. He nodded and smiled encouragingly at her, interested in her tale and sensing she was working towards a point. She smiled back and her next words were less stilted.

"I think you and I are nautiluses. We've outgrown where we began and we're moving forward to find a home that fits, just like the creature that used to live in here did." She lifted the shell for emphasis. "I want to cut it open and share it with you, so we can have half each. When I figure out how to do that, you'll see how beautiful it is on the inside." She poked the shell with another finger, her stubby nail tracing the inner swirl on the shell's side. "How it's like us," she said firmly, looking up into his eyes with that peculiar earnestness again. "We're moving through the worlds together now, carrying our pasts as baggage but only looking forward, seeking new spaces that fit us so we can live comfortably. Neither of us can ever go back; the change is profound and irreversible but we're stronger for it. We'll face lots of challenges while Wandering but I think we'll be fine as long as we stay together. We've got very different shells in our past but we're in the same one now. Different halves of the one whole, the one purpose. I think we can make it work," she enthused and her smile was beautiful.

Daeson released a soft sound of appreciation, delighted with her discovery and the eloquent explanation she'd given. It was heart-warming and showed him a sensitive side to her that he'd never considered. He had to stop drawing early conclusions about people and acting on them. Synjan had proven her depth.

"Me too."

They smiled at each other for a while before he remembered the other piece of information Hiyani had given him.

"There's a canoe building party happening soon. Either in three days time, or maybe tomorrow we'll make three canoes. Something like that."

Synjan re-pocketed the shell. "Where?"

"I think it might be on the islands where we landed."

"Makes sense. Are we both going? Or just me?"

"Both of us. I invited you."

"Are you going down the cliff?" she asked slowly, displaying her awareness of his discomfort.

"I'll have to at some point. I might as well see how I go."

"True. We need to meet the Portal."

He was pleased that she'd confirmed they would leave this place together. She'd shown she was willing to stave off a romance and made a large gesture about partnering with him. Her final statement was yet another affirmation that they would Wander together.

They just had to figure out the best time to get away.

CHAPTER SIXTEEN

The Briefing

HAWKE expected to be assigned a bed in the barracks except he ended up with his own room. Nakhari Base had special accommodation for visiting VIPs or high ranking officers... it was obvious they were trying to keep him happy. His room contained a double bed, a couple of plush armchairs, a dresser to store his clothes in and a curtained window. The room belonged in a well-run motel but without a turn-down service. He didn't mind making his own bed.

What he *did* mind was spending the first week waiting around. He'd used the gymnasium, slid down the deployment funnel until the thrill had gone and spent time at the library. He'd been notified that 'experts' were portalling in this afternoon to prepare him for his mission. He didn't know exactly what his mission entailed but he suspected he would be trained to behave like a slave.

It was logical to camouflage himself among enslaved men. Like most of the population, he was blonde and had Wanderer blood. Being a Shielder meant Intuits wouldn't be able to infiltrate his mind.

Three rapid knocks sounded at his door and Hawke opened it. An unranked female soldier stood in the corridor in full uniform—helmet, jacket and assault weapon carried high on the chest and aimed at the floor. She looked ready for an invasion.

"Sir! I am to escort you to meeting room two for debriefing."

"Yeah alright, hang on."

Hawke sat on one of the armchairs and pulled on his socks while the soldier watched from the doorway. After he was ready, he waved for her to lead the way and followed. Her boots thunked on the polished concrete floor while his sneakers made no sound.

She turned two corners and then stood beside a door with a black numeral two stuck onto it.

"Sir!" she announced but didn't open the door for him. Hawke gave the soldier a second glance before he went inside.

Four tables on castors had been pushed together to create a long one. Around it were six people, some sitting, some standing. Hawke made seven. Palua'a and his secretary stood at one end chatting with an older man Hawke didn't recognise. Ambassador Jinwa Woy sat at the other end. Hawke's presence must have been an indicator for starting the meeting as the others noticed his arrival and took their seats.

Palua'a approached him in long strides and reached out to place a hand on his shoulder. Hawke was uncomfortable with the touch; he liked his personal space and Palua'a's movement felt aggressive. If Palua'a detected any tension in Hawke's shoulders, he didn't react to it.

"Ah, Hunter Donovan. Take a seat and come find me after your debriefing."

At least the touch and proximity was short-lived. The Division Overseer saw himself out, his secretary trailing after. The door closed at their backs and Hawke selected the seat closest to Woy and opposite the supposed experts.

Introductions were made.

"I am Ambassador Jinwa Woy. I am a diplomat from the world of Demkoi, which you call Femme."

She'd spoken as though she hadn't sprung herself on him a week ago. He thought it peculiar—they would've been observed together, so why behave as though they hadn't met? He considered that it might be her habit of using the wrong tense in conversation but dismissed it. Her introduction was specific but it still didn't tell him what her role in all this was.

"I am Dr Vadri Fellows. I am a Femme-born psychiatrist presently working on Alpha Two." She was dressed in a stark grey business suit and her hair was pulled back harshly from her face. She reminded Hawke of his counsellor from Willets. Naomi... he hadn't thought of her in years.

The silver-haired man Palua'a had been speaking to was seated next to Dr Fellows.

"Dr Robius Garion," he said in a deep baritone. "I defected from Demkoi almost thirty years ago and studied engineering. I am now a lecturer on Othello and have lived there for over a decade."

Hawke guessed that Garion wasn't here for his engineering knowledge but rather for his familiarity with slavery. If he'd defected, wouldn't the Spy Division merely ask *him* all of the questions about how Femme worked? Why would they need Hawke to pose as a slave to bring back information? Were they after something more specific? He became uncertain about his upcoming mission.

He looked at the last person, someone he vaguely recognised though he didn't know where from or how. She was young and timid looking, the kind of woman who would never catch his eye. Under his scrutiny, she reached for the token on her necklace and toyed with it while she introduced herself.

"Emma Burrows," she said. "I'm one of, uh, Dr Kelly

Turner's assistants at the DOME."

Now Hawke remembered her. Whenever he'd seen her face, it was among many others. She and her peers had hooked him up to medical equipment or taken his blood.

"What the fuck?" Hawke looked back at each of them. The only person his swearing had affected was the Burrows woman. "Who's supposed to tell me what the fucking mission is, here? Is it you?" Hawke turned on Fellows, who carried herself as though she was in charge. She raised an eyebrow in response.

Garion spoke. "There is a location on Femme where you will be deposited by Ambassador Woy. From there you will make your own way towards Ning. At some point you will be collected by Demkoi Enforcers and we suspect you will be taken to a residence—"

"You suspect I will be taken to a residence," Hawke interrupted, repeating the words slowly. They felt sour in his mouth.

"We are not sure what the process is for Wanderers. This is why you are helping us," Fellows interjected.

Hawke looked between Fellows and Garion, galled by what they were asking him to do.

"You want me to pose as the kind of scum I hunt down," Hawke sneered. He glared at Emma Burrows who froze, meeting his stare with wide eyes. "And Kelly is good with this? She thinks it's a good idea to have *me* pretend I'm a fucking Wanderer?"

With a tremble in her voice, Burrows explained. "She doesn't have—"

"You *are* a Wanderer," Garion said.

Hawke leapt up, the movement launching his chair backward. Its subsequent clatter covered the sound of his palms as they smacked onto the table surface. The castors were locked but it didn't stop the tables from shifting forward as he leaned on them. Hawke could see the edge pressing firmly into Garion's middle, the discomfort shown clearly on his face. Hawke was surprised that soldiers hadn't stormed the room to find out what was going on. He could only surmise they hadn't because they had orders not to. Had these experts anticipated Hawke would lose his cool? Probably. Burrows had witnessed his rage often enough. Instead of yelling, he spoke normally to Garion—as normally as being furious would allow.

"Don't you call me that. Wanderers are selfish vagrants that lie, kill and steal. I don't use the bloodline as an excuse to do whatever the fuck I want, where I want, when I want. Everyone faces the consequences and that consequence is me. I'm the *opposite* of a Wanderer." After giving his bitter speech, Hawke straightened. Garion took the opportunity to move the table off his stomach. Its shuddering protest punctuated the silence and Hawke retrieved his chair. He righted it and sat upon it, leaning back with his arms folded, waiting to see who would speak next. He was surprised when it was Emma Burrows.

"Um, you asked about Dr Turner. She has put forward a formal protest on your being here but doesn't have the authority to stop it, since you signed the paperwork. She sent me to, um... look after you." The brief nervous smile and puff of laughter that she gave told him she also thought the idea of her looking after him was ridiculous.

"I hope your Shield is good," Fellows said, her single arched eyebrow still making its statement on her face. Hawke wondered what it would take to bring that eyebrow back down. "There are a lot of Intuits on Femme and that kind of passion against Wanderers would be noticeable."

"I'm not known for my apathy," Hawke countered.

"I don't know you at all," Fellows replied.

"Don't talk shit. You would've gone over my record."

"Do you prefer it when your reputation precedes

you?" Fellows asked.

"There's something wrong with your eyebrow. I think it's stuck."

"I beg your pardon?" Fellows asked, blinking. The lone eyebrow partnered with the other into a frown.

"Oh no, never mind, there it goes."

Woy made a noise beside him that sounded like she was holding back a sneeze. Hawke and Fellows both looked at her but she was composed. Hawke wanted this idiotic debriefing to be over. They'd dropped the big news; he had to pretend he was a piece of shit Wanderer and be escorted through the world of Femme. The only thing that made it palatable was that he would be experiencing the same thing as Synjan and her companion. When he caught up to them, he would be able to bond with them over the experience and earn their trust.

"My Shield will hold," Hawke countered, though he'd never gone into a world surrounded by the Wanderer bloodline before. His gaze flicked to Woy who stared at him with open interest. His Shield hadn't protected him from her visions and he felt vulnerable in the line of her unfiltered gaze. "What's your role in all this?"

"I am a diplomat for Demkoi," she repeated mildly.

"So I heard," Hawke countered, "but why the fuck are you here?"

He thought he saw a warning in her eyes.

"My purpose is to liaise between the Authorities and Demkoi officials."

"Who do you work for?"

"Both parties," she told him.

Hawke's eyes narrowed. Instead of saying anything to Woy, he returned his glare to Emma Burrows. "Kelly sent you here to look after me," he accused. "Does it sound like this—" he jerked his head towards Ambassador Woy in order to maintain eye contact with Burrows, "is safe to you? A Spy that works both sides on my 'team'?"

The diplomat in question bristled, sitting up straighter in her chair and drawing everyone's attention in the process. "Whether you approve or not, Hunter Donovan, I am a necessary addition. I am the only one that moves freely between the base and the surrounding world."

"And why *is* that?" Hawke asked nastily. "Because you make sure you tell both sides what they want to hear? Who gets access to your secrets?"

"Questioning my loyalty is an ineffective use of your time."

"Why don't *you* just tell them what happens when a Wanderer lands in this fucking world?"

"I am unable to supply those details."

Hawke was frustrated by the ridiculous secrets of this fucked up world. They corralled the Authorities into the small area of their base, allowing them in the world but restricting their access so that they had to resort to extreme measures to get answers. Anybody that colluded with Wanderers in other worlds were arrested alongside their asshole companions. Not here, where advanced technology held the Authorities in check. No, on Femme the conspirators got invited to diplomatic high teas so they could circle around and sniff each other's asses, hoping a nugget of information would miraculously fall out.

It was convoluted bullshit and a prime example of why he didn't have the patience for the Spy Division. Hawke gritted his teeth and tried to recall the way Kegan had looked when he'd begged him to save his friend's life. It worked to calm him but he couldn't resist a parting shot.

"You know this world helps Wanderers, right?" he goaded Woy.

"The Authorities are suspicious of Demkoi's actions and it is the same in reverse. I am assigned to negotiate the interactions between both parties. I am intimately aware of the web of misconceptions that each party holds about the other."

"Misconceptions? Are you here to make us one big happy family?" he spat, reading between the lines and hearing her say that, ultimately, she was powerless. "Why the fuck are we trusting this bitch?"

"Donovan!"

Hawke glared at Fellows but his response was cut off by Ambassador Woy.

"Excuse me," she said as she got up and walked regally out of the room.

"You're out of line," Fellows ground out.

"She's a double agent," he argued obstinately.

"She's just doing her job, as she has for the last *twenty* years," Dr Garion chimed in.

Hawke snorted. "Is that supposed to mean something?"

The other man's face tightened as he warmed to his defence. "Of course it does! It means she has the respect of her superiors and, most importantly, their *trust.*"

"Yeah, but if she's the only one in the middle and no-one else can do what she does, she's not accountable to anyone. She could be feeding both sides while working on her own agenda."

"Twenty *years*, Mr Donovan," Garion repeated, like the words were a talisman that would protect him from Hawke's doubt.

"So it's a long con." He shrugged, unperturbed by the length of time Woy had been milking her position.

"If the Ambassador had ulterior motives, it would surely have become apparent by now," Dr Fellows argued.

"You understand what 'long con' means, right?" Hawke mocked before he rounded on Emma Burrows. "What do you think? Do you trust her?"

"It doesn't matter what I think," she answered

crisply, her hands folded neatly on the table before her. "Or what you think. You signed the paperwork and we're all committed to the project. Ambassador Woy is an integral part and has proven herself a reliable emissary between the Authorities and the people of Femme for twenty years." She gestured at Garion as she repeated the number and he grunted his approval of her acknowledgement. "These are the facts and allowing emotions to cloud our judgement could compromise the outcome. That would be regrettable for *all* involved."

Hawke scowled, resenting the reasonableness of her answer and its ability to deflate his suspicion. It was unbelievable that a mousey little nothing would go from chewing her hair because she'd been put at the grown up table to shutting all debate down, but it had just happened. He should've known better than to dismiss a mouse trained by Kelly Turner.

"Fine," he sighed. "Let's discuss this brilliant plan, then."

The whole situation rankled but he knew when to keep his mouth shut. Just because he stopped questioning Woy's involvement didn't mean he'd trust her. The only good part about this plan was that he would find Synjan and her companion quicker than expected.

CHAPTER SEVENTEEN

Unwelcome Advances

SYNJAN rested her folded arms atop her knees and stared at the hive of activity on the beach before her. One hand pressed at her side, absently kneading aching muscles; Daeson's Healing hadn't much helped her seasickness, as they'd suspected. He also hadn't managed to climb down the cliff and was lowered via the pulley system. The Mukake had expected it this time so he'd been moved without fuss, allowing them to launch just after dawn and arrive two hours later.

Her gaze shifted to her travelling partner as he was relieved from his post. Six in their party were involved in carving out the inside of the freshly-felled trees that would become new Mukake canoes. The other four had hefted spears and run into the depths of the forest to secure some food. Everyone was taking turns at the logs, doing their best to get the canoes shaped while there was still good daylight. It had taken a couple of hours to get the three wooden giants scouted and chopped down, and the hunters still weren't back.

Reflexively, Synjan's gaze shifted beyond Daeson and settled on Bo, who hadn't taken a break yet. His head was down and he was gouging a sharpened stone along the guts of one of the trees with relentless aggression.

The tension in his powerful shoulders, the uncharacteristic scowl on his lovely face and the snappy way he was singing at everyone knotted her insides with guilt.

The night before, she'd taken Bo aside after dinner to deliver the news that she believed they were destined for different things. Daeson had taught her the word for 'leave' to help make her intentions clear. Unfortunately, he'd misinterpreted her courtesy and assumed she wanted to take him somewhere private to consummate the ardour they'd built up on the distant island that morning.

It hadn't ended well.

Once he'd finally understood, Bo's expression hardened into something fearful and he'd stalked away from her without another word. She'd followed at a slower pace, not missing the moment he reached the main area, turned to check that she could see him and purposely threw the shirt Daeson had given him in the dirt. Tagan had swooped in and picked it up. He'd greeted her wearing the too-big item of clothing this morning, also brandishing his teaspoon as if he was thanking her for some sort of endorsement. She hadn't the heart to dissuade him as well and had turned away.

Daeson sat on the sand beside her. "We're going to need a canoe," he remarked.

Synjan frowned, then understood what he was implying. Of course they'd need a canoe to get to the Portal once they were ready to make the journey, but she knew the Mukake didn't have any to spare.

"You're right. They're making three, do you think one of them could be for us?"

"I don't know how to ask," Daeson replied dismissively.

This morning, she didn't have access to her usual reserves of patience and she looked crossly at him. "Well, it's an important factor. Maybe you should figure it out," she snapped.

"We'll just take one when the time comes," he countered.

Synjan blinked and had to look at Daeson twice to be sure he was still the same person. "Did you just say we'll *take* one? You'll steal a canoe?"

"If the Portal's as far as you say, I'm not swimming," Daeson responded and then grinned—it echoed inside her, as it had every other time he'd smiled like that at her.

She was amazed by his ability to employ sarcasm at such a tense time. He was much more at ease since their open conversation the day before. He'd also been very kind when emotion had got the best of her; during her discussion of the disastrous separation from Bo, she'd cried. Daeson had comforted and reassured her that she'd done the right thing. Though many men would've been made nervous by such a show of weakness, Daeson seemed more confident and comfortable around her. He truly was remarkable.

"I didn't think you'd steal one, though," she clarified. "Shouldn't we ask them to make us one?"

"Well, two got stolen and they're building three," he shrugged, implying that he thought one was for them.

"We don't know that for sure," Synjan mused, her lips twisting thoughtfully.

"You ask them."

She stared at him, biting down on the urge to point out she could neither sing nor go to her usual Mukake friend. He knew. He seemed to be interested in goading her for some unfathomable reason.

Before she managed a response, Tagan interrupted them, miming the process of making a boat at Synjan. Thinking he wanted help with something, she got to her feet and allowed him to lead her away.

As soon as they reached a private area with a lot of foliage—and no trees to work on—Synjan realised she'd made a mistake.

"*Tagan*," she said his name warningly.

He turned to face her, making pleading noises and enveloping her in his arms. In an embarrassing mockery of her experience with Bo the day before, Tagan pressed his face against the curve of her neck and nuzzled his way towards her mouth, his hands tugging her downward.

Synjan went cold. Tagan believed she'd broken up with Bo because she was interested in being with him.

"No," she argued, fending off his groping hands in the manner a fish might try to subdue an octopus. She changed tactic to a very firmly stated, "Bin!" but the Mukake man was too absorbed by the process of seducing her to pay attention to the fact that she wasn't interested. Resignedly, she ploughed her hands upwards into his chin and hooked a foot behind his leg, dropping him onto his back.

He blinked up at her, unable to process how he'd got there.

"Tagan, bin," she told him firmly. "Synjan and Daeson piangi."

For the second time in as many days, her words turned a man's expression black and he scrambled to his feet to stomp away from her. She noted he gave her a wide berth on his way back to the others. She sighed, hanging her head and staring at the ferns surrounding her feet for a few moments, fortifying herself.

When she emerged onto the beach again, the sky had filled with dark clouds and a torrential downpour was imminent. As she approached the canoe builders, the clouds unleashed their promise. For some reason, everyone was complaining Tagan's name.

"What'd you say to him to make it rain?" Daeson asked as she reached him and sat down.

Synjan blinked. "Pardon?"

"Tagan."

"Made it rain?" she scoffed but when Daeson looked at her like she was being particularly obtuse, she understood. "He's an Elementalist!" she exclaimed, her eyes widening.

"That's the word for it. I forgot."

"You *knew*?"

"I thought you did."

"How would I?"

"He's fairer than everyone else, he's got green eyes and Wanderers drop off near here. I figure his dad passed through."

Synjan grunted, astounded by her own obliviousness. "I'm an idiot," she muttered, looking at Tagan briefly before she faced Daeson. The rain was very heavy and she had to wipe water out of her eyes. "Well, he just tried to 'marry' me."

"Ah."

"Yeah," she agreed pointedly.

Their moment of commiseration was interrupted by two of the hunters finally returning, shouting and beckoning the carvers. After an exuberant exchange, tools were laid down and the entire group ran into the forest. Synjan and Daeson hurried after them but they were bringing up the rear. By the time they emerged into a clearing at the opposite side of the island, things had already got out of hand.

The Techatachenti had finished tidying up the land that had upset Bo, Paki and Tagan the day she and Daeson had arrived. Five wooden huts had been carefully constructed in the centre. It looked to be the beginning of a village, judging by how much space had been made. The Mukake clearly saw the fledgling establishment as an offence. The other group's name was sung frequently as hunters and carvers together set upon the new buildings and tore them apart with malicious glee. First, the less substantial coverings on the rooves were ripped off, then cross beams and support posts were shoved over. What couldn't be torn, shredded or smashed was flung into the forest or carried away.

Daeson and Synjan hung back, watching. By the time everything was destroyed, the Mukake seemed buoyed by their unopposed victory and they left the area smiling, carrying souvenirs and slapping each other on the shoulders. The rain clouds hovering above them had dispersed as Tagan's spirits were lifted and the day's proceedings seemed set to continue in a figurative and literal sunnier atmosphere.

Feeling a mixture of guilt, embarrassment and disgust, Synjan exchanged an uneasy look with Daeson and then they also headed back to 'their' side of the island.

CHAPTER EIGHTEEN

Night Talk

HAWKE was resting on the bed of his assigned quarters when he heard a peculiar noise in the corridor. It sounded like someone sneaking around who could use more training in stealth. When the noise stopped on the other side of his door, he rose and reached for his weapon. It was an instinctive move that led to a dilemma—he was deep inside a fucking Authority base, who was going to attack him *here*?

Hawke went to the door armed, pointing his pistol at the floor. With his back to the wall he listened, but heard nothing. He reached for the door handle and pushed it down until he heard a click, then swung it open while peering around the doorframe.

Ambassador Jinwa Woy stood in the corridor, watching the space ahead of her. Her focus shifted to Hawke and she pulled a face of incredulity.

"I am not here to slit your throat."

"Is that a normal conversation opener for you?"

"Put your gun away."

"I'll hang onto it until you start being less creepy, thanks."

Her expression changed to something haughty before a smile flickered at the corners of her mouth. He waved her in and shut the door, returning the pistol to its spot on the bedside table as Woy claimed a chair facing the bed. Hawke sat on the edge of the mattress and waited for her to tell him why she'd come.

Her gaze dropped to his naked chest and then to his jeans. He was underdressed in comparison to her wispy, flowing garments.

"You can both look *and* touch, if you like," he offered. Her gaze dropped first to his bare feet before she met his stare, this time unperturbed by his forwardness.

"I have already seen much of you."

"You've seen me naked?"

She gave him a slow blink and he wondered if that meant she was embarrassed. Maybe she *had* seen him naked. He had no idea how her visions worked. It seemed an odd thing to predict though, the size of his—

"You will find Synjan."

Hawke felt all breath leave his body. Synjan? The Clairvoyant had a vision about his search for Synjan? He licked his lips and wondered what else she knew. He didn't even have to ask.

"The decisions you face in each outcome as you near her are... vital."

"Each outcome?" Hawke croaked, then cleared his throat.

"A person's life journey or destiny is already written, otherwise my talent would not work," Woy explained matter-of-factly. She could've been discussing the weather, rather than the fate of all things. "But there are many paths that can be taken, with many possible outcomes. If the future I see is close, then I am more accurate. If it is far-reaching, the myriad of choice could lead you away from what I have seen."

It made a horrible kind of sense. Suddenly he wasn't hating his Shielder talent. He could've been cursed with an unstable bloodline.

"Are you able to control it?"

"There are many ways to control something. What

kind of control do you believe I should possess?" Woy's gaze drifted to Hawke's chest again. It was funny—he'd never minded women checking him out, until now. There was something intense and peculiar about Woy's gaze that made him uncomfortable. He squashed a desire to put on a shirt or fold his arms. He didn't trust her and she knew it, yet she hadn't demanded an apology for his behaviour the day before. What was she here for?

"Can't you pick your way through the different outcomes and see what yields what?" Hawke offered.

"That is not how my power works."

"Because that would be too fucking useful?"

"Why do Authorities use that word in such a way?" Woy asked.

"What? Fucking?"

"Yes. Does it not mean sex?"

"It usually means getting screwed," he said with a smirk.

"Are those not the same things?"

"Uh. Double-meaning." Hawke frowned and shook his head, wanting to get back on track, but Woy's focus was fixed.

"You have sex with her." At Hawke's blank stare, she clarified. "Synjan."

Hawke felt his jaw slacken before he pressed his lips together tightly. He thought of Kegsy, who cared for Synjan enough to risk both himself and Hawke to get her back. He wouldn't approve.

"No. I don't."

There was a pause, then: "I have seen it."

"I'm not guilty because it *might* happen," Hawke snapped.

Jinwa Woy didn't lose her composure. "I thought you would ask me how to *make* it happen."

Hawke laughed. It eased the tension. "I don't intend on messing up my mission getting that close to her," he admitted.

"Finding Synjan is your mission," Woy repeated slowly.

With her help, he realised his mistake. Fuck, he'd thought the bitch had all the information already. She clearly only knew tiny pieces of what was going on… and even then she had the flakiness of potential outcomes rather than anything concrete.

She smiled at him, having won the upper hand.

"Do not worry, Hunter Hawke Donovan, I am not interested in your *other* mission. I will not interfere."

"So, no interfering beyond feeding me pieces of my own future to guide me towards a specific outcome?" Hawke asked wryly.

He watched as the Clairvoyant stood and unhurriedly approached him. He was aware when she was in grabbing range of his handgun, but he didn't think she was after it. She stood directly in front of him, between his jeans-clad legs, so that he had to look up at her. She reached down and took his hand, her soft touch caressing the calluses of his palm.

"Can you see more of my future now?" he asked.

"It helps me to see closer," she replied.

"How close do you need to get?" he murmured, his gaze running over her. "Will you end up in my bed?"

She puffed humourless laughter. "Not if you keep talking."

Hawke didn't reply.

Woy closed her eyes. He could see them moving behind the lids, like a dreamer. Her breathing deepened and slowed and she became very still. He was vaguely aware that he was Shielding himself from her, likely because she'd made him feel defensive and uncomfortable. He dropped his Shield and she spasmed.

"A platoon of soldiers… all of them dead. *You* are doing it, you kill them all. You… you do it for her."

Hawke suppressed the urge to snort. He smiled and

watched her frown. He expected her to start swaying and moaning, but she didn't. She just stood there, holding his hand.

"You throw... you are on a boat. You throw something overboard. It takes effort. You... *she* is there, she watches you do it. You look guilty, like you did something bad. She looks sick, her face turns away. You sicken her."

"That'd be right. Kill a platoon of soldiers for someone, get no thanks."

Woy frowned more deeply and her eyelids fluttered. Hawke remembered the threat about talking and decided to see where this nonsense led. Hopefully he wouldn't have to sit through too much more storytelling before getting his happy ending.

Woy's face changed into a sneer. "She is the seed of poisoned fruit," she hissed.

"Okay, that's enough," Hawke declared, pulling his hand away, rattled by the transformation of the Clairvoyant's expression and voice. Visions were one thing, the idea of her being possessed by them was too disturbing. She could do her weird shit in someone else's room.

Woy's eyes fluttered open and she looked at him in a way that he couldn't read—not that she'd been terribly easy to read before, but this expression was something different.

"Go on back to where you came from," he said softly. Woy's hands found his chest instead. "No more predictions," he told her.

"Do you think you can love the idea of someone?" she asked.

"Only if there's something wrong with you."

"So harsh," she whispered. She slipped the topmost garment off her shoulders, letting it drift to the floor at her feet. Hawke could feel it on his toes.

"Is that what you've done? Fallen in love with the

idea of me?" he teased, his fingers moving to the straps that held the rest of her dress. He'd expected it to slip off but it stayed frustratingly in place. She unhooked clips at her elbows and then wriggled out of her dress. There was nothing beneath except for her.

"I am not ever falling in love. Certainly not with someone like you."

He would've been offended except she started kissing him. He didn't care what kind of demented beliefs she had about love and sex, or whether he was good enough for one and not the other. There *was* a nagging suspicion that she was working him as some kind of asset... but her motivation wasn't important enough for him to deny himself the pleasure of her body.

CHAPTER NINETEEN

Woman Of Ill Repute

IT took the best part of three days to complete the canoes. During the third day, the hunters left with their spoils—a large pig and a generous collection of vegetation—so that a feast would be ready to celebrate the new canoes as soon as they arrived on the fourth.

They returned to Mukake Island when the sun was at the crest of its arc. Again, Daeson was winched to the top of the cliff but Synjan climbed it. She found the days away had hindered her speed because she'd fallen out of practice. Bo and Tagan shooting her weighted looks didn't help her keep her mind on task, either. As she ascended, she decided that perhaps she'd caused irrevocable harm to her reputation with the Mukake and thought about how nice it would be to leave that burden. When she reached the top, she sought Daeson out, talking with him as they stepped into the eating area together.

"You know, I don't think I vomited as much on the way back because I was rowing," she hinted.

"I wasn't keeping count, but if you think so, that's great."

She laughed, realising she'd have to be a little less ambiguous. "No, what I mean is—I think we can get to the Portal okay. I was thinking that maybe we don't have to wait for it to move."

"Didn't you say it would take months?" Daeson asked sceptically.

She couldn't bring herself to admit that the shame of ruining relationships on the island was beginning to outweigh the potential pain of rowing for an extended period of time and her shrug was part sheepish, part defensive. "Yes, but if I map it out carefully, we could find a route that could get us there efficiently."

"Can you make fire?"

"We have matches?" she offered in confusion, thinking inanely of the abandoned lighter in the Mukake's Wanderer shrine. She'd considered that Kahu might have tackled her if she'd tried to take it but if she didn't know...

"Oh. That's handy."

Synjan was disturbed by Daeson's sudden reluctance—he was looking for excuses not to leave, but she wasn't sure why. Was it just that the task was too intimidating?

"Are you worried?"

"Let's talk more about this later."

His dismissive words now had *her* worried and her mind turned over possible causes for his reticence. While they lined up to catch their baked vegetables and collected some meat, she tried to get a hint about what was going on in his mind by looking into his eyes. He seemed to be more interested in looking elsewhere.

Telling herself she was probably imagining it, Synjan settled at Daeson's side to enjoy her food, determined to remain calm and wait until he was ready to talk. Just after she took her first big bite, however, she was thumped firmly between the shoulder blades. Surprised by the attack, some of her food got caught in her airway and she started coughing violently as another shove came, now accompanied by a lot of loud, angry singing.

Blinking away tears and doing her best to clear her throat, Synjan hastily put her food aside. She scrambled to her feet, turning to face her attacker while she got her coughing under control.

"Paki?" she spluttered, looking up at the menacing countenance of the Mukake woman.

A tirade of singing abuse was flung at her in response. Among the string of rapid words were the names 'Bo' and 'Tagan'. Paki shoved her in both shoulders and Synjan flushed with embarrassment. Paki had made a habit of glaring at her during the twelve days she'd been with the Mukake and Synjan had tried to make peace. The warrior woman wanted nothing to do with her friendly overtures and had frequently sought to distract Bo's or Tagan's attention from her. She'd always managed to attract Tagan but Synjan sensed that he wasn't the man she was truly interested in.

"Hey, I don't want either of them," Synjan told her attacker soothingly, raising both hands palms out to show she was vulnerable.

Paki shoved her in the shoulder. Harder.

Synjan pressed her lips together and lowered her hands, shifting her footing so that she wouldn't be forced backwards if she was hit again.

"Paki, please, I don't want to fight you," Synjan said reasonably, lowering her hands between them. She did her best to keep her expression calm and neutral.

Paki swept her hands aside brutally, sneering at her and shoving at her again. She sang something obnoxious and looked around herself.

Synjan looked too, dismayed to see that nearly all ninety-three members of the Mukake had stopped what they were doing to watch the exchange. When she caught sight of Bo watching them with a troubled frown, she was hopeful he'd intervene on her behalf. She opened her mouth to call out to him but he turned away. It pinched Synjan's heart more sharply than his anger could have.

Seeing that she was distracted, Paki swung again, this time aiming for Synjan's face. Synjan caught the offending hand mid-swing and held Paki's fist at a safe distance.

"Stop it," Synjan warned through gritted teeth, hoping that the taller woman would realise that she wasn't dealing with a pushover, even if she appeared smaller and less capable.

Unfortunately, the island native became enraged and swung her other fist around in a punch.

Synjan blocked with her free arm and twisted the hand she held, pinching nerves and threatening a broken wrist—it was enough for Paki to abandon all thoughts of attack and drop to her knees, yowling like a stabbed cat.

"C'mon, it's not *that* bad," Synjan frowned, releasing her and stepping back just in case she made another dash at her.

Paki continued screeching, clutching dramatically at her wrist, tears welling in her eyes and a yelping tune falling from her lips as she scrambled away. She hobbled straight into the sympathetic arms of some onlookers. Into the breach stepped Hiyani, who had taken offence at Paki's treatment and now felt it was her job to be angry at Synjan and waggle a remonstrative finger in her face.

Before she could react, Daeson leapt to his feet and grabbed Synjan by the upper arm. His grip was strong and painful as he pivoted her to march her through the circle of gogglers and towards their tent.

"Hey!" Synjan protested, struggling to keep her feet on the ground and in step with his long, angry strides. He might think he was helping her but she felt like a naughty child, humiliated in front of her friends and trooped away to somewhere private for punishment.

When they reached the area they slept in, Daeson released her with an angry flick, his expression hard as he gave his assessment.

"That was excessive."

Synjan was outraged. "Hardly. She started it! I just ended it."

"I thought you wanted to leave your world behind."

"Excuse me?" she flared, her jaw setting in anger.

"You know how to fight. She doesn't. It was unfair."

"She pushed me multiple times. I tried to make her stop! You saw her, she wouldn't leave me alone."

"There are other ways to handle it."

"So I'm a bad person because I'm well trained and the way I chose to handle it is not the way *you* would choose to handle it?"

"If I thought you were a bad person, I wouldn't stay here with you. But that was a bad decision and I would've handled it differently. You handled it like you're on your own."

"That's not fair!" Synjan cried.

"I think it is. I think you did what you always do and you don't have to anymore." Daeson argued obstinately. With shock, she saw some sense in his statement. It left her momentarily mute.

She *was* trying her best to leave Trent behind. They'd had numerous pre-sleep conversations about how their lives were going to change and she'd admitted that she wanted to grow away from what Ellis had made her into. Only Daeson saw that here, in this awful incident, was the perfect lesson for her to realise that if she always reacted the way she previously had, she wouldn't find any different outcomes.

Her blood was racing and adrenaline was still jockeying it through her veins, making it difficult to see reason... but *Daeson* could see it. She needed to learn to trust him. She'd have to make conscious decisions to listen to him—against her honed instincts—but hopefully she could do it. With Paki, she should have looked to him for assistance or called for Hiyani when Bo couldn't help. Anything to have avoided the outcome she'd got.

Her perspective was precise: she'd contained the situation and stopped it from becoming bloody. She needed to start seeing things from other points of view and realise that they'd seen a situation unhinged and people getting hurt.

"I've... never had other options," she confessed, deflated. She hoped he didn't think she was making excuses.

"Now you do."

"I'm sorry," she whispered, ashamed of herself. She stepped forward and hugged him, closing her eyes and resting her face against his bare chest. His smell was comforting, his presence soothing. "I'll do my best to try things your way next time," she promised, opening her eyes again when his arms lifted around her to hug her back (somewhat stiffly, she thought, but she wasn't going to argue). "You may just have to—oh, *no*," she lamented, pulling away from him as she caught sight of the tent past his bicep. There was a hole almost the size of Daeson's fist halfway up one of the corner seams.

Daeson followed her over to inspect it. "The goats," he surmised.

"Yeah," Synjan agreed, feeling deflated. On top of the barrage of other emotions, she was almost ready to cry and admit defeat then and there. It wasn't a small amount of damage; it would have serious ramifications for the tent's air and water resistance, not to mention anything could get in. "I bought some tape that will patch it for now but I don't know how successful that'll be in future worlds," she said morosely. She went into the tent to retrieve the heavy-duty silver tape from Daeson's backpack.

They managed to stick up the inside and outside but

neither of them were convinced it would last through the next strong rainfall that passed over Mukake Island. Synjan tossed the tape back inside and zipped up the door to prevent insects from invading. She cast an assessing glance at the sky and saw it was filled with patches of cloud, as usual.

"I suppose we won't have to wait long for a water test," she mused, sighing at the ugly silver patch on the otherwise-neat domicile. "I guess we should be pleased that it took them this long to try it—and that they didn't like the taste enough to eat more!"

She turned to smile at him but stiffened.

"What's wrong?" he asked, alarmed.

"The Portal moved... *closer*! A Wanderer just left this world!"

Daeson blinked, processing this news. "They sent it closer to us?"

"Yes!"

"Do you know who it was?"

"The Portal was so far away, I haven't been looking at it. I'd have made myself too tired. Whoever it was, they could've been travelling towards it for weeks, I didn't check around it."

"How much closer is it?"

Synjan closed her eyes and mapped to be sure, her heart soaring. "Only a day or two!" she enthused, opening her eyes and jumping up and down before him. She gripped Daeson's arms, unable to contain her excitement.

"We should get ready. We'll have to go at night," he said quickly, his words conspiratorial.

"Yes but tonight's too soon—we'll need to get some food and plenty of water and we've already lost the best part of the day."

"And I'd like to say goodbye."

Synjan gave him a disbelieving look. "We're stealing a canoe, remember?"

"I still want to see them all one last time."

"Okay. We'll spend tomorrow with them and at night we'll get you down the cliff. Then we'll be on our way!" she squealed, her face alight.

He grinned back, looking just as buoyant as she felt.

CHAPTER TWENTY

Trust Mistrust

AWKE was pulled from sleep by a ringing phone, its shrill bell warbling in the stillness of his darkened room. Deep in the guts of Nakhari Base, Hawke's sense of time was forfeit. His sleep-fuddled mind could only recognise the sound as not being his watch alarm. A bleary stare at the shadowy lump on his bedside revealed a red blinking light on his landline, casting a crimson glow over his gun.

He picked up the receiver. "Yeah?"

"Hunter Donovan, your mission has begun."

The words scattered the last of his sleep away, dousing him with urgency.

"Acknowledged." Hawke dropped the receiver back into its cradle and sat up, rubbing his face with his hands. He swung his legs out of bed and turned on the light so he could dress himself. He'd readied his outfit by wearing jeans and a shirt for three days straight before setting them aside. They were comfortable, rumpled and smelly. He'd stopped shaving but had showered last night. The clothes would conceal any scent of cleanliness from him. His well-travelled messenger bag would suit his purpose, though he was reluctant to take it along in case it was confiscated and he couldn't get it back. Not many items had travelled through the worlds with him and this bag had served him well.

With a grunt, he grabbed it and flicked its strap overhead with practised ease. It irked him that the things he'd packed in there for his travels as a Hunter were also appropriate for him to use when posing as a Wanderer. He consoled himself with the knowledge that he travelled lighter than most of them. They tended to carry their own fucking world with them on their backs.

"Sir!" a soldier in full fatigues addressed him when he opened the door, startling him out of his reverie. Shit, he had to pull himself together, he'd become complacent on base. He hadn't heard her thumping her way to his door in her combat boots. "I'm to escort you to Area C."

Wherever the fuck Area C was. He was concerned about why a soldier was hanging around outside his door. It had been five days since Woy had visited him in his room. Had that been noticed?

"Were you stationed outside my room?"

"No, sir!"

"I'm walking right beside you, soldier. I don't need you at full volume."

"Yes, sir."

Her voice continued to carry along the stark corridor but at least it wasn't ringing in his ears.

They walked with matching strides to their destination. When the windows appeared they were black, reflecting his face back at him. He couldn't see out, though he knew soldiers were patrolling outside. Nakhari Base was run in a surprisingly militant fashion considering it was mostly bureaucratic and cosmetic. Maybe that was the point of headquarters with an ethos of deception; the exterior didn't match the interior.

"Area C, sir." The soldier who'd accompanied him pivoted and stood to one side of a metal door. There was no marking on it to tell him it was 'C' or any other part of the alphabet. It was just a brushed metal door with black and yellow hazard tape striped across the top and bottom.

He stared at the soldier as she faced the corridor they'd walked down, standing to attention. Just like the other soldier who'd escorted him to the debriefing room (or was this the same woman?). She didn't check beyond the door for him.

Hawke pushed the door open and exited the building.

He stood on a narrow strip of pavement, the chain link fence in front of him. It was dark here, the only light emanating from a small triangular wall-lamp farther along the building's exterior. He looked up and noticed that there was another one above the door.

"Donovan."

He'd seen her already, closer to the fence than to the building. She was a tall woman when standing. He couldn't see enough of her face to check if her eyebrow had got stuck high on her forehead again.

"Dr Fellows," he greeted, curious about how they were going to get him out. The fence had no gate here and he wondered if they were going to make him climb it. The razor wire coiled at the top didn't look inviting.

On cue, Fellows curled the fence back for him, like she was dog-earing a page in a book. It had already been breached. Her hands looked unwieldy in thick electrician's gloves.

"Is there a voltage I have to worry about?"

"Shut off temporarily."

Crawling through the fence awakened a distant memory of escaping a salvage yard into the desert. His stomach knotted and he hurried through, getting to his feet quickly and ignoring the gooseflesh lifting the hairs on his arms. Fellows pushed the fence back in place, doing a poor job of it but Hawke was certain there would be soldiers tying and welding it back in place as soon as he was safely away.

"Head south-west. Over the rise you should see her car." Fellows pointed. Hawke moved with purpose, not running but not ambling either. The hill was a small one and as he crested it, he saw a dark shape on the street that looked like two-thirds of an egg. He jogged toward it, his heart rate too fast and his tension too high. He felt isolated on the grounds.

A grassy knoll, his mind threw at him. It had been a turn of phrase during one of his Authority History lessons. He couldn't remember which world it came from but he associated it with an assassination. He didn't often feel the sick churn of vulnerability and he was disgusted by the sensation. He was grimacing by the time he approached the egg-car and had slowed to a strolling pace.

The car door slid upward into the roof. It was like watching an elegantly designed warehouse door rolling up, only those doors were loud and rattling while this had a smooth hum. Inside was a vacant seat and across the vehicle he saw a woman peering at him. She was wearing wraparound specs but he couldn't see much detail because there was no interior light.

"Hurry," she ordered. He recognised Jinwa Woy's voice.

Hawke dropped into the seat and she pulled away. The door was still closing—its hum was louder inside the car—and he hadn't found a seatbelt. He figured the egg-cars likely had a more advanced way of dealing with collisions and settled back awkwardly into the seat. He couldn't relax until they were a fair distance away from the base.

"Do not drop your Shield," Woy instructed.

"I won't."

"I saw an outcome where you have."

"Call that outcome a bad read because I won't drop

my Shield."

They drove on in silence. They'd had some contact with each other over the past few days but it hadn't been intimate. She'd watched him train for this mission, most of which involved roleplaying exercises that he'd thought were fucking useless. Among other things he'd had to feign surprise, lie convincingly and force genuine-sounding laughter. He'd been shit at everything. Hawke leaned forward, captured by the amount of stars he could see in the sky.

"There are no police cars overhead," she said.

"I wasn't looking for them."

"There is no moon tonight."

"Close. I was admiring the stars."

She smiled. "The emerald city doesn't wash them from the sky."

"The emerald city?"

"Ning."

"Right. So what makes Femme lights so special?"

"Different gas."

"What, like neon and halogen?"

"Different to them."

"But it doesn't matter if light comes from other gases. Surely if it's bright enough to cast a glow, it'll still interfere with the stars."

"I do not know exactly. I am Clairvoyant, not scientist. You should have asked Dr Fellows."

Hawke made a disparaging grunt. "She wouldn't know."

"Is she not a doctor of science?"

"Just the science of the mind."

"There are many Intuit Authorities that perform the same purpose more efficiently. Why study such a thing?"

Hawke looked over. Jinwa Woy was an intelligent woman; mature, poised and careful with her words. Her questions seemed harmless but they sought common knowledge in response. He didn't believe that she wouldn't already know the answers. To underestimate her would not only be arrogant, but foolish. She was training him to respond.

"Intuits just tell you what someone is thinking. Dr Fellows would tell you *why* they're thinking it," he said.

Woy glanced at him; whether it was because she sensed she was being watched or because she heard a change in his tone, he didn't know. Their eyes met for a brief moment before she looked back at the road. He felt an effervescent pull between them; a zing of attraction that hadn't been present until they'd had sex. He'd grown to admire her. She was intelligent and would outsmart him if he wasn't careful. He was sure she had a hidden ulterior motive, which would make her a triple agent; working for Femme while selling secrets to the Authorities but only the ones she wanted to. Lies built upon a foundation of lies.

"What does it matter why?" she said softly. He was momentarily lost, having forgotten what they'd been talking about. She continued and it reminded him. "If someone is thinking to harm or help you, motivation is irrelevant."

"Not when the circumstances change. If it interferes with their goal, a person would be motivated to change their plans."

"An Intuit would feel the transition."

"Only if they were actively looking."

"I imagine it would be difficult for an Intuit to stop looking," she said.

"Like a Clairvoyant?"

Her face held both a frown and a smile and her disappointment thickened the air between them. Was he off-track or had she disliked the implication? He looked out the window at trees blurred with speed.

"Where are we going?"

"We will drive away from the city for some hours

before you are to head back for Ning."

"Why does it have to be hours? Isn't that out of your jurisdiction?"

"I have free range."

"Like a chicken?"

She glanced at him, the impact of his joke obviously lost. Apparently free range chickens weren't a thing on Femme. Hawke's gaze left the windows and he focussed on the inside of the egg-car instead. The dash was a glossy flat brown. There were no instruments on it but he'd noticed her glancing down at the dash while driving, as though she could see something he couldn't. The specs must be working with the vehicle.

"I thought there weren't personal cars on Femme, that they were all self-driving or mag-levs."

"There are personal cars for certain ranks, like mine. They cannot be driven around Ning. I must park in a designated space and use the shuttles within the city."

He thought it was clever to restrict city driving but he wasn't going to verbalise his praise.

"How are you going to explain this trip on your GPS? Is there a way to wipe it?"

Woy uttered a short laugh and shook her head. "There is nothing to wipe. We are not being watched."

"So those specs don't feed into a giant computer system?" he scoffed. "You don't use specs when you come on base."

"These are for driving."

"But every woman wears specs. Aren't they a form of ID?"

"Is your mobile phone a form of ID?" she shot back, her eyes on the road. The thought of phones had him wondering about communication. Her hair was braided in such a way that her ears were covered, hiding the possibility of her wearing an ear-piece as part of her specs. Someone could be talking to her right now and he wouldn't know.

This mission was a stupid idea. He was going to get arrested. Why was everyone trusting this woman? Why had *he*?

"Mobile phones can be traced to a location and connected to an individual." Authority broadcasting technology wasn't a secret. "The only reason why you wouldn't be worried about being caught is if you had permission to come out here."

"I do not need permission; I am an Ambassador."

"But you have to report to somebody."

She looked at him for a lengthy amount of time and the car began to slow. He didn't know if it was a safety feature or if it had to do with her not paying attention—or both.

"If you believe I am setting you up for failure, why would I bother driving you all the way out here?" she asked. The car picked up speed again when she faced the front. Hawke noticed that her grip on the steering wheel had tightened. "A better question for you, *Hunter*, is why you would even be in this car with me?"

She spat out his rank in a way that didn't alleviate his concerns. He kept his mouth shut since he couldn't change anything now. As had been so succinctly pointed out (six days ago, as well as now), he was committed. If she really was working him as an asset, then she would find a way to smooth things out between them.

They were closing in on a mountain range when the car slowed to a stop and the door on his side whirred up. She hadn't spoken since her last words hours ago but now she turned to him and pulled her specs off so that she could meet his eyes without a barrier between them. Perhaps she thought the gesture would make her appear more genuine.

"I will not betray you. Do not betray me."

He stared at her before getting out of the car. Standing on the side of the road, he adjusted the strap of his bag to sit more comfortably on his shoulder and watched as her egg-car performed a u-turn. She drove away with the passenger door still up.

It was time to use his feet. He headed in the same direction she'd gone, ignoring her disappearing taillights in favour of the sky above. The trees he passed were like arrows, conducting his attention upward. His heartbeat slowed and his fingers unfurled, his steps a comforting cadence.

He'd heard many descriptions for his favourite view through the years but had never found one to his liking. Words failed to adequately describe the vastness of the worlds. Some saw poetry; some saw time. Hawke always saw the unknowable workings of the worlds in the stars. That people could see celestial machinations like those with the naked eye awed him.

Most of them didn't deserve to see such pure beauty and it was the least deserving of all—the Wanderers—that probably saw the most. He wondered how many of the scum understood the pattern he'd observed in the repetition of the constellations, how many they could name.

It was depressing how limited the combined imagination of mankind was. World after world Hawke visited, he looked up to see the same patterns of white in the sky only to find out that some idiot had had the gall to name the constellation merely for the shape it represented; a lion, a hunter, a crab. It was insulting to define arrangements he felt were unique and infinite by a single point-in-time perspective.

His perspective was ever shifting and though he'd memorised the names of constellations, he refused to let that limit his opinion. The stars were incandescent bodies fixed so far apart that it was laughable when small minds shaped them into galaxies and systems because they couldn't risk being overwhelmed by infinity.

People were assholes that liked their shit

predictable. Boxes and niches and stereotypes kept everything neat and able to be coped with. *He* didn't fit into anyone's category and he resented that all the different worlds he'd been on consistently worked to file and index every natural feature—especially the stars, which they couldn't get close to but still tried to own with labels.

His gaze shifted to his destination and his breath left his chest in a surprised exclamation. *This* view was unexpected and... humbling. He doubted any non-native of this shitty world had ever been afforded it. The emerald city was an accurate nickname; the distance allowed him to see the city's skyline outlined in a vibrant green glow. As he'd discussed with Woy earlier, that aura didn't become an obnoxious green cloche trapping the city in its glare, it was a softer, more limited outline that cloaked each building individually.

Hawke found it fascinating that the light didn't project far enough into the sky to interfere with the stars above and wished he knew how they did it. No doubt it had been manufactured for some functional purpose like not interfering with their flying transport. He bet they were all too charmed with their own accomplishments to appreciate the beauty they'd harnessed.

As beautiful as it was, the emerald city was still unknown territory.

The approach of dawn lightened the sky into a hue of blue-grey when Hawke spied a dark speck among the clouds. The speck became a triangle, then an imperfect diamond shape. Whatever it was, it was approaching fast. He felt a thrumming in his bones before he heard a deep note in his ears. When the craft hovered above him, its sound changed, reminding him strongly of the leaf blowers the gardeners had used at Willets. As it lowered onto the grass beside the road, Hawke moved away and turned his back as twigs, leaves and dirt were blown in all directions. He didn't turn around until he heard the noise winding down. Two women got out of the black diamond-shaped vehicle, dressed in identical silver dresses. Their specs were both black, hiding their eyes. One of them carried something in her hands—it didn't look like a weapon but the way she held it gave him the impression she could shoot with it.

The first policewoman addressed him in an unfamiliar language that sounded full of vowels.

"Sorry, I don't understand." Hawke made the effort to keep his voice light and his tone apologetic. If they were Intuits, his Shield would stop them from knowing what he was thinking, forcing them to rely on tone and body language. He kept his hands up and away from his body, presenting himself as unarmed.

"Where to walk you?" The first policewoman displayed her ability to communicate in Authoritan, if not very well. She spoke more of his language than he did of hers, so he couldn't criticise.

"Uh, I'm heading that way," he said, gesturing towards Ning.

"No! Where to walk you? Where to walk you?"

Her volume swelled in frustration. Hawke pressed his lips into a line and took a moment to check his patience. He didn't want to inflame the situation. If she didn't want to know where he was going, perhaps she wanted to know from where he'd come, though it should've been fucking obvious.

"I came from those mountains," he said, pointing at the hazy range behind him. "Now I'm walking this way," he said, gesturing at himself before indicating towards Ning. "That alright with you?"

He wondered if either one would catch his sarcasm.

He was doing a bad job of hiding his animosity. They weren't used to hostile men. The two policewomen made comments back and forth. Their tone was conversational. The one who'd spoken to him reached into the back of the plane and pulled out a flexible grey strap that was about two metres long. Each end finished with a white box and she plugged the boxes together, forming a large hoop.

"What's this shit, now?" Hawke asked, stepping back as she stepped forward.

"Stop." The policewoman with the hoop moved forward, her obvious intention to place it over him. Hawke ducked out of the way and she growled her frustration. "Stop. Help."

"Are you asking me to help you?" Hawke asked. After he spoke, he realised the question was too complicated for her to understand. "Help you?"

"Help you," she repeated, gesturing with the hoop. Her tone was softer, her posture no longer aggressive. He took the chance that this was something they needed to do before they would take him inside the plane. Perhaps once over his head, it would shrink to a size that would keep him contained but not suffocate him—hopefully a belt and not a collar. Femme technology was supposed to be impressive.

"Fine."

She held the hoop over his head and slowly lowered it over him, like a magician showing the audience that the floating assistant had no strings attached. She laid it on the ground at his feet until it bleeped, then picked it up, reversing its path. When it moved past his face, he saw pinpricks of light around the hoop. Was it some kind of body scanner? Had they scanned him? Was he going to get a 3D figurine of himself as a prize?

The policewoman finished her scan and stepped away. They both stared at one another, waiting in silence until the hoop bleeped twice. She unplugged it, turning the hoop into a strip again and tossed it into the plane like it wasn't a super-expensive piece of equipment. What the hell?

"Inside larmeur," the policewoman ordered, stepping aside and waving at the plane.

Hawke hesitated, every part of him wanting to refuse. Had Woy sent them to pick him up? She'd promised that she wouldn't betray him. Why the fuck not tell him if she knew this would happen?

"I'll just walk," he argued, shaking his head. The overconfident tone of his words gave him pause; he'd heard it from Wanderers trying to bluff their way out of a vulnerable situation. It snapped him out of his paranoid thinking. Of course no-one had warned him that the police would pick him up. No-one *knew* what happened when Wanderers arrived, hence the fucking assignment. This was what happened. Instead of fighting the process he should probably start taking notes or something.

"Inside larmeur!" The policewoman's face was all sneer. He believed she was capable of hurting him if he denied her again. Wanderer or not, she wasn't having his refusal. Peripherally, he was aware of the other policewoman casually lifting her weapon. What kind of effect would that weird thing have on him? It looked like a kid's extravagant bubble-blower.

"Okay, yes, alright," he said, hoping she understood at least one of those words of agreement. He moved towards her and she gestured at his bag.

"Give."

Fuck you, he wanted to say. His grip on the strap tightened and he took in a breath. He held it, on the precipice of denial, his heart hammering as he considered his limited options. If he refused, he would be shot with the bubble-blower and have his bag taken off him anyway. He'd seen how fast the plane was, he wouldn't be able to outrun it—the bitches would probably land it on top of him. There was only one choice.

Hawke handed his bag over. Tension left the policewoman's shoulders and she waved again at the plane, this time not barking her limited vocabulary at him.

There was a cramped space behind the pilot's seat. He made himself fit in it and then both policewomen were sitting in front of him. If he wanted to lose his shit, they were vulnerable. Maybe. He didn't know their technology—they could have rigged his seat to send thousands of bolts up his ass with the press of a button. The doors closed and Hawke braced himself for flight. The engine started, followed by a whooshing sound.

The car shuddered and bounced and he felt vibrations through the seat. He had a moment to consider that Authority flight was smoother before he became aware of forward movement without lift. He couldn't see anything; there were no windows. They must be operating the plane with their specs. The ride smoothed out and he felt the turn as they drove onto the road. The plane was less of a plane and more like one of the flying cars Woy had mentioned. Hawke shifted around on the back seat, wanting to catch up on his sleep. He expected to be yelled at for his fidgeting but the policewomen said nothing. He found a position that gave him the least discomfort and closed his eyes.

Sleep didn't come.

He heard a one-way conversation and reasoned the specs acted like a phone after all.

Hawke could hear the sounds of the city when they entered it but he couldn't see it; it was another disappointment and one he should've realised before now. There would be no information for the bureaucrats about the route they took. He felt the car slow down and pull over. Both policewomen got out. Hawke unfolded himself out of the car and stretched, pleased to be given his bag back. He slung it over his shoulder, surprised that they hadn't rummaged through it. Maybe they'd scanned it?

His view of the city street was brief but interesting. Blonde women in shimmering gowns turned their heads at the spectacle of his arrival but soon looked away. He had a brief glimpse of his surroundings; blue painted streets and odd little bubble cars, white curved buildings and vibrant green spaces. The policewoman who knew Authoritan grabbed his upper arm and forced him to face the building they were parked in front of. Her grip was strong and he fought his instinct to shake her off. Looking up, he saw the awning was fashioned to look like thousands of leaves. Either side of the door were pillars carved like tree trunks. Small rodent-like creatures and vines were sculpted in the hollows.

"Walk," the policewoman said, releasing her hold. Hawke was flanked as the trio walked into the foyer. More conversations died but talk resumed after that brief lapse of silence.

"Nothing to see here, apparently," Hawke muttered. The policewoman didn't react other than to speak with a uniformed man behind the front counter. He addressed Hawke directly.

"Do you speak Authoritan, brother?"

Hawke nodded mutely.

"Welcome to the Clio hotel. I am Palo, the concierge here. An usher will show you to your rooms shortly." Palo gave him a broad smile. The policewomen strode away, speaking to one another in their vowel-heavy language. He watched them leave without a look back and a mixture of emotions battled for dominance within him. Relief won.

"Does that always happen?" he asked.

"I beg your pardon, brother, do you mean the enforcer escort?"

Enforcers. It suited them better than 'police'.

"I do."

"Escorts are normally diplomats, not enforcers. You will be joined by a diplomat shortly. In the meantime..." the clerk looked over Hawke's shoulder as someone approached from behind, "...if you could please follow our usher to your rooms?"

Rooms. It was the second time the word was pluralised so Hawke expected a suite. The hotel foyer looked much like any other glamorous hotel of ostentatious styling. The only thing that made him feel displaced were the locals—all of them wore similar fashions with similar hairstyles and every one of them was blonde. He'd known of it, he'd been told about it, but seeing it made him feel trapped in some kind of cloning experiment. Femme's strict immigration laws allowed no room for diversity.

The usher's uniform was a simple burgundy shift dress that ended at his knees. Hawke supposed he would be given a similar outfit to blend in with the locals. He followed the usher into a lift that operated in the usual way.

When they stopped outside his rooms, the usher unlocked door 848 by peering at a small square screen. He then held the door open and gave a small bow, waiting for Hawke to enter first. Once he did, the door was pulled closed, leaving him alone in the room. Hawke blinked in surprise then tried the handle. It was locked.

Well, fuck, there were worse prisons. Maybe this was what they did with Wanderers who travelled; locking them in somewhere luxurious before they were moved on. Perhaps they would even try and talk him into staying so he could experience all the delights that slavery had to offer.

He tossed his messenger bag onto the sofa and investigated the suite. It was a swanky, modern affair that made him feel like he was in an Authoritan hotel. The outstanding differences were some weird symbols projected on a wall and a strange lamp in one of the bedrooms that had a slot for something. The master bedroom had an impossibly sized bed... bigger than a king size, he thought, but it was hard to tell in the vast space of the room. With floor to ceiling windows, he finally had a view of the city.

There were more impractically-shaped white buildings than the standard rectangular type. He could see large patches of greenery down median strips, along footpaths, on blocks of land big enough for more buildings... their green space meant a lot to them. He grudgingly admired that. It looked like a hopeful artist's rendition of what a future city looked like, with clean, crisp lines and elevated mag-lev trains and bubble vehicles. Every woman wore specs and most of them had a man trailing behind them. If it was cultural, then so be it, but slavery wasn't culture, it was oppression. The men here were no better off than dogs or cats; the notion that they could be loved and treated well or abused and discarded like common pets was repulsive.

His bitter thoughts were interrupted by the sound of the front door opening and closing. His diplomat had arrived. Now he had his very own woman to trail after.

He went out to meet her and received a shock when he saw who it was. Fucking Jinwa Woy. He pressed his lips together and glared at her, pondering the implications of her presence and the consequences for his mission. *Missions*. Part of him wasn't surprised it was her—she'd imparted enough of her special brand of crazy that he should have expected it—but mostly he was angry that he didn't know which version of her he was getting.

Was she Femme-faithful Ambassador Woy, sent by someone in the Wanderer-loving department of Femme to meet him? Or was she Authority Lackey Woy, uptight, Spy-hugging bureaucrat conspiring against her Demkoi home team to help her adopted family get some answers? It was just as likely she was neither and he wasn't clever enough to figure out what the third option might be.

"Do not look at me this way," she instructed him. A manicured finger rose in the air and he expected her to waggle it at him but it remained between them, like a shushing gesture.

"How *should* I look at you?" he growled.

Her finger lowered and she glanced around the suite with deliberate intent. She'd have been in rooms like this before so there was no need for her to take in the decor. Was she indicating the room might be compromised and he should be careful with his words? He curled his lip because nowhere on this fucking world was safe.

"With pleasure that you are meeting me."

He snorted. "So you're a diplomat?"

"Rarely. I am Ambassador, not diplomat. I hold greater title."

"So why are you lowering yourself today?"

"Do you not have a brain, miette-hudondi? I am Clairvoyant. I have seen this outcome. I knew I would be assigned to you."

His brain stuttered as he tried to process her implications. She believed they were being watched so they were performing for an invisible audience, yet she'd just openly declared she had prior information on him and she was speaking in a very familiar way. He thought it was too familiar but he supposed her last message meant she knew him because of her foreknowledge. His head hurt from all the 'coulds' and 'might bes'.

"Clairvoyant, eh? Tell me my future or are you only here to fill in paperwork?" Woy's stare could've frozen snow.

She hurriedly closed the distance between them so she could hiss in his face. He instinctively held her by her upper arms, thinking she was going to shove or slap him. "What do you think I could do, great Hunter? Anything I say about you comes back to *me*."

Since it appeared to be okay to have a close-quarters whispering conversation, he thrust his nose near hers, glaring right back.

"If this is something you've already done for Wanderers, you know the process. Why not just share that information? Why send me here and make me do all this?" he asked hoarsely, seeing that this whole endeavour was just pointless bullshit—though it *did* conveniently keep him in place while looking for Synjan.

"Because I want to remain on Demkoi and I am not Shielder," she ground back in hushed tones. "There are Intuits everywhere; it is a common bloodline. If I betray a world secret, I will be discovered. They know everything I share with the Authorities. I am unable to keep straightforward secrets so I must be careful how I help. Everything I do is bluff."

"Then why do it at all?"

"Why are *you* doing it?"

"My reasons are not the same as yours and that's a fucking sidestep, throwing my question back in my face."

"No. I illustrate that we both have reasons. You do not wish to share your reasons and I do not wish to share mine. We are at an impasse. You have no choice but to trust me. I have no choice but to trust you."

It made a horrible sense and he was pleased to have received an explanation he could have faith in. He got the feeling that he might never know where her loyalty ultimately lay but at least she was vulnerable... just not as much as he was. He had more to lose. He was a man on a world that enslaved men, an Authority on a world that mistrusted Authorities and a Hunter in a world filled with Wanderers.

"Nothing changes. Beware what you pretend with your expressions," she said quietly.

Hawke pulled his face away from hers and moved to the couch, placing his hands on the low back. He leaned forward, thinking. It was a strange phrasing but he understood the message clearly: he was a shit actor and should take care with the lies he told. Were there cameras to contend with as well, though? How much was he masking here? He couldn't think properly when he was looking at her. She was calm when facing his frustration and it gave her the upper hand. He had to remain in control.

"What happens now?"

"I ask you what power you have."

He grinned at her, standing up straight. "Shielder. Then what?"

"I show you around the suite," her nose wrinkled. "I will show you the shower, first."

He leered at her. "Will you be joining me?"

"I have to."

He blinked, his plan to make her uneasy backfiring. "Is that an extra service you provide to all new Wanderers?"

"We will be having sex while we are here. I have seen our intimacy."

Hawke chuckled, liking her matter-of-fact delivery in spite of himself. They needed to have sex now that they'd officially met, to cover up the fact they'd done it previously, he supposed. Apparently he had no say in the matter. Was this what slaves went through here? Too bad if they weren't attracted to the woman who demanded such things. It wasn't a problem he had to deal with.

Hawke looked around at the empty room before his gaze settled on Woy. Her stare on him was unwavering.

He made his way over but he only got halfway before she held out her palm, stopping him.

"First, you shower."

Hawke laughed. "I bet you say that to all the filthy Wanderers you help."

She waited a few heartbeats before she spoke, staring levelly at him. "I told you. I do not generally perform tasks such as these. Clairvoyance has brought us together."

"Convenient," he smirked.

"That is how you like your women, is it not?" she asked lightly. She moved past him, walking silently down the corridor to the master bedroom.

Hawke remained where he was, swallowing down the curious mix of fury, guilt and despair the comment had aroused. She hadn't said Brita's name but her meaning was clear. He should've prepared himself for the fact that her powers weren't limited to his future but it had still hit him hard.

When he followed her, she showed him an ensuite with a two-person shower. As promised, she joined him.

CHAPTER TWENTY-ONE

Controlling Interest

ELLIS awoke to the sound of mortars firing and bombs exploding outside the building he was in. It was a typical lullaby in Baldemaris, rattling the foundations and shaking plaster loose from the cracked ceiling. He was reclining on a stiff chair that supported his entire length, a pulse monitor on an index finger and patches on his forehead and chest to keep track of his vitals. There were no windows in this room—it was an underground bunker—so his view was less than enchanting.

"That sounded close," he observed, wiping plaster dust out of his eyes and pulling the patch off his head at the same time. The patches on his chest went next, causing a nearby machine to beep in protest. He sat up in one movement, swinging his legs over the side of the chair. Finally, Ellis removed the pulse monitor from his finger and withdrew his glasses from his pocket, giving them a quick wipe before he put them on.

"Mm, generators got 'em stirred up," Vex agreed, twirling a finger to indicate the machines above them. "How you feelin'? You done disconnected me," Vex chastised, reaching over to flick a switch. The angry beeping stopped abruptly.

"Alright. Alive." Ellis grinned wolfishly and the

expression felt foreign on his face.

It had been eleven days since Synjan had left him and he'd had no cause to show pleasure in that time. He'd told Freddie everything and Hawke had been deployed to rescue her but nothing had come of it. For almost two weeks. In his misery, he'd seen no reason to put off his bi-monthly visit to his holdings on Baldemaris, the second world the Authorities had discovered (but certainly *not* shaped). He wouldn't stay long. However, now that he was here and the usual sense of desperate abandon had spiked the adrenaline in his system, he was glad he'd come. It would take his mind off things.

"Aye." Vex sighed and stood up, turning off the machines splayed before him. He was short, fair skinned and bald. He had intelligent blue eyes behind a set of gold-framed glasses and an ornate-looking set of goggles strapped around the top of his head. Once all the machines were off, he grabbed a helmet and bullet-proof vest from the chair beside him and stepped around the bank of machines, the lapels of his long leather coat flapping at his shins. He took broad, high steps over the myriad of cables and cords snaking between computers and the chair Ellis was in. "Ready soon?" he queried, placing the helmet on the foot end of the chair while he disposed of the patches and cords Ellis had been holding.

Before he got a chance to respond, another explosion sounded outside, though it was farther away than the last. Either their attackers' aim was less than stellar or they were just letting off munitions to keep the occupants lively until they exited the portal bunker. It was a typical act of this world; a place that had evolved beyond the point of sustainability and fallen into total disarray through the millennia since the Authorities discovered it.

Of the thirteen unofficial portals Ellis' affiliates

controlled throughout the worlds, three of them were on Baldemaris. The opportunities afforded by a world bent on the annihilation of all opposition and the accumulation of wealth were unparalleled. The company that operated them no doubt made an excellent return from all three stations. None were exclusive; part of the reason the shells outside weren't encroaching on the portal bunker was fear of being prevented from using it if the owners found out. Ellis had made it his business to control the area closest to this one. It was situated in mountainous terrain only a few hundred kilometres below the northern polar region; hard to attack in, easy to defend.

"Soon. It sounds necessary," Ellis chuckled, rebuttoning his shirt. His outfit was far less refined than usual. Practicality was key in a war zone and he always dressed for the occasion, foregoing suits for cargo pants, steel-toed boots and armoured button-downs with crew necks and lots of pockets.

Vex grunted, waiting for him to fix his shirt before he pushed his way between Ellis' knees and reached around to strap him into the kevlar vest. Ellis lifted his arms and allowed his assistance, finding he was still weak from the world travel to do too much heavy lifting just yet. Besides, he enjoyed having the muscular bulk of the technician between his thighs; another distraction he was looking forward to when everything was settled.

"How is everything faring, Vexatious?" he asked while he was dressed.

As Estate Supervisor, Vex was in charge of all of Ellis' holdings on this world. It was an esteemed position and one Vex had more than earned in his fifteen years of loyal service. They'd built their empire together and now dominated the resources in a two hundred and fifty square kilometre stretch. Such an area of sovereignty was unheard of in these parts.

Ellis watched his employee avidly while he extolled the changes that had occurred in the two months since Ellis had visited, his shorthanded manner of speech challenging but not impossible to follow. The man was a very rare combination for this world. He was intelligent enough to attend to the estate's technical requirements (including running the requisite diagnostics on machinery *and* humans after inter-world portal transfer), diplomatic enough to govern its constituents in Ellis' absence and savvy enough to know when each skill was needed. His compassion would be a detriment to most in this world, but it was one of Vex's most endearing qualities.

"Helmet?" he now asked, rubbing his hands along Ellis' legs in a tender gesture.

Ellis covered his hands with his own, smiling more naturally. "You do know how to take care of me," he mused.

Vex snorted and picked up the helmet he'd placed on the end of the chair, lifting a set of goggles out of it first. He held both items towards Ellis, watching him put them on. It was more likely Ellis would need the safety equipment in this bunker—to protect them from the deteriorating ceiling—than on the drive to the castle, but it paid to be cautious.

When Ellis was ready to walk, Vex put an arm around his waist and helped him out of the bunker, shutting down the generators and leaving them in darkness as they went. Their night-vision goggles showed them the way to the adjoining garage. Their vehicle crouched inside like an angry animal waiting to be set free. It was heavily armoured, fully spiked and sported huge tyres and suspension fit for climbing mountains.

Vex opened the back and shuffled Ellis in before he climbed into the front. Although there was room for three on the backseat, there was space only for one in the single bucket seat in the driver's section. It was surrounded by a dizzying array of screens, toggles, sticks and buttons that proved the cockpit of this vehicle was more complicated than that of an aeroplane. Vex buckled himself into the powered seat—it had full rotational flexibility—and tied his own helmet on.

"Feelin' ready?" he asked, looking at his boss in the rear-view as he powered the vehicle up.

"Think they'll follow?" Ellis asked curiously, clicking his seat harness in. It had been a while since they'd experienced a road ambush. The prospect sent a thrill of excitement through him.

"Chancin'," Vex said and pressed the ignition button. The engine sprang to life, snarling and roaring as Vex tested the accelerator and watched various needles on his dashboard. Ellis' eardrums were further assaulted by the sound of some very loud, very fast music pounding out of the speakers either side of him and his blood leapt as the vehicle edged forward, pressing up the ramp that led out of the garage. As they approached, the thick metal barricade that protected the entryway split apart, allowing a gradually-widening view of daylight to be seen through the slitted windows that constituted the windscreen. The car vibrated agitatedly as it was forced to wait for the barrier to disappear, the thrill of it rolling through Ellis' chest and into his bones.

The instant the metal door was down, Vex gave the vehicle its head, roaring up and bursting out of the garage so hard that they collected air at the top. They landed with a bouncing jolt and screeched across the pitted cement roadway, turning a hard left onto a rutted dirt track that seemed to ascend into the sky itself. Ducking his head, Ellis could just catch a glimpse of Harliss Estate, a blurry black dot squatting atop the next ridge over, some distance away but with the best vantage point in the area.

The day was bleak, the sky covered in dark clouds spitting intermittently at the world below. The rain made the road perilous and they lost traction a few times, sliding briefly along the incline before Vex worked his magic and got them moving forward again. Each time, Ellis' heart had to be swallowed back to where it belonged, exhilaration rocketing upward to take its place in his throat immediately afterward.

They descended the first ridge and begun a more stable path winding through the nature-choked remnants of a long dead city when Vex turned the music down. Through the ringing in his ears, Ellis heard a distinctive beeping that he knew wasn't good.

"They creepin' us soon," Vex warned, indicating a screen that showed the view to their rear in high definition. Every now and then a black vehicle twice the height and girth of theirs was visible, catching up with them now that its greater bulk was less of a handicap on the flat ground.

"What do they want?" Ellis asked, not expecting an answer.

"You," Vex replied, making eye contact with him in the mirror.

Ellis laughed. "That will never happen. Let them come. I'll take care of it," he promised.

"Got rockets," Vex suggested but there was no conviction in his voice. He knew how Ellis would prefer to deal with this situation.

"Don't waste the ammunition," Ellis responded negligently, doing his best to peer through the slatted windows around them in order to figure out where they were. "Are we close to the quarry?"

"Ten minutes 'til."

"Alright. Stay ahead of them for another five and then let them get closer," he instructed.

The music didn't get turned up again but it became a sibilant companion to their drive through the heart of toppled skyscrapers, around fountains blown into decorative pieces across now-savage parklands and along the derelict reminders of what roadways once were. As they reached the outskirts of the city, the whine of their vehicle's engine decreased noticeably and Ellis unbuckled his harness in order to turn and look out the back window slit.

"Shouldn't," Vex condemned his actions and—as if to prove his point—they went through a pitted hole that had looked to be little more than a sore in the roadway. Ellis bounced out of his seat and hit his head on the roof.

"That's what this is for," Ellis scoffed, rapping his knuckles on his helmet. He tuned everything else out, watching carefully for the black monster vehicle to close the gap behind them.

At first, the sight of it was fleeting, little more than a looming shadow cut off by trees growing out of the skeletons of buildings or half-eaten cement pylons. Into the second minute, the shadow took form as the truck came into full view. It was a magnificent beast. Its wheels were taller than their vehicle and barbed for sidelong protection. Along its hard shell top it had a fan of spikes forming a spine with black ropes, hooks, blades and flags swinging from them. Its front plate sported a massive triangular grill that jutted out, pushing every obstacle out of its path. Several arms of encouraging passengers were visibly banging the sides as the distance between them closed. The best thing about it was that there was a fairly clear view of the driver, who thought himself protected because he sat high and far back from the nose.

It was an exercise in patience.

Finally, when they were within a hundred metres, Ellis made his move. He regained visual contact and jumped the gap into the mind of the driver of the truck behind. Their cabin was a cacophony of sound, the excited hoots and curses of numerous men ricocheting around him like the waves of the ocean. He looked at them, counting two beside him and another five on the bench seats in the back end of the truck, their faces alight with bloodlust and the scent of imminent victory.

"Slam 'im, Georgio!" the man jostling against his side screamed lustily and his cry was echoed with rising fervour. "Get him!" they all howled in one form or another and Ellis laughed at them all as they bayed for his blood.

He noticed the patch on his passengers' jackets—all of them bearing the insignia of Baron Tenacious. The mark was familiar, though the man's estate wasn't even close to his so he wasn't sure why Tenacious had decided assassinating him was necessary.

"Let's show 'im we're winners!" someone in the rear shouted.

"Gentlemen," Ellis shook his head, aware that many couldn't hear him and even if they did, they weren't really paying attention anyway. "The winner in any given circumstance is merely the one who has the least to learn from the situation. This will be your last lesson."

The man beside him turned a puzzled squint on him but Ellis ignored his scrutiny. He had learned enough. His grin only grew as a familiar turn loomed. They'd begun the climb that would lead to his fortress and though it shouldn't have been, the heavier vehicle was still gaining on the one in front. No-one questioned it until he slowed down briefly in order to take the right turn towards the quarry and even then, it took them far longer than it should've.

"Hey! Where you goin', Georgie?"

"What the?"

"Fuck, take care, high here!"

Their words bled into one another, the pitches escalating deliciously. At the last moment, strong hands grasped his arms and tried to change his course but the road was short, the drop was sudden and they didn't try soon enough. His last act in the mind of Georgio was to press the accelerator to the floor and direct the vehicle straight at the gaping mouth of the quarry, gouged deep into the heart of the mountain in order to extract all its mineral treasures. The front wheels had just found open space when Ellis snapped back into his own body, the melody of their mingled screams still ringing in his ears and the kickstart of imminent death tingling falsely in his veins.

He laughed long and loud, settling back into his seat and reinstating his harness, a broad grin on his face. Vex merely watched him in the mirror, not asking if he'd been successful.

Hours later, Ellis lay in his bed in the highest turret of Harliss Castle, half sitting against the headboard and watching lightning streak through the night sky. His bed was positioned in the middle of the circular stone room, between two sets of glass doors that were open to the night, their curtains billowing in and out as the frenzied storm ebbed and flowed across the mountainside. The occasional spray of rain was refreshing and he was loathe to get up and close out the elements for the sake of staying dry. Vex was sprawled beside him, face down and dozing, the intermittent lighting illuminating his beautiful, naked body to dazzling effect. Ellis trailed a reverent finger across the bunched muscles of his shoulder, thinking.

"I have a request," he mused airily.

"Mnm?"

"I need a bedroom—or one of the dungeons—converted."

Vex swiped his face across the pillow and wriggled so that he could peer up at Ellis. Without his glasses, he looked far younger than his forty years.

"For what?"

"I might need to bring someone here. A woman. It's not certain but... she's travelling and I don't want her to. She might object to my wishes so I'll need somewhere to... *contain* her. I'll likely have to bring her back to safety via the portal anyway, depending on how far she gets. Might as well come here until things settle down."

"You stayin'?" Vex asked hopefully, his expression alight with the news.

Ellis smiled lazily at his lover, amused by the part that he'd chosen to focus on in all of that. "Yes. When she's caught. I'll stay too."

Vex rolled up onto one elbow, using his other hand to cup Ellis, causing him to suck in a hasty breath. "With *me*," the bald man asserted jealously, apparently only now realising that Ellis had told him he'd be bringing a woman to the castle.

Chuckling, Ellis eased Vex's grip and entwined fingers with him instead. On Baldemaris, Ellis only ever chose Vex and he never spoke of the countless women and men that graced his other beds, out of respect. Truthfully, it was also to encourage Vex's love for him, to cement his loyalty. Having Synjan in the castle wouldn't upset their physical relationship but Ellis knew the dynamic between his Trent number one and his Baldemaris number one would be combative at the least. He would deal with that later.

"Yes, with you," he agreed, raising his eyebrows as a flash of lightning and a crack of thunder landed at the same time, illuminating Vex's expression clearly for him. "But she will need a nice room and a good bathroom behind a strong door. Can you see that it happens?"

"How soon?"

Ellis sighed, disappointed by the ache in his heart that hadn't lessened in his journey here; it had only been suppressed until this moment, when he was forced to pick it up again. "I don't know. It could be weeks, it could be longer." His mind balked at defining 'longer' and he knew he would go insane if it remained thus. He couldn't bear to sit idly by, waiting on others to restore his heart to whole once more. He wasn't used to not being in control. A reckoning would come. "You will have at least two weeks, probably more," he told Vex sadly, suddenly unable to find comfort in the man's touch or his concerned expression. He let go of him and stood up, walking out the open door and onto the balcony beyond, unconcerned by his nudity.

Leaning on the battlements, he looked down at the township clustered at the foot of the castle between its solid stone and metal walls and the extraordinarily high fence that protected them all. In sporadic flashes he observed the fields that fed the few hundred people of Harliss, the houses that sheltered its servants, the spiked and rutted moat of rusted machines and stone. The only lights he could make out in the lulls of darkness were the flames of the guards atop the wall and one or two candles in windows below.

He expected there'd be reprisal from Tenacious on the morrow and all of it would come under fire but he was confident they wouldn't fall. Not with him here.

Vex padded out beside him and tried to wrap an arm about his shoulders but Ellis shook him off. "I'm tired," he explained, not looking at the shorter man. "And I suspect we'll be seeing more of Baron Tenacious' men tomorrow. You should get some sleep. In your own bed. We'll talk again in the morning."

He didn't need to look at Vex to know that when he walked away silently, his expression was wounded. It didn't please him necessarily but part of him exulted in the sharing of his misery. Sadly, that was the way it

would be until he found Synjan again. Everyone would
just have to get used to it.

CHAPTER TWENTY-TWO

Discretionary Interference

A unique tension flowed through her the moment Synjan opened her eyes. Part excitement, part dread, she was energised by the knowledge that today would be their final day with the Mukake. The rumbling of thunder and push of turgid winds against their tent echoed the storm of emotions inside her, promising a memorable finale to their stay. The patch in their tent was holding... so far.

Two weeks had changed them a great deal. Idly, she brushed her cheek against Daeson's arm. He was wrapped around her as he slept, despite his nightly assertion that he'd keep to himself. She'd learned to smile and agree, not telling him that she'd be disappointed if it stopped now. He'd read too much into it.

She closed her eyes again, seeking out the Portal with her mind. There was a feeling of grandiosity in pulling away from her body, elevating her senses until she had a topographical view of this world. Defining it in its simplest terms—the peaks and troughs—allowed her to Navigate with less strain.

The Portal was a beacon pulsing north of where they were now; life and light atop the grid. She slowly worked her way backwards from it, mapping the islands she and Daeson would have to negotiate to reach their destination. If the tides were with them, they should leave this land of imposing heights and endless water in the next two days; the prospect was both a relief and a dirge reverberating in her soul. Despite the tribulations of this world, it would always be the first she'd Wandered to and it had forever marked her heart.

As she neared her physical position, Synjan was distracted by movement on the larger of the Exclamation Islands. She shifted focus and her mind swooped lower, startled to find three dozen people moving around the area where they'd destroyed the huts six days before. She observed them carefully. The patterns were unfamiliar and so numerous that they could only belong to the Techatachenti. Of all the days for the Mukake's adversaries to invade, it had to be the one on which she and Daeson were planning a strategic retreat.

With a new sense of foreboding, she rolled over so that she was facing Daeson and rubbed her hand along his arm to rouse him. "We have a problem," she told him quietly.

Daeson's eyelids fluttered and he gazed at her with such open innocence that she almost believed everything would be alright.

"What is it?"

"Thirty-six Techatachenti are on the hunting island."

He blinked a few times. "What?" he asked again.

She repeated her statement.

He sat up, fighting off the last vestiges of sleep. "This is a problem."

"Yes. Should I tell the Mukake?"

Daeson opened his mouth but closed it without speaking and gave her a thoughtful look instead. His next words were cautious. "Uh, they're going to find out eventually."

"Yeah, but that could be after we're gone."

"Oh."

Synjan watched him silently. She doubted it was necessary to talk about how such a revelation would explode through the Mukake people and result in overreactions that would certainly ruin their final day. His understanding was in his eyes.

"Don't they ask you every day if there are people on the island?"

"Yes."

"So what are you going to say?"

The magnitude of the decision overwhelmed her. "I can lie."

Daeson's eyes widened and he shook his head slightly. "No, we should tell them."

Synjan took a breath and nodded.

Once they'd committed to the decision, events unfolded swiftly. The weather pummelled them as they exited their tent, the driving rain soaking them as they made their way towards the gathering area. Synjan had mapped Hiyani conversing with the Shinu in their shelter so she led Daeson on a storm-battered path straight to them. They hunkered beneath the lean-to as much as they could, crowding the small space.

"Techatachenti," Synjan told them abruptly, pointing in the direction of the island in question. A grim expression immediately settled on the faces of both Shinu. Hiyani merely nodded, like she'd expected such a thing. Synjan doubted she was prepared for such numbers though, so she started flashing the fingers of both hands until she'd numbered thirty-six. Daeson watched her display and reached over, his large hands covering both of her fists.

"Sho, sho, sho, kinucka Techatachenti," Daeson interpreted.

Hiyani sang something at Daeson that prompted a thoughtful look from him. He replied haltingly but the old woman waited until he'd finished. More rapid questions came from Hiyani and each time she waited for Daeson to respond but once she was satisfied with his answers, they were disregarded. Synjan tried not to be offended by the negligent manner in which they were waved away—or the fact she was ignored during the exchange. Once they were dismissed, Hiyani turned and spoke urgently with the Shinu, mentioning Tagan's name.

As they retreated, Daeson told her, "They're sending people over there."

Synjan frowned, a sinking feeling gripping her heart. "They're going to try to move them away? That will likely end in a fight!"

"We shouldn't have told them."

"It's too late now," she sighed.

"They've landed," Synjan told Daeson and sat up, instinctively clutching his hand as she turned to face him. They were knee to knee in their little canvas haven.

After hiding themselves away for the last three hours, the tent was pristine. With time on their hands and a storm battering the world outside, they'd had nothing to do but organise and pack their gear. Their bedding was put away because they were planning to leave in the night. The process had been dragged out as long as possible but, inevitably, they'd been left with nothing to do but wait.

The Mukake—with predictable righteousness—had dispatched twenty-four of their fiercest warriors to row to the hunting island to confront the Techatachenti invaders. Tagan had been summoned first and commanded to control the storm.

Synjan and Daeson had ventured out of the tent when the quality of the sounds outside changed, and emerged to find a circle of clear weather encompassing the small pillar. Synjan had seen tanks of fish in expensive houses on Trent and, looking up at a blue sky surrounded by a surreal border of roiling, seething clouds and furious rain, she felt like she was in one of those tanks. The storm had been cast beyond Tagan's influence and once he'd climbed down the cliff (it was slippery and terrifying to watch them all descend), the patch of blue sky stayed with him.

Within ten minutes of the warriors setting off, the storm returned, sending Synjan and Daeson scurrying for cover. They could've spent their time huddling with Hiyani or Kahu—both of whom had had a profound impact on their stay—but they had never felt more like intruders. In addition, Synjan wanted to watch what happened and she could tell from the tension in Daeson's shoulders that he wanted to know, too. His intent expression prompted her to continue narrating, though she closed her eyes to map more easily. Hovering close by made her feel like she was one of them, their familiar patterns the lights illuminating her darkness.

"They're not... they're streaming out of their canoes and onto the beach. They'll go through the forest and straight across, like they did wi—*oh*," she cried in dismay, doing what the Mukake had failed to do and looking ahead of their incensed friends. "There are scouts. The Techatachenti are running back first, warning everyone," she explained, opening her eyes briefly to share a saddened look with Daeson before closing her eyes again.

Of the twenty-four patterns now barrelling blindly through the forest, Synjan knew three well and the rest in passing. They were a mix of men and women, twenty of them the younger adults and four of them in their forties. Kahu would have gone, had she not been obligated to stay for her daughter's sake. Synjan had never been more grateful for the brat than when she realised Kahu would remain behind.

Instinctively, Synjan watched Bo's pattern first, checked Tagan's second and Paki's third. Her heart was thumping fast enough to drive her alongside her companions but she was compelled by fear for their safety rather than anger. The Techatachenti would be ready for them by the time the Mukake got there. They were no military geniuses; their blood was up and they were swarming towards their target blindly. The outcome was unlikely to be good and the longer she watched, the more certain of that she became.

It took some time for the Mukake to get through the forested width of the island and she moved compulsively amongst them the whole time, watching silently and sipping from the water flask she had at her knee. When she finally broke the silence, it wasn't with good news.

"They've reached the Techatachenti compound. They're all over the place."

From the Mukake's movements, she gathered that the Techatachenti had been rebuilding their destroyed huts. The Mukake were channelled into four groups. Synjan tried to hover behind them. To her left, Paki stood with one of the older men in a huddle, arguing with a lone Techatachenti pattern. Towards the middle was a group of five Mukake members facing off against six Techatachenti members; Bo was at the back of that group, holding his own counsel. As the groups shuffled closer together, Bo became separated, letting the other four strut forward and yell their message while he remained behind.

The show Bo's companions put on was obviously very loud because the next group over swarmed in and merged with them. The Techatachenti six also gathered more supporters, creating a festering clump of adversaries in the middle and two smaller collections either side. Tagan had joined the central group, in front of where Bo stood. Synjan didn't look at anything else.

For a time, it seemed that the middle patterns were only interested in posturing and shouting. They jostled and waved arms at one another, their mouths open and their fists closed. Physical contact was made when someone pushed someone else and chests were pressed against each other. Tagan cockily walked the man in front of him back a few steps before his opponent drew a friend to help him stand his ground.

"What's happening?" Daeson interjected and the anxious tone of his voice told her that she'd been quiet and watching too long.

"Sorry," she said hastily, "It's a mess. There are different conversations happening everywhere. There are three groups but the main group is the biggest and they're shoving each other now."

She backtracked and explained to him how the two groups had merged so he could picture it.

"It's..." she frowned, watching the relations between the opposing groups in the middle disintegrate. "They're jostling each other, some of them are yelling in each other's faces, others are—there's a fight. Two of them are throwing punches, going pretty hard at it. Fuck, that was a big hit, the Techatachenti guy almost went down but they helped him up again. Everyone's circling around them, they seem to be cheering their man on."

Bo chose that moment to walk towards the group, catching Synjan's attention because he'd kept himself apart for so long. The Techatachenti also noticed the largest Mukake warrior's movements and a cluster of them broke away from the fighting in a swirl of panic. They were a blur of pushing, shoving and grabbing and then one stepped forward boldly. Synjan's mouth went dry as the man turned his body in a telltale pose; one arm forward for balance, the other drawing back... his pattern flared with concentration as he released a spear with savage accuracy. Bo took one more step before his pattern staggered, teetered... and blinked out.

Synjan screamed, her eyes flying open and her mouth covered by her hands as she stared at Daeson. An intense ache blossomed in her chest, brandishing tears and stealing her breath.

"What happened?" Daeson asked.

She tried to speak but it took her a moment before she could get anything out and even then, it was minimal: "Bo."

Daeson scooted closer so he could hug her but she couldn't bear to stop watching. She needed to know how much worse it would get.

By the time her mind returned to the distant island, it seemed that everyone had got over their shock at Bo's death. The two fighters had become ten, fifteen, even more... and everyone's patterns were throbbing with shock and adrenaline.

The pattern of the Mukake man standing beside Paki started to strobe and fade and Synjan saw the Techatachenti person pull an arm back. A slash to the throat had been delivered— a very effective one, because the pattern faded quickly. The Techatachenti murderer didn't have time to relish his kill before Paki avenged her partner and cut him down with her sickle. She stood over him as his pattern blinked out.

Coming to her senses, Paki ran for the rest of the group. Her motion spurred the Mukake into action and they retreated. The group sped away in bedraggled clumps, helping each other if they couldn't walk properly and cowering away from the victorious actions of the Techatachenti.

Synjan saw Tagan crouched in the sand with another Mukake member. The two of them were dragging something; she realised they were trying to take Bo's body with them. Without warning, the pattern helping Tagan arched backwards, stiffened and toppled, blinking out in seconds. Tagan dropped what he was holding and ran. Synjan didn't blame him.

Taking a few breaths to steady herself and wiping her eyes before she opened them, Synjan looked at Daeson with a wobbling chin, steeling herself to speak. She had to clear her throat before she managed it successfully.

"They're leaving now. Three of them aren't coming back but Paki got one of theirs."

Daeson pulled back to look at her. "What do you mean she 'got one'?"

Synjan swallowed and blinked at him. "She killed one of them."

Daeson sighed heavily. "This war's been brewing for a long time. Looks like it's here."

"*War?*" She was devastated by the thought of more Mukake deaths in the near future. They were so few compared to a people of so many. Their suffering was already exponentially worse than the Techatachenti's would be, how could they consider adding to that misery?

"The Mukake consider that island sacred. They're not going to let the Techatachenti live there," Daeson explained.

It explained why the Mukake didn't live there but was not a good enough reason for suicide. "They don't have the numbers!"

"I don't think that matters."

"How can you *say* that?" Synjan cried. She was offended that he seemed to be wiping his hands of the outcome, yet he knew the tragedy would continue to unfold if the Mukake returned. They would smash themselves to pieces against the overwhelming numbers of the Techatachenti.

"Because Hiyani is no longer Shinu and the new ones will want to fight."

"That's insane! They'll all die!"

Daeson's expression cracked from the reasonable mask he'd been wearing and he withered, shrugging helplessly at her. Synjan realised he wasn't apathetic; he was barricading his feelings in an effort to fend off the powerful emotions bombarding them. He was being hit as hard as she was, he was just dealing with it differently.

A horrible thought surfaced in the maelstrom of her emotions and she looked at Daeson fearfully. She almost didn't dare give it voice. Almost. "I can... make sure the Mukake win," she offered hesitantly.

When his gaze hardened it was clear he understood she meant her guns. Synjan braced herself for accusations of violence being her only answer, for him to condemn her once more as a product of her world. But they didn't come.

"I need some time to think," he said instead and left the tent.

Synjan nodded in his wake, drinking some more water and then curling up on the floor of the tent to bury her face in her arms, to mourn and to oversee the returning Mukake members.

Daeson returned an hour later, his expression reflecting the seriousness of his thoughts. He sat across from her and took his time before he responded. His voice was measured and sombre.

"There's a lot to think about. Not just about this war but also the world. We've come into it and we're going to leave it. If we stayed, that would give us more right to be involved. But we're not staying, so I don't think we should interfere."

She understood his reasoning but it clutched at her heart. The Mukake had become their friends, their companions, their almost-lovers. The memory of their precious patterns blinking out was not something she could stop replaying and to give up on those that still lived felt like an unnecessary betrayal.

"But it'll be a slaughter," she argued weakly.

"It'll be a slaughter either way. Them killing each other or us killing them."

She appreciated his use of the collective 'us'. The fact he was willing to accept responsibility with her summoned more tears; this time, of gratitude. She sobbed into her hands, her head hanging as she mourned the future Mukake losses.

"We don't want to be like the Authorities," he said, attempting to soothe her with a hand on her shoulder. "I imagine this is how it starts. First they protect, then they teach, then they take over."

Synjan lowered her hands and sniffled as she frowned at Daeson. "We're not taking over the Mukake people."

"That's right, because we're leaving. We have to go tonight. Did you notice they took all the boats?"

She nodded, wiping her cheeks and sighing resignedly. "Yeah and if they only come back to regroup like you think they will, we won't have another chance," she agreed.

Their course was set. Their only option was to flee while they could. Synjan was not surprised but she was disenchanted that the decision had, once again, been taken out of their hands.

CHAPTER TWENTY-THREE

Combating The Cliff

WITH a churning stomach and dry mouth, Daeson slipped the lasso tether over his head and spun it around so the line holding him was at his back. He double-checked the post that held the tanga vine, confident it was secure. The knot was also firm—he yanked and stretched it as hard as he could, preferring it to break before he banked his life on it. It held. Daeson shouldered his backpack and looked at Synjan.

She was checking her own harness but must've felt his stare because she turned to meet it.

"They don't climb while carrying things," he said, his voice carrying in the stillness of the night. A goat bleated in reply.

Neh-neh-ma jun juwa piku-buh, his brain immediately threw at him. Goat-Man now climbs down cliff.

She didn't reply, nodding instead. He was telling her something they both knew, though his anxiety had urged him to give it voice. There was no other way to get the backpacks down and to climb together. Operating the pulley system would force them onto a more difficult section of the cliff and Synjan had assured him that climbing down the tribe's sleeping side was their best chance to arrive at the bottom safely.

"Do you think they'll stop us?" Daeson asked, wanting more guarantees even though he knew Synjan couldn't honestly give them.

"Hopefully they'll all be asleep," she whispered back.

"And if someone isn't?"

"Then we'll deal with it when it happens. Are you ready to go?"

He didn't like not having a plan but her tagged on question suggested she thought he was stalling. Perhaps he was. He wanted to say he was ready but couldn't. It took him a few tries to get out the truth.

"I don't feel like I'll ever be ready but we should go now."

She nodded, her expression lost to black. It would be harder to see her when they were climbing down the cliff-face.

He followed Synjan to the edge and watched carefully as she turned and crouched. She stepped backward and gradually disappeared until he could only see her head.

"You can do this, Daeson," she urged, her soft voice reminding him of the time on the bridge. He'd crossed it with her help and her belief in him gave him the courage he needed. Synjan had dropped out of sight; he imagined her working her way down the cliff. She was getting out of his way, he presumed.

Daeson turned and dropped into a crouch, fingertips settling on compact dirt. It was strangely easier to begin this climb than it had been to step out on the rope bridge, perhaps because he wouldn't be looking at where he was going. His seeking foot found a place to step and he gradually put his weight on it. He found a handhold quickly and step-climbed down again. He was grateful for Synjan's suggestion and her experience on the cliff-face.

Unlike the bridge, she wasn't talking him through it.

He was aware of people around him, he could sense them hanging inside their roosts.

His foot slipped and he tensed, hands clawing on rocks until he found a new place to stand. He couldn't lose his concentration during this climb.

"You okay?" Synjan whispered to him from somewhere below and to his left.

"Yes," he said, surprised that he could answer her so bluntly. Gravity's fingers were gripped on his backpack as though it wished to peel him off the cliff. He hadn't been greatly bothered by the sensation but he thought it was because the climb had been easy so far. How far down did the sleeping area go? Would the handholds be this easy all the way to the bottom? He hadn't asked and suspected Synjan might not even know.

Focus. He had to focus.

Hand, foot, foot. Hand, foot, hand. It was monotonous, slow and difficult. He passed very closely to a sleeping roost, seeing three bodies hanging inside of it—two large and one small. It had a disturbing feel, as though the people within weren't sleeping but were corpses, hanging up like bled pigs. Bile rose in his throat but then it went away, only to be replaced by a potent thirst. One of the bodies sing-murmured groggily, as though they sensed they were being watched or perhaps they'd heard Daeson's clumsy movements. He held his breath but couldn't do it for long while climbing. He blew it slowly and took another careful breath through his nose.

The hanging family were above him now but his thirst remained. It didn't help that sweat was pouring off him and fear made his palms slippery. It took him a few goes each time to get a good hold. He felt like he'd been climbing for many hours but it was still dark. Time was immobile.

After passing the last group of sleepers, the lasso tightened and refused to let him climb farther down.

He'd reached its end. He fumbled his way out of it, feeling vulnerable once it was over his head and hanging loose on the rock. After a few deep breaths he got going again, mentally encouraging himself with each step and handhold downward.

After an age—when the cliff-wall felt wetter—Synjan whispered, "Come left now."

He followed her advice, working his way left instead of down. He was surprised at how much harder it was to move across. He was more aware of the constant pull on his backpack, it had greater influence on him. He sensed that he wasn't as closely pressed against the wall of rock, that he'd tired over time and was reaching farther, taking more risks for faster progress. It also felt good to stretch out; his arms and legs had cramped during the climb.

Daeson reached for a jutting rock on his left that looked perfect for holding onto. He went up on tip-toes and his fingers curled around the rock just as his foot slipped off the edge of his narrow foothold, causing his other foot to follow. He cried out, unable to contain his voice as he lost his second handhold; he hung onto the jutting rock by fingertips alone. He was strong; strong enough to hold himself this way until he found another handhold... but his backpack full of equipment was too heavy. His fingers trembled as he scrabbled for purchase.

"I'm coming," Synjan said. The urgency in her voice revealed her awareness of his predicament but she was a couple of handholds away. Too far to help. Daeson's other hand sought cracks, bumps, anything. His boots scuffed against the unyielding rock of the cliff. Synjan reached out just as Daeson's fingers refused to hold him any longer.

As he fell away from the wall, he didn't try for her outstretched hand, knowing his weight would just take her with him. As he dropped, he saw the cliff's great mass above him in detail, he saw Synjan's eyes widen and her mouth open, he saw the roosts peppering the cliff above them. The sound of wind and ocean filled his ears. He would smack into the water below at such a great speed that it would pulverise him—there would be no time to Heal.

The impact forced out any breath he might've thought to hold but the freezing water shocked a gasp from him, offering a minimal amount of air. He'd heard and felt the splash before being enclosed in the chilly capsule of the ocean. Salt stung his eyes and he screwed them shut; the water was an inky blackness he couldn't see in anyway.

There was momentary elation that he hadn't fallen from as great a height as he'd thought. He'd survived! His celebration passed when he continued to sink.

For those two visits to the holiday world of Mwavey, he'd played in the surf and learned how to swim. He'd picked it up quickly, the mechanics of sweeping arms and kicking legs was a skill he'd been good at. Except he hadn't been clothed then, nor carrying equipment—it felt cumbersome. He considered dumping his backpack but thought of Synjan's protectiveness of their equipment. He thought he should at least try to surface with it. A losing battle would see it off his shoulders, sacrificed to the ocean depths.

Daeson got his bearings by swimming in the opposite direction of the tugging water. He felt like he was making progress, though it was difficult to know how far he'd sunk. His lungs burned for air and he didn't have much in reserve. The pressure was unbearable. He needed to know if he was going the right way so he sacrificed a bubble. He felt it slither past his face before it easily outpaced him. He had time to wonder if he should've dumped the backpack after all and if his hesitation in doing so would undo him now.

He broke the surface and took in big gulps of air and

seawater, coughing the latter out. He heard his name being called out by Synjan but nothing more than that—his ears were clogged. His backpack threatened to drag him under but he fought it, determined to keep it now he'd reached the surface. Synjan would be pleased that he'd saved their stuff. His pack held their tent and all of their money.

Daeson swam around to where he thought the platform was but he couldn't see it. A row of boats were floating on the ocean's surface farther away, attached to hooks in the cliff-side. Synjan didn't move to them, instead she stepped down into the ocean. Daeson's frantic mind didn't understand what she was doing until he saw her walking across the ocean-surface, her boots kicking up splashes. The tide must have risen and covered the platform in shallow water.

It didn't take him long to reach her. He pulled himself up onto the platform as Synjan helped him, throwing her arms around him and squeezing him once he was safe.

Daeson hugged her back, realising it must've been frightening for her too; to have seen him fall and perhaps drown, leaving her to deal with this world and Wandering by herself.

"It's okay, I'm alright," he said.

"They're coming. I shouted when you fell." Synjan pulled back and wiped an arm across her eyes before pointing at the nearest canoe. Daeson could hear a few voices singing but not as many as he'd expected. Perhaps an alarm hadn't been raised.

Daeson waded over to the canoe and dumped his pack into it before following its line to a hook in the cliff. He worked the knot as Synjan pulled off her pack and placed it in the centre of the boat, adjusting Daeson's sopping one alongside it. His clothes were uncomfortable and heavy but he didn't have the time or anything dry to change into.

"Hurry," Synjan prompted as she stepped into the canoe, but there were already two Mukake men wading over. Daeson faced them and they stopped. They didn't look angry, more concerned. Being able to see their expressions made Daeson aware that the sun was rising. The Mukake people should've been out fishing already, working on breakfast and setting up the weaving mats. Their routine had been abolished in preparation for the war that would begin today.

"Ma-ma seh kapu, Wandruh piangi," Daeson sang.

The two natives looked at one another and then back at him. They were silent until Daeson threw the line into the boat.

"Bin, ma-ma duwa kapu jun," the taller one protested.

"What's being said?" Synjan whispered behind him.

"I told them we're leaving, that we need the boat. They don't want us to take the canoe. I'm going to tell them they don't have a choice. Hiyani tentaya bulu."

The two Mukake men, neither of whom Daeson recognised, looked at one another again as Daeson instructed them of their duty; not to interfere with Wanderers. It was a rule that Hiyani had set in place when she'd been Shinu decades earlier.

Daeson took the second paddle from Synjan when she passed it to him and then he stepped into the canoe, careful not to tip it as it rocked violently from his movements.

"Iyabi! Iyabi!"Daeson ordered. One of the Mukake men stepped forward and gave the canoe a push, sending them on their way.

"Did you tell him to do that?" Synjan asked, her disbelief apparent.

"Yes but I didn't think either of them would. I tried because they looked uncertain."

They paddled away.

Their silence lasted an hour before Synjan's stomach couldn't handle the choppy waters. The sky was cloudless, though white caps on the waves promised and delivered a constant roll. They ended up beaching on the side of an island opposite to Mukake Island. Daeson took the opportunity to unpack everything to dry upon the rocks. He avoided placing his clothes on sand wherever he could.

"Over there are oysters," Synjan announced, pointing at a small peak in the sea. "Kahu and I dove for them the other day."

When he didn't comment, she filled in the silence. "Not far past it is Wanderer Island."

"How do you know that?" Daeson asked, impressed that Synjan had learned something that he hadn't.

"There was stuff there from the Wanderers who came before us."

"So they didn't call it Wanderer Island. You did," he said.

She shrugged like it wasn't important. Daeson reflected on why he'd wanted to make the point. Did he feel superior to her because he'd learned the language and she hadn't? He hoped not, he didn't like what it implied about his character. He'd always thought of himself as a good man, loyal and open-minded.

"Do you think of me as open-minded?" he asked as Synjan lay flat on her back on the sand, obviously relishing the lack of motion. She squinted at him before shading her eyes with a hand.

"Kind of. I don't think of you as closed-minded."

Daeson thought it wasn't the same thing.

"Why?" she prompted.

"I learned more about myself than I expected."

"You learned that... you're open-minded?"

"I always thought that I was. I don't think I am, anymore."

"You think this world did that to you?" Synjan asked, her tone sombre and her expression changing to concern.

"No. I don't think I ever was, looking back. Change was forced on me and I resisted it. That's not being open-minded."

Synjan smiled at him but said nothing. The way she pressed her lips together made him think she was holding back.

"Tell me," he demanded, because orders worked better on her than requests.

She giggled and shook her head.

"What? Why not?"

"You'll take it the wrong way," she said.

"You can't know that until after it's said."

"Anybody would take it the wrong way," she countered. Her statement sat in a strange place in his gut, where metaphors lay. It wasn't a lie but the words were too general to be an exact truth.

He didn't pursue it and she didn't relent.

"How many days do you think we'll be rowing before we reach the Portal?"

"If we get good weather and flat seas, I don't see why we can't reach it in a couple of days. Three is more likely, if we have to stop. Speaking of, as soon as your stuff is dry, we'll be good to go."

"Are you sure? You still look..." *sweaty* was the word he was going to use, but he didn't want to use it. No other word seemed to fit.

"Queasy?" she offered. "My stomach has settled."

They checked his things. After an hour under the hot sun, most of his clothes were dry. His backpack itself was cold to the touch and his jeans were still soggy, so Synjan organised his pack in such a way that the clothes that had dried weren't touching the ones that were still wet. She had patience for such things.

The wind shifted and brought with it the distant sound of voices singing together. It was a chanting that Daeson didn't recognise but suspected it was a war-song. The wind shifted the other way and he could no longer hear it.

He wasn't going to tell Synjan what he'd heard, except she stood up straight and stared at him with pain in her eyes.

"They're leaving to go fight," she said.

He refused to look over his shoulder at the pillar. It felt appropriate to keep it behind him. Synjan started turning and he spoke up so she wouldn't finish her action.

"I heard them when the wind changed. They must've raised their voices in a chant."

She stared at him. "You've got good hearing, Daeson."

"I can't hear them anymore. The ocean carries sound farther, anyway.

"I thought that was only when the water was really calm."

"It *is* calm," Daeson said. "It's better than calm. It's been Tagan-ed."

Synjan looked out at the sea. "I wonder how far his influence carries."

"We should take advantage and head off," he said. He didn't want Synjan to map the Mukake people if all she was going to see were their deaths. She wasn't showing her emotion over Bo but he suspected the pain of losing him was still with her.

CHAPTER TWENTY-FOUR

Taking Control

ELLIS took a moment to stretch his limbs and assess the colours streaking across the late afternoon sky over Bardon City. He'd been driving for hours to get here by evening and his ageing body knew it; he hadn't given it enough time to recover from portalling back into Trent before inflicting this extra punishment on it. With a few final cracks and a heaved sigh, he closed his car door and walked up the path to the nondescript suburban brick home. Apart from being two levels, it didn't stand out as anything different to the other homes in the street, yet its occupants were anything but ordinary.

As a matter of courtesy, he knocked on the glass-panelled front door, choosing not to use his key because he hadn't pre-warned the residents that he was coming. As their benefactor and landlord, he was also mildly curious to see the state of things when he surprised them.

Amara answered the door, her eyes wide when she caught sight of him. "Ellis! What are you doing here?" she asked, her voice loud enough to carry through the house.

Ellis smirked at the sound of furniture scraping across polished wooden floors and dishes hastily being collected and rushed to the central kitchen. She kept the door mostly closed but he saw the outline of a figure hurrying past.

"I have some business I need to discuss with Michael and Fyfe," he answered mildly, knowing she would sense his intentions or thoughts on the matter anyway—as a full blood Intuit, it was her duty to protect those in the house with her talent.

"Uh... I'll see if they're here," she agreed, opening the door for Ellis to enter. She closed it behind him. "Do you want to wait in the lounge?"

From the doorway, a great deal of the open plan ground floor was visible—a sitting area, dining table and a games area at the other end of the house. Since there were six residents in the home, it was difficult to find privacy. A small, wary face peered around the corner from the kitchen, watching him with large dark eyes. Beside the front entry was a formal lounge with double doors that could be closed to give seclusion.

Ellis nodded. "After I use the facilities," he agreed. "It was a long drive. A cup of tea would also be welcome," he hinted as he headed for the nearest restroom. He wasn't especially thirsty but the beverage might help to settle his stomach.

"Of course," Amara demurred politely and scurried around him to do his bidding.

As he waited in the lounge some minutes later, Ellis reclined in the armchair—he'd positioned it to face the couch squarely, wanting to make eye contact with the men he would speak to.

He had returned from Baldemaris despairing. His home felt empty without Synjan and Freddie had no news for him—more intent on chastising Ellis for Omerri being in hospital than worrying about what Hawke wasn't accomplishing. Freddie's insistence that there might be no news for some time was offensive and unacceptable. It spawned a renewed sense of determination.

As he saw it, Hawke had positioned himself on Femme and was waiting for Synjan and Daeson to turn up and draw attention to themselves so that he could catch them. It had been sixteen days since the pair had departed Trent and nothing was happening. From experience, Ellis knew what the Authorities did not— there were worlds in between those that had been tagged by them, worlds that could only be reached by travelling the natural way.

Either Synjan was on one such world, between Trent and Femme, or she was as smart as Ellis and Freddie had trained her to be and she was eluding Hawke's vigilant overwatch. Ellis needed to be sure it wasn't the former, because she might never emerge if the world was good enough. He couldn't continue to live in existential limbo, not knowing.

He looked up as the door to the lounge opened but was disappointed to see Amara carrying the cup of tea he'd requested.

"Fyfe's not here but Michael is coming," she informed Ellis as she set the cup down on the table in front of him.

He wondered if he detected a tone of superiority in her voice. Perhaps she was pleased he wasn't immediately getting what he wanted because he hadn't called ahead.

"Do you know where Fyfe is?"

Amara snorted. "At the shops."

It was obvious that Ellis was supposed to glean something from that tidbit but he had no idea what it was.

"I saw Patience loitering in the kitchen. Perhaps she should utilise her young legs and collect him for me?" he suggested.

Amara opened her mouth to say something then seemed to think better of it. Ellis knew she was old enough to be the Ghost's mother and acted accordingly, but he was glad she didn't try to argue with his suggestion; Patience was sixteen years old and not as helpless as she liked to appear. Amara nodded and walked out of the room, doing an awkward half dance with Michael in the doorway as he entered before she could exit.

"Ellis," he greeted simply, nodding his bearded head as he waddled into the room and obediently settled his bulk on the couch opposite. "What's gone wrong?"

Ellis would have liked to reassure the man that his cynicism had got the best of him but he couldn't. *Everything* was wrong and he realised, as he looked at the forty-eight year old's increased rotundity, that this was not the man that could help him right it. Obviously he'd been keeping his Wanderer residents in excess because the Navigator sitting across from him was far too fat and old to be of any use.

"I was just thinking—have you ever visited Gredann?"

"No. Is there a reason to?" Michael asked gruffly.

"Not really, I was wondering if you'd ever met Synjan, my number one," he answered mildly. Ellis knew very well that the residents of this carnival house had never met his heart because he'd deliberately kept her away from them all. He'd begun collecting the six people that lived here after he'd found her as a child, for no solid reason other than to assure her she wasn't alone and encourage her to stay, should she ever decide she wanted to Wander. Now they needed to serve a different purpose.

"What would be the good of that? Is she single?"

Ellis was secretly appalled by the thought of Michael getting his hands on Synjan.

"No, she's missing."

"You need me to find her?"

"If you've never met her, how could you?"

"I couldn't, but it's your brainy idea, isn't it?"

"Do you ever make statements?"

"If I did, you think anyone around here would listen to me?"

Ellis pulled a face. "Thank you for your time, Michael. I apologise for summoning you unnecessarily."

For a moment, his portly companion continued sitting there, staring at him like a toad from a drain pipe. "Okay. Let me know if you change your mind," he said before he heaved himself up and left the room.

Ellis breathed a sigh of relief and lifted his tea to his lips, pleased to find it hadn't got too cold. He wasn't sure what he was going to do if Fyfe had changed but one thing was certain; he had no other option so neither did his charge.

He'd finished his tea and had begun contemplating ordering another when Fyfe finally showed up. Something frantic inside Ellis was appeased when the tall, dark-skinned, twenty-one year old waltzed through the door flashing a cocky grin.

"Hey," he greeted laconically. He manoeuvred into position to sit on the couch but remained standing, his rear hovering over the cushions as he reached a hand out. His limbs were so long that he easily covered the distance over the coffee table to make contact with Ellis without his benefactor needing to stand.

Ellis raised a hand to shake, only to have his hand folded into a fist and his knuckles rapped by Fyfe's. The younger man chuckled like he'd successfully duped his elder and then flopped onto the sofa, his gangly body sprawled across most of the piece of furniture.

"Hello, Fyfe," Ellis said, feeling put off by the odd hand ritual he'd unwittingly participated in. Perhaps it was a Bardon City custom but he rather suspected it was more a generational difference. It didn't bode well but his choices were too limited to let that interfere. "Thank you for coming to speak with me. I know my visit is unexpected and my request will be surprising but, rest assured, you *will* be generously compensated for your contribution."

As expected, the word 'compensated' had Fyfe's light blue eyes twinkling with interest. He was a handsome young man and he was well aware of the effect he had on others. He might be arrogant and youthful but his beauty would be an asset that Ellis could use to advantage.

"I'm listening."

"I need you to Navigate for me."

When Ellis finished the sentence succinctly, Fyfe frowned, his mouth twisting into a thoughtful shape. "I gather you mean off world?"

Ellis was pleased. "Very astute. I believe you have observed my second in command in Gredann. Synjan?" he prompted. "She came into my office once when we were talking, not long after you Wandered into Trent."

It was a reference more than three years old, so it took Fyfe a few moments to remember but then a light of recognition lit up his face. "Oh yeah! I remember her! The cranky one. Blonde," he snickered lecherously, cupping both hands in front of his chest to imply large breasts, "and short. Brown aura," he finished, tapping his head to indicate how he'd seen her as a Navigator.

Despite being annoyed by his crass gestures, Ellis was immensely relieved that Synjan had made enough of an impression on Fyfe that he remembered what she looked like externally *and* using his talent.

"Yes. She has Wandered with another and I fear for her safety. I plan on following after her to bring her back."

Fyfe gave him a dubious look. "If you're planning on *us* Wandering after her, aren't you worried about *our* safety?"

"No. The Authorities' best Hunter is also helping me find her. I'm confident that, between the three of us, we'll catch up with her and the gentleman she's travelling with in no time. Our safety won't be an issue."

"You seem real confident about that," Fyfe drawled, narrowing his eyes at Ellis like he wasn't sure whether to believe him or not.

"I am. And there's something else I'm willing to disclose to you, as a further assurance and sign of my commitment; I'm a Controller."

Fyfe's eyes widened in amazement. "Oh *shit*, man! Controllers are fucking *nasty*!"

Ellis wasn't sure he approved of the description but he got the impression it was a positive term of reverence.

"Regardless, I'm confident that the two of us will be able to complete this mission in a safe and timely manner. When we're finished, I'm willing to return you to whatever world I have the power to reach, with compensation, as I said. Do you agree to these terms?"

Fyfe pursed his lips, making a show of thinking it over but Ellis could tell he was already swayed. "Sure, I agree. When are we going to get this freight *moving*?" he cried enthusiastically.

Ellis smiled his pleasure. "Wavering heart; empty hand. We'll leave as soon as we are organised."

CHAPTER TWENTY-FIVE

Arrested

JINWA Woy possessed an understated beauty. There was nothing particularly memorable about her face, everything was well-defined and proportionate. Her composure and elegance did more to attract Hawke than her outward appearance, though he didn't think that would've hooked him had she not availed herself. Perhaps she'd predicted that.

She'd instructed Hawke to braid her hair after they'd woken and showered, and now she coiled the plait around her head, pinning it in place. He watched her do it, propped against the bathroom counter with his arms folded, assessing her ability to create her own hairstyle. He knew the slaves here were trained in hairdressing but she did well enough on her own.

"Do you have a man stashed somewhere?" he asked her.

"I do not own a slave," she replied.

"Because he'd enjoy too much freedom while you were away?" The words had come out bitterly and Woy didn't acknowledge them. He'd expected one of her cool stares.

"You should sit and allow me to see for you again." She made her declaration calmly, facing the mirror. Then she turned to him for his response.

Hawke felt ambivalent about the offer. Having a genuine Clairvoyant was handy but her talent couldn't be controlled. Getting a straightforward answer out of her was like trying to catch the wind with a fishing net. Still, there might be more about Synjan in amongst her babbling.

"Alright."

They moved to the living room. She sat in an armchair while he perched on the edge of the coffee table. He leant forward and held her hands, feeling vulnerable as he dropped his Shield.

"This would've been more fun in bed," he commented.

"I would have been distracted."

Hawke chuckled, knowing the flirt was for his benefit. It only added to the sense of being played.

She closed her eyes and did some slow breathing exercises. He smelled mint on her breath.

"I can see paperwork. Someone is signing paperwork."

More paperwork in his future was not a surprise.

"I see your name on the pages. There is..." she frowned and twitched her head to the side, as though listening. "He is making more of you because of your success. When you hide, it delays his plans but when you return, your efforts will see you rewarded."

"What?"

She said nothing, her cryptic words lingering between them as he tried, and failed, to analyse them. Hiding could be a metaphor for Shielding. Who the crap was making more of him? What did that even mean? Did she mean Ellis? Was he sending more people after Synjan? That would complicate things.

"The man that sends you after her wanted to raise you both."

That settled it, she was talking about Ellis. Because the message was about a past she couldn't possibly know, he was finally impressed.

"The wheel of your death has recently been turned by your hand."

Fuck that. He didn't want to know about dying.

"Tell me about Synjan. What can you see?" Hawke insisted. Jinwa expelled an air of frustration and frowned, her face moving through different expressions before she looked peaceful again.

"Yes, yes I see her. She stands with a slave in a garden. They are talking together. She looks around and... Goddess of Stars, she is in the High Palace Courtyard! How did she—?" Jinwa lapsed into silence, testing Hawke's patience. He held tightly onto her hands. Was this the present or the future? If Synjan was in the High Palace at this moment, how was he supposed to get her out of there? The palace would be impossible to penetrate. "She is watching... she is watching..."

"What? What is she watching?" Hawke pressed, knowing that his outburst was more likely to ruin her focus than to enhance it, but he couldn't help himself.

"She sees them blending together. If I... oh!"Jinwa's lips parted and she went deeper into trance, or whatever it was that she was doing when she had her clearest visions. "No wonder she watches, he is divine..." she whispered, then she frowned and her eyes moved rapidly beneath her lids. "Everything ripples."

He had time to wonder what she meant when Jinwa's hands were wrenched out of his grasp and her armchair flipped up and over. She catapulted backwards across the room, sliding and then rolling across the floor until she stopped at the wall six metres away. Hawke leapt to his feet, looking around for the threat but seeing nothing. She'd been shoved backwards by an immense invisible force.

Was it a Ghost? Had one of them pushed her? If he hadn't seen the Wanderer Ghost fading in the prison cell in front of him, disappearing through walls, he wouldn't have understood the advantage those freaks had. Nothing was safe from them.

No, something *was* safe. The DOME. His Shield had created an effective prison for Wanderer powers. He wished he could project his Shield onto this room, but the most he could do was slide it over himself, over his own skin.

He ran to her, half-expecting her to be knocked out even though she hadn't bumped her head. What the hell had made her fly across the room? Ghost or not, even if Hawke was twice as strong as he was now, he wouldn't be able to deliver that kind of blow.

"What was that?" he asked when her frightened gaze found his.

"I... I do not know."

"Are you okay?" he helped her stand and she held onto him with both hands, even after she'd found her feet.

"I do not believe I am hurt," she said. "Possibly a few bruises."

He led her to the couch and sat with her, a flurry of questions arising that he didn't give voice to because they were all theoretical. He settled on the facts.

"What did it feel like?"

She took a moment to respond. "I do not wish to talk about it."

"What? Why not?"

"Because it felt like someone was listening and disapproved."

"If someone's listening to us, we're both screwed."

Jinwa's gaze found him and she didn't comment, though Hawke got the sense that she was disappointed in him again.

He had no idea why.

Jinwa shook him awake when it was still dark. He reached for his gun but there was nothing on the nightstand. He felt vulnerable and instinctively Shielded himself.

"We must depart," Jinwa hissed. She'd taken the time to get dressed, collect her specs and braid her hair while he'd slept, so they couldn't have needed to get away that quickly. He shot her an annoyed glance that she missed because she was throwing a tunic at him. "Hurry."

He compressed his lips to stop himself from making a scathing comment. She looked panicky and the urgency of the moment was catching. He didn't want to waste time arguing about things he couldn't change. Taking care of herself before waking him was evidence she was concerned with her own skin.

Once he was dressed and presentable, she made him place his messenger bag inside a large, unwieldy silver gift box, adorned with an excessively-curled purple ribbon.

"Our disguise is that we're going to a birthday party in the small hours of the morning?" he asked as they headed for the suite door.

"Midnight parties are popular now."

"Where are—"

She shushed him and his eyes widened before he pressed his lips together again. He wanted to snark a comment at her but swallowed it as they entered the corridor. He didn't want to fuck up their getaway.

It would've been nice to have been told why they were fleeing. He could only assume that she'd had some kind of vision. In the lift, he chanced a question.

"Is it Synjan?"

"What?" Jinwa asked, her momentary confusion

answering the question even before she had a chance to shake her head. "No."

"Me? Something I did?"

"Not yet."

The lift doors opened and they entered a hushed lobby. He counted three women in the foyer, two of them accompanied by their silent slaves. The hotel staff had swapped waiters for cleaners, though Hawke recognised Palo at the front desk. He must be the night manager, to be here at this hour. He didn't like the glint of interest that Palo had in his eyes when he looked their way.

"Ambassador Woy, may your night be filled with much pleasure."

Hawke released a puff of laughter before Jinwa locked a steely gaze on him. She said nothing in return to Palo—it was obviously fucking customary to be rude to men. He kept in step with her and she was walking fast. They exited the hotel together and she got into one of the self-driving bubble cars. He followed obediently. She said something in her language and the car reacted by sliding the door shut and silently accelerating.

"Where—?"

He stopped when she held up a finger. He looked out the window instead, regarding the green lights. They weren't so spectacular up close. They looked like regular lights tinged green, though they didn't leave an after-glow behind his eyes. How could such a thing work? He puzzled over the science of it.

The shuttle brought them to one of the plain buildings. It was a giant block of white, though the corners were curved and there were cosmetic strips and wedges on the facade to make the building look more interesting. He saw it was a parking lot due to the silhouette of egg-cars behind the open-air windows.

Jinwa led the way into the building and he followed, tucking the silver gift box under his arm. He felt his bag shift inside and it somehow made him feel better. It was irrational for him to grow attached to it. He was less possessive of his guns, but then, he was always upgrading his weapons so he never had them for longer than a year.

Jinwa approached a pale green egg-car and punched in a code. It was one of the few times he'd seen a panel used instead of a retina scan.

"That's not as secure as an eye-scan," he observed. Jinwa flashed a warning look his way and said nothing. Was he still not allowed to talk? The door rolled up but there was something different about this egg-car that he couldn't figure out. It bugged him even as Jinwa climbed in and made the passenger door roll up. Hawke sat down and the shape of the seat was what finally made it click.

"This isn't your car."

"This is my car but it is an older model." She took off her specs and put them in a slot beside the steering handles. It was funny how the older model looked more futuristic than the other car... which had a regular steering wheel. This car looked like she would be using resistance bands, the kind that would enhance her biceps as she turned left and right. Who'd decided it would be a good idea to combine gym equipment with a car?

"Your expression tells me you have something to say."

"No, I'm good," he said, not needing to share his current thought.

"You have been interrupting me all night."

From the centre console, Jinwa took out and put on a different pair of specs before pulling back on both handles to make the car reverse. She yanked twice on the right handle and the car turned as it backed up. She performed a peculiar gesture and the egg-car moved forward.

"Steering wheels are better."

"Steering wheels are an Authority invention."

"So where are we racing off to?" Hawke unpacked the gift box and tossed the container into the back, holding his messenger bag in his lap. Beyond it, he had a clear view of his bare legs and slip-on shoes. He looked ridiculous. It was comfortable in the same way that being naked was comfortable; the material of his tunic dress was too soft, too light.

"To the Portal. The real one."

"The real one," he repeated, his voice dripping with contempt.

"Yes, the one that is not artificially made. The one that occurs naturally. The real one."

They left the car park and pulled onto the street. There were a few bubble cars and pedestrians around, but not many. Midnight parties might be a thing but Ning wasn't a city that buzzed with life at all hours.

"How many people live here?" he asked.

"Just under three million."

"I thought Ning was supposed to be one of the largest cities on this world."

"It is the largest city in this hemisphere, but it is not sprawling."

"So there is a bigger city in the south?"

"Yes, but southern cities are harder to..." she took her time searching for the appropriate word, "...define."

"How so?"

"There are townships that the city outer limits have spilled into. The cities do not wish to claim the townships as an extension of themselves, but the townsfolk insist they have been absorbed."

"They want to be a part of city life?"

"Living in the city qualifies a citizen for extra credits."

"Ah. And the Priestesses don't want to give their citizens more money?"

"The *High* Priestesses," Jinwa corrected, "are aware that a citizen in a township does not commit work towards the running of the city, but to their town."

"How does that work?"

"It is not straight forward but for the purpose of this conversation, you may understand that each citizen supports only their local area."

"You know a lot about the political setup."

"I am an Ambassador."

"I thought that meant you mediate between Femme officials and Authorities?"

"That is one of the jobs, yes."

"And this town-city thing is another?"

"Yes."

"You have your fingers in a lot of things."

"I am overworked, yes."

He grinned at her when she didn't take offence at his accusation. She glanced over and he saw a slight pull at the corners of her mouth.

"So is this normal? Taking off in the middle of the night in an old car that is no longer associated with you?"

She looked at him in surprise and the car reacted pulled to the left. She corrected and faced the front again.

"It's not hard to figure out something's gone wrong."

"I... there is an outcome that I did not foresee until it was... closer."

"So the mission is fucked?" Even though he asked it, Hawke didn't believe it. They'd lolled about in the apartment for a grand total of two days, not even making it all the way through the third night. It had been an exercise in sex and prophecy. He didn't feel like he'd learned anything.

"What happened when you were taken to Clio?" she asked.

"Who's Clio?"

"The hotel."

He thought it over. "I got picked up by police. By enforcers. They squashed me into their plane's storage space and drove me to the Clio."

"You are missing detail."

"They aimed a bubble gun at me the whole time."

Jinwa glanced over before looking back at the road.

"They scanned me with a hoop thing."

"They scanned you!"

"That supposed to mean something?" Hawke asked, his heart sinking.

"They never believed you. From the beginning they never believed you are Wandering, even though you are Shielder."

He was angry. This stupid mission had been doomed from the start. Either he'd been spotted leaving Nakhari Base or somebody had leaked information or having him walk into Ning was so dumb an idea that they'd laughed as they'd collected him. If it was the former, Jinwa Woy would be in a lot of trouble. Or perhaps she wanted him to think that way and she'd been the leak.

"Is this car registered to you?"

"Nobody would register this car is mine," she replied, misunderstanding his question but answering it anyway. In hindsight, Hawke realised that registration of vehicles was typically an Authoritan thing to do. Femme seemed to recoil from paperwork. He liked that idea.

"How many cars do you have?"

She smiled at him and didn't respond. Hawke settled back and closed his eyes, missing the soft bed but not needing it to catch some more sleep.

When he woke up, he was able to discern by the dull early morning light that they were close to the mountains. Tall, grassy fields lay on either side and the road stretched on ahead. While relaxed, he sensed something was amiss. The realisation had him tense in his seat and glare at Jinwa.

"You lied," he seethed.

"What? Go back to sleep," she said, amused.

"We're not going to the Portal. You lied."

She stared at him, shock on her face. The car began to slow; it must have had the same safety feature installed.

"How can you know that?" she asked, her voice weak.

Meditation helped, but being relaxed was usually enough for him to get a sense of the Portal's direction. Theories had been put forward to him and he'd been asked about his uncanny success at Hunting many times, but he'd never confirmed that it was his Wanderer blood helping him hunt down illegal Wanderers. He attributed it to his instinct, to his training, to his skills. Sensing the Portal didn't make him a better Hunter, it just helped him know which direction to start looking. To admit his blood gave him an advantage would devalue his accomplishments.

The car stopped and both doors rolled up. Hawke looked at Jinwa as she threw her specs on top of the blank dashboard. She lunged towards him and he reacted instinctively, his arm blocking her. She grabbed his forearm and peered over it at him, her eyes wild.

"Don't go to the Zed Plateau," she said, then released him and threw herself out of the car, almost slipping on the road. He watched, stupefied by her sudden transition from elegant woman to panicked creature. She reached into the car and grabbed her usual specs out of the compartment she'd put them in. Then she circled around and disappeared into the fields on his side.

"What in the...?" Hawke looked at the place where she'd vanished and had to give her credit for not disturbing the grass. He could only see where she'd gone in because he'd seen her do it. Someone not as observant or untrained wouldn't see the slight bend of grasses and a growing breeze was busily pushing them back into place.

A familiar base note that he felt rather than heard accompanied the wind as it swirled around the cabin of the car. Hawke set his messenger bag into the footwell and climbed into the driver's seat, aware that he was revealing a lot of himself as his tunic rode up. As long as the stupid clothes didn't get in the way he didn't care, but underwear would've been nice. He grabbed Woy's driving specs and put them on but saw nothing beyond a green line of light. The light disappeared and the specs sent a jolt of electricity into his temples.

"Fuck!" Hawke yelled, smacking them off his face. The shock had been more of a deterrent than a punishment but it had the desired effect. He couldn't drive this car because he hadn't passed the retinal scan. He wasn't going to put the specs back on and figure out a way to get them to work, either. He didn't have the time.

A wedge-shaped plane landed in front of the egg car. It was a touch bigger than the one that had first collected him. Two enforcers got out, their silver dress uniforms glinting in the dawn light. Both of them were pointing bubble guns at him. To show he wasn't hostile, he raised his hands out of the car first, then followed them. His tunic fell and covered him as he stood, which was good because he didn't want to offend these bitches with his male genitalia.

He waited for them to bark an order at him but they didn't bother. The one closest to him lifted her bubble gun a little higher and he only had time to register that she was going to shoot before his head was covered in some weird slimy shit.

He reached up to wipe it off but it was hard in an instant; the slime had moulded to his face like a plastic mask. He couldn't draw in breath and he couldn't take it off. Hawke lost his footing and went down, landing hard on the road. He tried cracking the shell of his mask on the bitumen but it did nothing. He scratched at it with his fingers to feel for the edge was but there was no seal. He couldn't get it off without breaking it... and he couldn't break it.

The world had muted and now it was darkening. Fucking Woy had added herself to the list of Wanderers that had betrayed him by running off to save herself. She hadn't given him a chance to escape. Now he was going to die inside a fucking pseudo-plastic mask while two enforcers watched.

The indignity was the worst. Wearing a dress in a world that considered him unimportant because he was male. His body might not even make it back to the Authorities. He wouldn't get a decent burial.

The world went black from the outside in.

He didn't want to die.

CHAPTER TWENTY-SIX

Together

LUCK was with Daeson and Synjan on the third day of their row. By mid-morning, white fluffy clouds had gathered, covering the sun's harsh light. A cool breeze blew at their backs; light enough not to influence the ocean's waves and a wonderful relief from the burning sun. Daeson couldn't smell the ocean like he'd thought he would; in Dockside and on Mwavey, the smell of salt had been strong and persistent. The smell in the middle of the ocean was of nothing at all. He'd expected at least *something*.

Synjan paddled with single-minded determination in front of him. She had developed a golden tan after he'd Healed her sunburn every evening. Daeson's own skin remained lightly bronzed, as though being a Healer protected him from colouring further. He wondered about it, about the benefits his Healer ability afforded him. He'd never been afflicted by disease, had never suffered the itch of mosquitoes or had reactions to plants or foods. Everyone had the sniffles in winter except him. How had it escaped his notice on Kharltae? How had his father not noticed?

His father. He could have lain hands on his father and saved him. All he'd had to do was wish the disease away and he wouldn't be here now. He'd probably be married and with a child on the way, running a thriving farm with his father to help. Instead, he'd Healed criminals after they'd hurt themselves doing bad things to other people. It didn't seem right or fair; he hadn't saved a person he loved, only those he didn't care about. Even Marcus, whose death had impacted him, wasn't someone he missed. He'd been a friend, yes, but not a close one. Marcus had made his decision to follow Nick, though he hadn't deserved to be killed by him.

Synjan's life had come at great cost but she was here with Daeson, helping him, seeing the worlds with him. He no longer felt angry at her but he was still wary. It would take him some time to trust again. He wondered if having a suspicious nature was part of gaining experience or if it was Omerri's direct influence.

It hurt less, to think of her now.

Something smacked against the bottom of the canoe, interrupting his reverie. Daeson looked down and around and his eyes widened at the sight of a large shadow beneath the water.

"Synjan, look," he whispered, not wanting to alert the thing near them. He had no idea what it was but it was following the boat. When she didn't react, he hissed: "Synjan!"

She twisted around to look at him, holding the paddle across the bow of the canoe to keep it secure. Daeson gestured at the shadow beside the boat and Synjan searched the water with her gaze, but the lapping ocean waves must've hidden it from her because she didn't react—or the sun was in her eyes.

"It's huge, can you map it?" Daeson prompted, his own paddle stilled because he didn't want to disturb the water's surface. The boat was bumped again, a low thud that didn't have much impact. Synjan's expression shifted before she closed her eyes and faced forward. After a moment she turned back around to face him.

"I can't see anything. Nothing close to us is big

enough to map."

"It's bigger than the boat!" Daeson argued.

"Maybe it's a bunch of little somethings," she suggested. They both stared at the ocean and were rewarded with the sight of the sea-creatures as they surfaced together.

"There must be hundreds," she said in awe.

Daeson had never seen or heard of creatures like these; they looked like over-sized glass marbles with a peach-coloured ball in the centre, big enough to fill his palm. After he watched them bobbing about, he noticed a single blue tentacle trailing after them, like a tail. It was their tentacle-tail that made a noise as it bumped against the canoe because their soft marble bodies were silent when they squished against it.

"They're beautiful," Synjan smiled.

"I wonder if you can eat them?"

She gave him a crooked look, then released a peal of laughter that matched the warmth of the day. He liked her laugh, it was natural and buoyant and contagious. He grinned back but didn't scoop up one of the marble-creatures to test if it was edible. He and Synjan had enough food packed in their bags and his question was borne of curiosity rather than desire. This moment, surrounded by the marble-creatures as they swam beside the boat, was the first time Daeson was glad he'd Wandered into this world.

"Is this what you imagined Wandering would be?" Daeson asked Synjan as they lay on the sand together, looking up at a moon-less sky. The island they'd stopped at was little more than a sandbank, though a few trees and scraggly bushes grew on the grassy part of it. A small hillock was the only nub of height on the island, promising safety from an encroaching tide. They'd shored their canoe and lashed its tether around one of the trees, just in case the tide rose higher than expected. There was no flat ground for the tent but there was no need for one—the night was warm. It would've been silent except for the handful of nattering seabirds roosting in the tops of the trees, squawking their dislike of invaded territory. Daeson had tried shooing them away but they'd only taken flight and returned. Synjan hadn't bothered, collapsing onto the ground instead and massaging sore muscles.

"Something like it, yes. Only with less ocean."

He chuckled but sobered as he wondered how to phrase his next question. "What if the next world isn't Femme?"

"I don't know. I don't even know what this world is called."

"J'Bdyamn."

"Sha-biddy-what?"

Daeson smiled and sang it for her; the three notes that made up the world made a nice melody. "It means 'A Collection of Land and Ocean'."

"Oh yeah! I remember Bo teaching me that 'amn' was 'ocean'."

Daeson looked at her, seeing her smile fade as she thought of Bo. He'd been killed before the war had even begun and it wasn't right that she didn't even have hope he'd survived. He wondered if she'd checked, to see if there were any survivors. There were times when she could've instead of scouting ahead, she could've looked behind and seen the repercussions of war.

"I'm sorry," he said.

"Yeah. Me too."

"Do you..." The question was hard to ask and he hesitated, unsure if he wanted to know the answer. "Do you regret not helping?"

"Yes and no. I agree with you about not interfering

but they welcomed us and looked after us. We were already interfering just by being there."

Daeson sighed. "It's hard to know what the right thing to do is."

"Next time we should just do what we think is best."

"Even if that means killing someone?" Daeson asked warily.

"I don't want to stand aside and let others be killed."

She had a point but he felt a niggle of untruth in her words; perhaps she felt conflicted. Her doubt made him feel better about her. She meant well and had a good heart. She wanted to protect others, to help them... and she was ruthless enough to do the worst even if she didn't like it. He needed to travel with someone like her, who could do what he couldn't. Or wouldn't. He didn't like that part of her but he saw the use for it. Even though he needed her to be this way, it was a part of Synjan that he would never like.

"If you found a world where you no longer had to defend yourself, would you stop Wandering?"

"Defend myself," she mused aloud, giving the words some thought. Instead of objecting to them—which he thought was about to happen—she answered. "Sure, eventually."

It was the truth but it was the 'eventually' that he noticed. If the next world was one that she could stop at and be safe in, he had no doubt that she would continue on. He didn't need her to say it out loud to know that was true.

They dragged the canoe out early in the morning of the fourth day, eating some cereal bars that had fallen to the bottom of Synjan's bag. The morning was already warm.

As they finalised their gear, Daeson noticed Synjan crouched by her bag, staring into its depths.

"What's wrong?" he asked her.

The look she gave him was hesitant. "I'm going to change my clothes before we go. Put my gun bra back on and wear my gun into the next world. Under my shirt. In case."

She'd surprised him with the gun upon entering this world but he could see the wisdom of it. If they'd been discovered by the Techatachenti, who knew what their greeting would have been like?

When he nodded, she changed her underwear in front of him. The holster looked obvious between her breasts and it drew his gaze repeatedly for all the wrong reasons. He was glad that it remained empty but he knew that would change. Once it was covered, it would be easier for him to forget about. It was too hot for her to put on a shirt when they still had rowing to do.

The seas were rougher today. It wasn't long before Synjan was feeling unwell. They'd discovered her Navigator talent gave her some reprieve; when she scouted ahead, she didn't get nauseous from the movement of the boat. When this happened, her paddling became erratic, her mind purposefully distracted. Daeson preferred her poor paddling to the noise and smell of her retching.

After a couple of hours he heard her murmur, "So close." Daeson was surprised he'd even heard her over the splashes of the waves and the cry of seabirds overhead. Now that she'd alerted him, he lifted his head and heard the familiar call of the Portal.

"I feel it too," he replied. He thought they were still paddling north because the rising sun had been on their right and he was fairly sure they'd travelled in a straight line. Even though the sky was a washed out light blue, he could see the beam of light that was the Portal; the brightness of the day couldn't match it. He squinted at it, his emotions towards it bitter-sweet. It had tricked him out of a world he'd loved but now it offered an escape from a world he found unbearable.

He could see the Portal was in the middle of an island.

"It's on an island!" Synjan told him. Daeson chuckled. She might not have realised he could already see it. He reflected that he'd previously been annoyed with her statements of the obvious but was now giving her some credit. She was mapping and didn't know that it was visible just by looking. His irritation at her previously had been his problem, not hers. It was a relief to finally let go of his anger.

The island was bigger than the sandbank they'd stayed on the night before. This one had a jungle on it—its diameter wasn't so big but the trees were huddled together in a dense pocket of green.

The waves were pushing them towards the island so they reached it quicker than expected. When they beached the canoe, Daeson noticed Synjan was rubbing her shoulders again and he approached.

"Need a Heal?"

"Nah, better to save the water we have before we go into the unknown." She grinned at him, her eyes dancing with excitement. She looked like she was thrumming with energy. With a last dip into bags, she holstered her small gun and they both put on shirts. He helped her put her backpack on and she helped him in return. They checked there was nothing left behind in the boat.

"I wonder if anyone will ever find it here," Synjan mused, her tone sombre as she regarded the abandoned canoe. Daeson looked past the boat at a trio of flat black rocks—except they were moving.

"What are they?" he asked, pointing them out.

"I don't know. Crabs, maybe?"

Now that she'd identified them, he could see their little legs scuttling and a large claw held close to their bodies.

"Can we go now?" Synjan prompted as he dawdled. He turned back to her and shrugged.

"What? You don't want to go?" she teased.

"I do want to, yes. I just don't want to rush this time. The first time I used it, I didn't know what would happen. The second time I used it, I didn't know *you* would happen." He smiled at her sheepish expression. "This time, I want it to be deliberate. Expected."

"I can understand that," Synjan said.

He moved towards her and reached out a hand. She took it and they walked into the jungle together, helping one another to avoid strange prickly plants and stepping over mossy logs, until they arrived at the Portal.

Their beacon of light.

He stared at it, feeling warm and tingly, hearing soft noises like whispers, smelling and tasting the moisture in the air and the greenery around them. He dragged his eyes away from it to look at Synjan, staring up at it in uninhibited wonder. It looked like she was in love.

With his hand tightening slightly around hers, to make sure they were together, he lifted their combined hands into the light... and they were gone.

OTHER TITLES BY THE AUTHORS

By Delia Strange
Femme: Light (A Wanderer Novel)
Blue Shift

By Delia Strange & Linda Conlon
Axiom: Wanderer of Worlds 1
Untethered: Wanderer of Worlds 2

**Anthologies featuring
Delia Strange and/or Linda Conlon**
Unspeakable Crimes
Obliquity

ABOUT THE AUTHORS

Delia Strange

I have always been addicted to strange and unusual stories. It's known as speculative fiction nowadays. I am also enchanted by all manner of fantasy—from dark to epic to contemporary. It's only natural that I would write it. I remember fondly those black and white TV episodes of The Twilight Zone.

Once I discovered that not only could I read such stories but also write them...! I haven't looked back since.

In my private life I'm married and have a young daughter. I've also got two cats—one that sleeps on my desk as I write and the other who likes to tap random objects off flat surfaces.

Linda Conlon

As a child, I was a voracious reader. Whether I was on one of our numerous family holidays, travelling to my younger brother's incessant sporting events or just lazing around at home, I was reading. It was a running joke in our family, that I never had my nose out of a book. My parents eventually learned not to pester me about the life I was 'missing' beyond those beloved pages; I didn't care. I was living hundreds of lives vicariously.

When I met Delia, that changed. She opened the

world of writing for me and I experienced for the first time the wonder of creating, rather than just experiencing.

Now, I don't read nearly as much as I write and I'm very much looking forward to publishing the stories Delia and I began together as seventeen year old ingénues. It's time we told them to someone besides each other.